LADYSTINGER

LADYSTINGER

A NOVEL BY CRAIG SMITH

CROWN PUBLISHERS, INC.

NEW YORK

Published by Crown Publishers, Inc., 201 East 50th Street, New York, New
York 10022. Member of the Crown Publishing Group.

CROWN is a trademark of Crown Publishers, Inc.

Manufactured in the United States of America

Library of Congress Cataloging-in-Publication Data

Smith, Craig (Craig Bradford), 1947–
    Ladystinger : a novel / by Craig Smith.—1st ed.
        p.   cm.
    I. Title.
    PS3569.M5168L34   1992
    813'.54—dc20   92-6131
                                                            CIP

ISBN 0-517-59012-3

Book Design by Lenny Henderson

10 9 8 7 6 5 4 3 2 1

First Edition

For my father
RUDOLPH Z. SMITH
(1920–1985)

LADYSTINGER

*A*ccording to the plastic program card atop the television set upstairs in his hotel room, a movie called *Spanked by Satan's Slaves* was coming on at eight-thirty on one of the adult channels.

It sounded like just the kind of thing Bob Sarcominia would enjoy.

He consulted his new Benvenuto Cellini Collection Rolex and found he had ten minutes to spare. More than enough time to knock back another Scotch and water. He signaled the bartender by thumping his empty glass, then swung away from the mahogany bar to take another look around the crowded lounge.

It was an impressive establishment, the LeHigh Room of the old Warwick Hotel on Baronne in New Orleans's Central Business District. A big, dark, Victorian saloon, it offered a high stamped-tin ceiling, gaslight fixtures, a massive, carved bar fitted with a solid brass railing, heavy velvet drapes, even a black marble fireplace. On this evening a very young, very thin black man in a tuxedo was playing a Steinway.

Hell of a place, he thought.

The bartender brought him his drink and, while he was handy, Bob Sarcominia ordered another, a double.

He particularly admired the walls. The upper two-thirds were covered with some kind of ornate, rust-colored fabric, while the lower third featured a dark, cherry paneling. There was a name for that kind of paneling, and he tried to remember what it was, but he couldn't come up with it. This frustrated him. It was a common name, something he ought to know, seeing how that was, roughly, the business he was in.

The company of which he was the chief financial officer was the world's second-largest manufacturer of prefabricated log houses. Last fiscal year, sales had topped fifty million dollars. The owners were an extremely tough old man and his two brain-dead sons. Bob Sarcominia's background was strictly accounting and finance, and he'd only been with the company for eight months, but still he felt he ought to know the name of that goddamn paneling that goes along a wall, just about waist high. It was just the sort of thing that would come up in conversation. The idiot sons were always talking about post-and-sill construction and expansion gaskets and crap like that, all the time cutting their eyes at him, like he didn't know what they were talking about.

He propped his foot on the brass rail and swallowed the last of the Scotch. The bartender hadn't brought his double yet.

What the hell was it called, that paneling? It was really starting to bother him. He wanted to ask the bartender, but thought better of it. He'd just make a fool of himself, trying to explain it.

He was looking at the paneling, concentrating, following it all around the lounge, when he happened to notice a young woman seated alone at a small table near the piano player. He wondered how he'd managed to miss her before. She must have just come in. She was dressed in a simple black dress, rather low cut but not immodestly so. In the soft light of the bar, her skin seemed very pale, almost translucent, and her long blond hair almost white.

She smiled at him.

Bob Sarcominia smiled back.

And immediately sucked in his stomach. He was not accustomed to young women smiling at him like that, certainly not young women who looked as good as this one looked. The secretaries at work smiled at him, but they more or less had to. It was part of their job description. Outside the office, walking in the mall with his wife and kids, say, women never gave him a second glance. Or a first, for that matter. It was like he was invisible.

He looked back at the girl, but this time she was staring off toward the entrance. No doubt waiting for her date. She was certainly well put together. She reminded him of an actress he'd seen in a movie on cable last month; it was a gangster movie and she'd been taking a bath in a big clawfooted tub with steam rising out of it and there was this one terrific shot of her standing up in the tub, stretching out to reach for a towel, all wet and naked. He couldn't think of the name of the movie.

He couldn't think of the name of anything tonight.

The bartender finally brought him the other drink. It was eight twenty-seven but he didn't want to go up to his room just yet. Satan's slaves could wait a little while. They repeated the movie all night long anyway.

He checked out the blonde at the table again, couldn't help himself. And there she was smiling at him like before. Big smile.

What the hell was she smiling like that for?

Bob Sarcominia smiled big right back at her, nodding his head in acknowledgment. Then he lifted his drink, like a little salute. He wasn't sure why he did that, but he was glad he did because she answered him in return, hoisting her own glass, something with a parasol in it.

Jesus.

She was awfully good-looking. It was fun just sliding his eyes over her. He hadn't tried to pick up a woman like that since . . . ever. In fact, it had been close to five years since he last cheated on Ellen, and, come to think of it, that had been at another convention like this.

What the hell. He picked up his drink, buttoned his jacket, and strode through the crowd toward her, watching her face to see if she seemed alarmed at his approach.

No alarm, that was for sure. She had a wide, happy grin on her face.

That was when he remembered about his wedding band. Trying to make it appear casual, he jammed his left hand inside his jacket pocket. It was awkward, because he missed on the first try, but the blonde didn't seem to notice.

"Care for some company?" he asked her. It was the first thing out of his mouth, and it sounded twenty years out-of-date.

He started to pull back a chair, but hesitated. There was something in her expression that said he definitely needed permission.

And she didn't say a thing, just started looking him over. It was like he was at a job interview and he wasn't sure he had the necessary credentials. There were three or four little paper cocktail umbrellas on the table in front of her, indicating she had been sitting here longer than he'd thought. At this angle, he could get a pretty good peek down her dress, but he didn't think that would be smart at this stage, so he made a point of keeping his eyes on her face, which was no problem at all.

Finally, she spoke, "That a Rolex?"

"Yeah," he said tentatively, gazing down at his watch. "Yeah, it is. Rolex."

"It's so . . . big," she said.

Say what?

"Yeah, well. That's the way they make 'em."

"Guy with a Rolex like that, I guess he can keep me company." She gestured for him to have a seat.

Whatever works.

He noted that she was slurring her words. A good omen, he felt. And it was gratifying that he was sober enough himself to pick up on it. His adrenaline was pumping furiously. Suddenly, he wondered if she was a hooker. Must be. Hookers were different here in New Orleans. A high-class call girl like this you didn't see at home in Lansing. But right now, he didn't give a damn. He would certainly pay for a woman like this. Hell, he'd trade his Jeep Cherokee for a woman like this.

"I'm Bob Sarcominia," he said, reaching over to shake her hand. She smirked at him, like she thought it was silly, shaking hands.

"Sarco-*what?*"

"Sarcominia. Sounds Italian, but it's Spanish." Actually, it was Sicilian but he didn't want to get into that. Maybe later. Years ago, when the first Godfather movies came out, he'd found the word *Sicilian* turned women on. But he didn't want her thinking he was some kind of mafioso.

"Sounds like a tumor," she said.

Keeping his hand in his pocket, he tried to remove his wedding band. His fingers were a little swollen and it wouldn't slip off too easily. He gave it up because he was afraid she might think he was playing with himself. But then, if she was a hooker, it wouldn't matter anyway, being married, would it?

"So what's your name?" he said, trying to keep the conversation flowing.

4

"Maggie."

"That's my sister's name. Margaret."

She didn't seem to care. Her head was bobbing to the music. She had interesting eyes, a light, icy blue, flecked with gray.

Bob Sarcominia started moving his head to the music, too, grooving to it. To show he was a music lover himself. A passionate man. A devotee of all the arts.

But he really couldn't keep his eyes off this woman. Maggie. He edged his chair closer to her, ostensibly to get a better view of the pianist.

After a moment, she looked back at him, and smiled again. Almost like she was surprised to find him sitting there.

He was thinking it was pretty much a dream scenario: alone in New Orleans with a gorgeous, tipsy blonde.

He said, "Are you . . . uh, a . . . professional girl?"

At once, he knew it was the wrong thing to say.

"A professional girl?" she said. "You mean, like a *whore*?"

Probably the best-looking woman he'd been around in twenty years and he'd already blown it, even before the drinks had arrived.

"No, no," he said. "I mean, like a working girl—er, white-collar worker. You know, your *job*. I'm asking what you do for a living."

Couldn't get any lamer than that.

Her smile ratcheted down a notch. In a flat voice, she said, "I'm associate systems analysis director at Inskip Technologies in Cleveland."

"Oh."

"Why, do I look like a whore?"

He really wanted to get out of this line of conversation.

"No, no," he said. "I didn't mean that. You misunderstood me. Jeez, you look terrific."

That seemed to please her. "Here's my story, stud," she said, and giggled for some reason. She then paused and inhaled deeply, steadying herself for the challenge of getting the next few words out in the correct order. "I'm single, I'm in town for three days, I'm really, really bored, I've had a couple of drinks and I want another one bad . . . and you're kinda cute. You play your cards right, don't go calling me a whore, you might get lucky tonight. Maybe. No promises."

Bob Sarcominia looked around for a waitress.

But she placed her hand on his, leaning into him as though to confide some important news. He had an absolutely stunning view of her breasts and discovered to his great elation that she wasn't wearing a bra. "It's too busy," she whispered. "Why don't you go up to the bar, get us the drinks there?"

"We could have one in my room," he said, but he knew it sounded too eager. He had to get the twelve-year-old kid out of his voice.

She laughed. "Don't push it, honey."

"What are you having?"

"Ladystinger."

"What's that?"

"The bartender knows."

He shrugged and left for the bar.

There, waiting to catch the bartender's eye, he finally wrenched his goddamn wedding band off and slipped it in his pants pocket. Every so often he would look over at Maggie, verifying she was still there.

On his return, as he placed the drinks on the table, she said, "Do you mind going and getting me a pack of cigarettes, Bob? There's a machine near the entrance." She picked around in her big purse, prowling for money. "I'm afraid if I try to walk I might fall down or something. I think I may have to stop drinking this shit before long." She held out a five-dollar bill but he waved her off.

At the vending machine he glanced back at her. He couldn't get enough of looking at her. Her purse was still open and she seemed to be fiddling with the drinks, rearranging them or something. Goddamn, she looked good. He tried to imagine exactly how she might look with her clothes off. He couldn't.

Just then, she noticed him ogling her. Very deliberately, she stuck out her tongue and licked her lips at him.

He couldn't believe his luck.

Half an hour later Bob Sarcominia was opening the door to his room. In the elevator she had clung to him, one arm tight around his waist. It was hard to hold his stomach in so long, but he managed. He had held her close and sniffed the lemony shampoo scent of her hair and gaped at the swell of her milky white breasts. His greatest hope in life now was that he would be able to achieve and maintain an erection. Under normal conditions, there should be no problem about this, he assured himself. It was just that he'd had a lot to drink and sometimes that affected things. And if anything went wrong tonight, he would never forgive himself. But he wouldn't even consider that possibility. It was a mistake to put that kind of pressure on yourself. Just relax, dummy, go with the flow. Enjoy the experience.

He flipped on the light switch and then bowed exaggeratedly, allowing her to enter first. She strolled unsteadily across the threshold, taking in the suite and its furnishings, then giggled. He admired the sway of her hips in that tight black dress.

It was then that he began to feel a little odd. A little . . . fuzzy. He was thinking maybe he should have stopped drinking before he did.

He picked up an ice bucket and said, "I'll get some ice." He figured they would probably want something to drink before the night was out, even if it was a soft drink.

But then he felt very light-headed, like he needed more air than there was around him.

She could sense there was a problem. "What's the matter, honey?" she asked.

"Nothing," he said. But he knew something was screwy. His head was swimming. Of all the times in his life to get sick, now wasn't the moment. He couldn't permit this to happen.

Feeling very shaky, he rubbed his forehead. What the hell was wrong? Was it just the booze?

He pursed his lips and blew out air.

"You don't look so good," she said. "What's wrong?"

"I'm okay," he said. But he was afraid that if he didn't lie down soon, he might fall down. He'd never passed out before, but that was what this felt like. Like his brain was shutting down on him.

"You sure?" She seemed agitated, worried about him.

"I don't know," he finally said. "I just feel kinda weird all of a sudden."

He heard a thumping sound and realized he had dropped the ice bucket on the carpet. This was crazy.

Heart attack. It came to him that he was having a coronary. Panic overtook him. He expected a pain in his arm, that was what happened on TV. An uncle of his had died of a heart attack when he was only twenty-seven after getting in a fistfight at a drive-in movie. Bob had never known him.

"You feel like you're going to be sick?" she asked.

"I don't know," he said, sitting down on the bed. "I don't know what's wrong with me."

"Why don't you lie down for a second?"

She yanked a pillow from beneath the covers and propped it under his head as he lay back.

Now she seemed extremely apprehensive. He watched her chew the inside of her mouth. He was reminded of a biology class from long ago, a film on insects, watching their mandibles grind mechanically away.

"I'll get you a washcloth," she said.

Wainscoting, he thought. That was the name of that kind of paneling in the bar downstairs. Wasn't that it?

She said something else to him but her voice didn't seem in sync with her lips; it seemed to come to him from somewhere else in the room, somewhere else on the planet.

Wainscoting.

Bob Sarcominia could feel himself slipping away and it occurred to him that his last living thought was of wainscoting. It was a goddamn stupid thing to think about as you were dying.

2

*N*ine minutes later, as Maggie Rohrer strolled from the bank of elevators across the lobby, a doorman rushed to open the heavy glass entrance doors. He smiled at her, but there wasn't any edge to it; it was just your basic doorman smile, the one he offered to all the guests. Maggie was acutely sensitive to the facial expressions of doormen. Sometimes they gave her a smirking, wiseass look, like they thought they knew something about her.

Like they thought she was a whore.

"Taxi, miss?"

"No, thank you." Her smile to him was demure and impersonal, the kind she imagined might be delivered by a tight-assed associate director of systems analysis.

Of course, she didn't give a flip what doormen thought about her. What concerned her, when she received those little looks, was that maybe she was dressing too showy and needed to tone it down. It was a fine line. Gradually, though, over the time she'd been running this particular scam, she felt she had determined what worked best for her. The Little Black Dress, crepe-backed satin, the hem just above the knees; a tasteful diamond pin perched on the shoulder. And, naturally, a pair of black patent fuck-me heels.

Outside, the New Orleans air was fetid and heavy, redolent of fried food and carbon monoxide and vomit and God knew what else. Across the street they were hosing down the sidewalk in front of a little hole-in-the-wall restaurant. The sign said HUNGARIAN-CAJUN DELIGHTS. She tried to imagine what that would be.

Halfway down the block, she opened the passenger door of a

parked mud-gray 1986 Oldsmobile Delta 88. Seated at the wheel was a beefy man in his middle-fifties, dressed in a loud sports jacket and an open-necked white dress shirt. His name was Barry Landers.

He tossed his cigarette out the window and started the engine, engaging the gear before Maggie could shut the door.

Maggie said, "Hi, honey, I'm home."

Her companion wasn't much on sarcasm. "How much cash?" he said, jerking the car into traffic.

"Don't you want to know how my day went?" she asked.

"Cut the crap, okay?"

She looked at him. He smelled of whiskey, tobacco, and sweat. Attached to one lapel was a professionally printed name tag that read: HI! I'M DON D. DONALDSON. Barry had found it years ago in the men's room of a bar. Now he wore it regularly because he felt cops wouldn't roust him if they thought he was in town for a convention.

"Four hundred and forty," she told him.

"Yeah?"

"And over five hundred in traveler's checks."

"No shit?"

Actually, the take was a little better than that. Bob Sarcominia had been carrying more than a $1,000 in cash. Of that amount, Maggie now had $585 stashed inside her panties. Tomorrow or the next day, whenever she found time, she would purchase a money order and send it to her aunt in North Little Rock, Arkansas. In turn, her aunt would take $50 for herself and place the rest in a safe deposit box at Twin City Bank.

"So, give it to me," Barry said, at the first light.

Without warning, she dumped the contents of her handbag into his lap. Everything—wallet, checkbook, traveler's checks, Rolex, the wedding band she found in Bob Sarcominia's pants pocket, even a big, heavy can of unsalted macadamia nuts she raided from the mini-bar.

"Hey! Come on!" he yelled. "What's the matter with you?"

A good question, she thought.

They turned onto Canal, heading toward the river. Maggie stared out the window at the wandering, wide-eyed civilians, sheep soon to be sheared. She was tired of this scam; maybe it was time for another. But she couldn't think of anything else that paid as well.

As he drove, Barry quickly and expertly counted the bills.

He was excited. "Teach that asshole to carry so much fucking money around, huh?"

She said nothing, continuing to stare out the window.

He handed over her cut. Although she was sure Barry understood she was skimming, he never said anything about it. Maggie knew he made up the difference when it came time for him to split the income from what he'd run up on the hot credit cards. That generally came to five bills apiece from the banks. But she was aware that Barry also spent a good amount of time inside department stores charging whatever he could later hock or sell on the street. All of that money was supposed to be divided between them, but Barry's accounting was sloppy. This way, by taking cash off the top, she didn't have to keep reminding him.

Barry kept a shoe box in the trunk to hold all the plastic they accumulated in their travels. Every couple of weeks the box would fill up and he'd send it by UPS to a fence in Miami who paid him three dollars a card. By that time the only value lay in the account number itself, but there were people who would pay for that. They'd use the number on applications to open new credit accounts so that when those cards came in, they could begin the cycle again. It was for precisely that type of fraud that Barry spent all of 1977 and most of 1978 inside the federal penitentiary at McNeil Island, Washington.

"I was thinking maybe we could hit the Acadian," Barry said, tucking his wad of bills inside his jacket. He left the traveler's checks on the car seat. "I drove by. It looked busy."

"I don't know."

"You don't know, huh?"

"I'm tired. I think I just want to go to my own room and go to bed."

"You ever get over thinking you're too good for me," said Barry, "we could maybe do that sometime, you know. The two of us, climb into bed."

She gave him a look like she'd just swallowed a spider and Barry's leering smile evaporated. He pulled into a parking spot down from the Acadian, bumping into another car as he did so.

He turned to her. "Hey, we're in this for money, right? Well, there's three big goddamn conventions in town. There's optometrists and building contractors and something else, I forget. So go make us some money."

It was either that or lying in a motel room, she thought, watching cable TV. Right now, she didn't much care either way. She sighed, picked up her purse, and retrieved a few personal, untraceable items of her own.

Along with a small plastic squeeze bottle.

"I could get caught, Barry. You ever think of that?"

Barry hooted. "Bullshit. Guy's gonna be out till morning, right? Half the time they don't even go to the police, they're so embarrassed. You know that, Maggo. Time he looks himself in the mirror, wondering what the shit happened, we'll be on I-ten to Houston."

Barry shook loose another cigarette, putting the near-empty package up close to his glasses so he could peer over the rims and check inside.

"Easy for you to say—you don't do anything. I'm the one puts it on the line."

"What do you do?" asked Barry. "Guy buys you a cocktail, you go up to his room, you watch him fall asleep. *Ding!* Nine hundred and forty bucks."

Maggie wasn't up to the argument. If she wanted, she could push it and they both knew she'd win. She held all the cards. But he was right: they were in this for the money. Wasn't that what she was in this for? She reached into the glove compartment and removed a large glass bottle with the label peeled off. Uncapping it, she inserted the tip of the squeeze bottle and drew in a yellowish liquid.

Barry watched her with a grin. "Think you're the only one knows how to do that?"

"I don't make mistakes, Barry."

She slipped the squeeze bottle into her handbag and returned the bottle to the glove compartment, along with her stack of cash.

Barry leaned across and opened her door, trying to move her along.

"Look, think of it this way," he said. "A lot of people, they never find out what they're good at in life. This is what you're good at, Maggo. You think of it like a career, you'll enjoy it more."

"Career girl, that's me."

"Knock 'em dead," he said, but his attention had already turned to the loot on the car seat. He was holding the Rolex to the light from the streetlamp, checking for an inscription.

"Don't touch my goddamn macadamia nuts," she told him.

Maggie walked away from the car, leaving the door wide open, forcing Barry to stretch across the seat to close it.

3

A jazz trio was playing "Three Little Words." The bass player, an old black man with a grizzled beard, nodded to Maggie occasionally. It was a knowing, penetrating look, as though he recognized her as a fellow creature of the night.

The lounge at the Acadian was not ideal for this sort of thing. Brightly lit and cavernous, it lay between the lobby and a shopping arcade that led to Canal. Guests were always trooping back and forth. Most of the patrons at the tables looked like they were waiting for the rest of their party to arrive so they could all depart for the French Quarter.

She checked her watch: ten after ten. If nothing developed in the next fifteen minutes, she would be heading out the door.

Maggie liked the way her watch, a Patek Philippe, sat on her wrist. She had come upon it last Christmas in the suitcase of a prone airline executive. It had been beautifully wrapped in gold foil and she had torn open the package like a child. Since then, it had been appraised twice: once for $8,500 and another time for $12,000. The second jeweler, a young man who also cast several appraising glances at Maggie, had told her the bracelet was eighteen-karat gold. Normally, she thought expensive watches were an absurd vanity, but she found she loved wearing this one. It was her favorite possession.

A pair of clowns had hit on her right after she entered the lounge, aggressive young twits bursting with testosterone. One of them was obviously still in college, out for a night on the town with pop's Gold Card. He was wearing a Casio.

She yawned. The alcohol, no doubt. She always laid out a few parasols on the table, to make it appear she was drinking heavily. Even so, tonight she'd put away—what?—three Ladystingers?

Guys seemed to prefer women who ordered drinks with umbrellas in them. That had been her experience. A Ladystinger was her favorite cocktail, but it was hard to find bartenders who knew how to make a good one. It was essentially a gin sling with a pony of cherry brandy. It looked frou-frou but had a nice kick.

A man sat down at her table, just like that. He was holding a drink and he smiled at her like he'd known her all his life.

He said, "Mind if I join you?" He was a big man with a dark, angular face and a sleepy grin, like he thought it was real funny, asking permission after he'd already done what he wanted to do. Cop, she thought. This had happened to her only once before with this scam, just after she met up with Barry, at the Excelsior Hotel in Tulsa. The bartender had called the police, thinking she was a streetwalker. The cop hassled her halfheartedly, telling her to move on. The next day she went out and bought two new outfits, charging over two thousand dollars on some guy's American Express card.

"Yes," said Maggie sternly. "Go away."

Besides being a cop, he wasn't the type she was after. He was a nice-looking guy, but kind of scruffy and untended.

"You waiting for somebody?" he asked, still smiling, like a man with no intention of moving.

A cock of the walk. Her least favorite category.

"Yes, I am," she said. "As a matter of fact."

She tapped out another cigarette. He reached over to light it— and Maggie couldn't help but notice that he was wearing a big, heavy Rolex.

"So maybe I'm the guy you're waiting for, huh?"

Maggie smiled.

He noted her interest in his watch. "What? You like Rolexes?"

She sipped her drink. "They're okay."

"I bought this one off a guy on Bourbon Street," he said. "You wouldn't think they could make any money, selling them so cheap."

She knew he was kidding but she must have given something away in her face. He laughed.

"Relax," he said. "It's real. See?" He held it in front of her face. "What are you, anyway? A jeweler?"

She said, "I'm associate systems analysis director at Inskip Technologies in Cleveland."

He did not seem overly impressed. "I'm sure you'll make director someday," he said.

She had picked up the title from a bearded gentleman she had knocked over in St. Louis, at the La Salle. It had a nice, meaningless ring to it, she thought. It made her sound serious and smart. If anyone ever questioned her about what kinds of systems she analyzed, she was confident of her ability to make something up. So far nobody had inquired.

"And what do you do . . . ?" she asked.

"Shanks. Jack Shanks. I'm from Milwaukee. I'm a mortician."

She made a face.

"Now don't be that way," he said. "Morticians are people, too, you know. It's not all formaldehyde and internal gases. So what brings you to New Orleans?"

Throughout all this, there was something a touch unsettling about Shanks's delivery. He was very deadpan, like he might possibly be putting her on.

"Convention," said Maggie. She was sizing him up. After he flashed the Rolex, she no longer thought he was a cop. They wouldn't go to that kind of trouble.

"No kidding," he said. "Me, too. A lot of exciting new advances in mortuary sciences are going on these days. So what do the other associate directors call you back in Cincinnati?"

"Cleveland."

"Right. What do they call you back in Cleveland?"

"Maggie," she said.

He stroked his chin speculatively, as though pondering the name *Maggie* and how it fit into the world order.

"Yeah," he said. "You have a Maggie look about you."

She didn't know what the hell that meant.

Shanks opened his wallet and Maggie observed that it was bulging with cash. Mostly fifties, from what she could tell.

"Care for another drink?" he asked.

It was like the trapdoor opening up. She had her mark.

"Why not?" she said.

He looked around for a waitress and Maggie started to speak. But he took the words out of her mouth: "Probably better if I go up to the bar, huh?"

He rose, smiled again, and departed, leaving his own half-full drink behind on the table. Maggie didn't hesitate. While his back was to her, she pulled out the small squeeze bottle and quickly passed it over his glass. Two long squirts.

Then, watching him lumber up to the small bar, she gave the drink another dose, mixing it with his swizzle stick.

After she'd gotten the squeeze bottle back in her handbag, Shanks made a ridiculous little kissy face at her. She gaily waved her hand in return.

Asshole.

Back at the table, he lifted the half-full drink to his lips—and nodded at the bass player. Maggie glanced over at the old man, who had the look of a terrapin, something that had been around forever. When she turned back to Shanks, he was delicately wiping his lower lip with a finger. The glass was empty.

He said, "So . . . ready for a little action?"

4

*B*arry Landers liked to tell people that he was tending bar at Jack Ruby's Carousel Club in Dallas on the afternoon the president was shot. It was a good dodge for hustling drinks in bars, which is where Barry spent most of his time when he wasn't sitting in the car.

There wasn't a word of truth in the story, of course, but Barry had spent countless hours regaling his fellow drunks with extravagantly detailed stories of Ruby and his strippers and that strange little fellow Lee Harvey Oswald, who used to slip in the back door and whisper in the corner with Ruby. Barry's more flagrant inventions involved the sexual preferences of Marina Oswald, to whom he had once written a love letter while housed inside the Connecticut State Prison in Wethersfield. He had received no reply.

Nowadays, he didn't bring up the story much. People his age were starting not to believe him, and Barry was afraid he was losing his ability to lie successfully, which is what happens to grifters right before they drop into the grave. With the young people, Barry knew not even to try it out anymore. It took too much time explaining things; they didn't know who the hell Ruby was and they tended to get their Kennedys confused.

Waiting for Maggie, he rummaged through Robert Michael Sarcominia's collection of plastic. He turned over an ATM card, hoping to find the PIN access code scribbled somewhere on the back, but there was nothing there. Half the time, a mark would write down the number in tiny print somewhere in his wallet, like he thought a thief wasn't going to notice it, or wouldn't pick up on what it meant. Barry searched the rest of the billfold but couldn't find anything.

He removed all the credit cards and shoved them in the side pocket of his jacket, along with the traveler's checks. The rest of it, the photos and receipts and video club membership cards, he left in the wallet, which he would toss in a trash receptacle at the first opportunity.

Around ten-thirty, his hemorrhoids flared up from sitting around and doing nothing all day, so he locked up the car and went inside the Acadian. He found a pay phone in the shopping arcade and dialed a long-distance number, charging it to Bob Sarcominia's AT&T card.

A woman answered.

"Mrs. Sarcominia?"

"Yes."

"Mrs. Sarcominia, I'm Don D. Donaldson, vice president of credit operations at First National Bank of New Orleans. Are you the Sarcominia who resides at fourteen-oh-one Old Bear Road in Lansing, Michigan?"

"Yes."

"Good. I wanted to make sure I had the right person. I'm calling because I believe one of your family's automatic teller machine cards has been misappropriated here in New Orleans. Is your husband Robert M. Sarcominia?"

"Yes he is." A note of alarm crept into her voice. Now she was thinking that maybe this wasn't a nuisance sales call after all.

"Is he visiting here in New Orleans?"

"Yes. He's there for a convention. Is anything wrong? Is he all right?" He had her complete attention now.

"Oh, I'm sure he is, ma'am. No reason to suspect otherwise. But it seems someone has tried to use your husband's bank card here in New Orleans at one of our metropolitan bank locations. The card was issued by First National Bank of Lansing. Do you have your checkbook handy, Mrs. Sarcominia?"

"Uh, yes. Just a minute."

Barry lit a cigarette. Over the phone he could hear children yelling in the background and Mrs. Sarcominia telling them to hush.

"Yes," she said. "I have it."

"I want to verify that account number. Should be at the bottom of your check. Five-five-one-zero?"

"Yes."

"Two-two-one-zero-dash-six—is that correct?"

"Yes. Did someone steal it from my husband?"

"Well, it's possible that he just misplaced it, ma'am. Set down his wallet in a restaurant or other public place and some lowlife person picked it up and ran away with it. Anyway, someone attempted to get cash out of one of our Bank of New Orleans ATM machines—through the AVAIL network? Not knowing the access code, they just popped in some random numbers apparently. Well, of course, the machine wouldn't accept it, so they evidently tried again. That's when the machine jammed. Normally, the machine is supposed to keep the card in an incident like that, keep it and not return it, you know? But in this instance there was a malfunction and the machine jammed. That's why I'm calling. I need for you to provide me with the access code so that we can remove the card. Then we will either hold it here for Mr. Sarcominia or mail it to your Old Bear Road address, whichever you prefer."

"You want the code?"

"Yes, ma'am, to release your husband's card from the machine. You're really quite lucky the thieves weren't able to misappropriate any money out of your account. I don't know your bank's regulations, but here in New Orleans the customer is liable for the first five hundred dollars charged from a stolen ATM card, unless of course the customer notifies the bank that it is stolen. Incidentally, I can take care of that for you, if you like. We can fax a card loss report to First National Bank of Lansing. Then you won't have to worry about it."

"But maybe my husband tried to use the card and the machine messed up or something. Maybe it's not stolen."

"That's entirely possible, Mrs. Sarcominia. It certainly is. However, he hasn't notified us if that's the case. I think, if I were you, to play it safe, I would notify your bank of the possibility that the card is stolen."

"I think I should call my husband."

"Certainly. But before you do that, could you please give me the access number? That way we can remove the card and hold it for your husband to pick up tomorrow morning."

"Yes, that makes sense. Uh, let's see, the code is four-one-four-four."

Bingo!

"Four-one-four-four?" he said.

"Yes."

"Well, thank you, Mrs. Sarcominia. If you will ask your husband to call me tomorrow at our main branch in downtown New Orleans, I will personally arrange for him to retrieve his card."

Barry then spent a minute spelling his phony name and giving out his phony telephone number.

Afterward, he found the gift shop was already closed, so he couldn't buy any cigarettes. He decided to take a tour of the lounge, to see if Maggie was still there.

On his way, Barry reflected that Mrs. Sarcominia was now calling her husband at the hotel. When Bob failed to answer, she would probably wait a while and call again, then keep calling through the evening. But it was possible that she might notify the hotel management after the first try and ask them to check on her husband. Unlikely but possible. Then the hotel would call an ambulance and the police and, eventually, in about an hour or so, word might spread to other downtown hotels. By midnight they might even have a description of Maggie from people who saw her in the lounge.

But by then they'd be on the way to Houston. In any event, Barry knew he had plenty of time to work his mischief with the bank card. No reason to hurry.

The Acadian's bar wasn't doing much business and Maggie was nowhere around. That was good. It meant she'd hooked her fish and was upstairs gaffing him. Lushwork, they used to call it, a long time ago when he was a kid growing up in Newark. That was when you beat up a drunk in an alley outside a bar and stole his wallet. They didn't call it mugging then. There were a lot of bars in his old neighborhood and a lot of alleys, but Barry never indulged. He preferred not to touch his victims.

Soon Maggie would be back down, sashaying to the car with that go-to-hell look on her face and a pile of cash, cards, and jewelry in her purse. Plus all that candy and crap from those little refrigerators, if they had them in the rooms here.

Barry ordered a whiskey neat and gulped it down, then returned to the car to wait.

An hour passed.

In that time, he watched dozens of people come and go, but no Maggo. She'd never stayed in a room with a mark this long before, and it was making him very antsy. He tried to imagine what had gone wrong.

5

*I*t was the first time Maggie had ever made it to the upper floors of the Acadian. Last summer, she and Barry had hit the hotel but there hadn't been much going on then. Maggie had sat in the bar for close to two hours, sipping a banana daiquiri and chewing honey-roasted peanuts. A tiny Japanese businessman kept winking at her, but never made any kind of move. The next night she hit the River Plaza and raked in over a thousand dollars from a thin, wispy Texan who said he was the heir to a fortune made in the manufacture of turbine ventilators.

Shanks had a corner suite. Although it wasn't particularly spacious, it was quite stylish and comfortable. The bed had been turned down with a little mint placed on the pillow. She noted the amenities: a hair dryer, a complimentary bathrobe, even a telephone in the john. And, to her delight, a mini-bar.

They'd had another drink in the bar before Maggie suggested they go up to his room. This, of course, was the toughest part of the hustle. It was practically impossible to tell how long it would take the mark to drop. She'd given Shanks a big dose, but he was a big man.

Sometimes they began pawing on her as soon as they got inside the door. She had to push them off and force them to settle down, have another drink. It usually took anywhere from ten to thirty minutes for the drug to take effect. Once they started getting groggy, she had to get them to the bed fast, so they wouldn't crack their head on the way down. Often, they mistook this for the signal to begin foreplay. It was tricky. A couple of times she'd started peeling off their clothes, drawing it out. So far, she'd never had to take off her own clothes—and she knew she never would. She'd walk out the door before she'd do that. That wasn't her game.

Shanks took off his jacket and automatically mixed another drink for them both. No funny business. He sat down on the chaise lounge by the window, kicked off his loafers, and set his feet on the glass coffee table, nudging aside a tray holding a bottle of Evian and two small porcelain bowls of candied pecans.

Maggie sipped her drink, a screwdriver too heavy on the vodka, and watched Shanks closely, looking for the first signs.

"How do you feel?" she asked him.

"Feel? I feel wonderful." He patted the chaise. "Why don't you come on over?"

"Let me finish my drink first," she said.

"Ah, why don't we just go ahead and jump each other, huh?"

She smiled at nothing, then looked out the window. They were twenty-two floors above the city streets, overlooking Canal and the Quarter. It was a very clear, very starry night. She liked to watch the stars, wished she knew the names of the constellations. She'd never had any real education. One of her ambitions, when she quit this life, was to buy a very expensive telescope and sit out on the deck of the beach house in Florida she was going to buy, and study the stars and listen to the ocean.

Shanks smiled agreeably. And then it happened: he shook his head distractedly, as though trying to clear away cobwebs. A telltale sign.

"What's wrong?" she asked him.

"Wrong? What d'ya mean?" He was beginning to slur his words. It wouldn't be long now.

"You don't look so good," she said. His position was okay. She'd prefer to have him on the bed, but this was good enough. The way he was sitting, his head would fall to the right. She could lift up his legs, slip him down to the floor, prop him on his side so he wouldn't swallow his tongue, then go about her job.

"Well, it's funny you say that," said Shanks. "I don't feel so good either. I feel . . . hot."

"Maybe you should lie down."

"Maybe I should," he said. But he made no attempt to move.

This was her favorite part. She felt like a big-game hunter who'd just shot a rhino full of tranquilizers and knew it was finally working, that she wouldn't be trampled to death, that she would soon have her way with the big beast. Only Maggie wouldn't be checking Shanks's teeth or banding his leg tonight.

His head dropped back, but the eyes were still open. Not particularly glassy, though. That surprised her. Usually, they turned a little glassy right about now.

He said, "Now, you did say that if I played my cards right, we'd get to fool around, didn't you?"

"I remember."

Men were amazing, absolutely amazing. A hairbreadth from being comatose, his mind was fixed on sex. She remembered something a veterinarian had once told her. Around his office when they had to neuter a dog, they called it a lobotomy. That's the way it was with men: all their thinking was between their legs.

"Well, did I?"

"What's that, honey?" she said, searching her purse for a cigarette.

"Play my cards . . ." his eyes finally clamped shut, like a doll's, ". . . right."

His head fell back. Down and out.

Maggie lit her cigarette. And then a highly satisfied look brightened her face.

Gotcha.

She watched him for a moment, giving him a little time. He wasn't bad-looking, actually. Rough around the edges, kind of . . . rugged. A big man, but there didn't seem to be any fat on him. He sure didn't look like any mortician she'd ever seen. She wondered if he had been kidding about that. Probably. Guys in bars always lied. But usually, they made themselves into bank CEOs or professional athletes or CIA spooks. Why would someone say he was a mortician when he wasn't?

She went over to him and felt for a pulse. Counting off, she studied his hand. Large and callused, not the sort of hand you imagined popping out eyes or removing entrails or whatever morticians did exactly.

Sixty-eight beats. Close enough. She started removing the Rolex.

And as she loosened the watchband, Shanks's hand opened up and grabbed hers. Very tightly.

She gasped and tried to jerk away but his grip was like an animal trap.

He blinked his eyes and smiled slyly at her. "Short naps," he said. "That's my beauty secret."

His demeanor had changed. He was no longer the fun-seeking mortician from Milwaukee, and they both knew it.

Still clasping her hand, Shanks turned his wrist to check the time on the Rolex, twisting her arm in the process.

She tried again to pull away but he yanked her down on the chaise next to him. She knew there was no escape from his grip, no wriggling away. She was not above gouging an eye, but something about him told her that wouldn't work, would only make him mad. He was not a man she wanted to make mad, not at this proximity.

Slowly, his other hand moved up to her face. Very deliberately, he withdrew her cigarette and mashed it out in a nearby ashtray.

"You shouldn't smoke," he said. "It's bad for your health."

He released her hand and she sprang to her feet instantly.

Taking his time, Shanks also rose. He strolled across the room to the dresser, with his back to her, seemingly unconcerned.

The door was about fifteen or twenty feet away. The problem was, she had on spike heels. Kicking them loose would throw her off a second. And then she'd have to fiddle with the lock on the door.

"Don't," he said, his back still to her. He was searching a drawer. "You won't make it to the door because I'll stop you. And if I should happen to trip over some heavy object, like my Rolex, for example, and you do manage to make it out the door, I'll pick up the phone and the lobby will be crawling with hotel managers and"—he turned around to face her—"*associate* hotel managers ready to snatch you up."

He had found what he had been seeking: a small, leather-bound notebook.

"You know," he said, "you're bad PR for the hotel industry."

He eased back down on the chaise, setting the notebook beside him, then poked around inside Maggie's purse.

Maggie said, "Are you a cop?" She didn't like the sound of her voice. It was unsteady. She was afraid he might misinterpret it and get the idea she was going to cry. She didn't think that would be the way to play it, not now at least.

But he ignored her. He had found the squeeze bottle.

"What is this stuff, anyway?" he asked, lifting it to the lamp.

"I want you to read me my rights." She was sure he was a cop now, and it scared her. Because he wasn't acting straight. He wanted something out of her. What?

He laughed. "Seriously," he said. "What is it? Chloral hydrate?"

"Apivan," she said.

"Apivan?" he said. "They use that for childbirth, don't they? To ease the pain? I remember right, it can cause heart attacks, if you screw up."

"I don't screw up."

"Right now, I'd say that's open to debate."

"How come you know so much about Apivan?"

"I used to be in pharmaceuticals," he said, tossing the bottle aside. "Before I fell into undertaking. Sit down. I'm not going to hurt you."

Spoken like a true cop. She remained standing as he continued to dig through her purse.

"How'd you work it with the drink?" she asked. "Did you pour it on the floor?"

"Something like that," he said, not even looking up.

"Who are you?" she asked again.

"I'm Jack Shanks, remember? And you're Maggie Rohrer."

She felt her heart crash against her rib cage. She knew she hadn't given him her last name. She never told the marks her last name.

"What do you want with me?"

"No cash," he said, putting away the purse. "Girl like you, with your income, you'd think she'd carry some cash around. Sit down."

Maggie sat gingerly on the edge of the bed.

"What's going on?" she asked. *"Tell me."* There were only two things she could think of: one, he wanted her to drop the dime on Barry; two, he wanted her to jump into bed with him, on the promise he wouldn't arrest her.

Instead, Shanks went to the bar and poured two more drinks. He held up the squeeze bottle.

"You want yours with or without?"

Playing with her.

"I'm not thirsty," she said.

He handed her a drink anyway. As he returned to the chaise, she slipped off her heels, pushing them under the dust ruffle of the bed.

"You know, Maggie," he said, "you're in what they call an exposed position. You rolled that gentleman over at the Warwick an hour ago, so the NOPD would like to meet with you. And since you unfortunately do this trick across state lines on a regular basis, the Federal Bureau of Investigation would also like to make your acquaintance. And we're not just talking robbery. We've got, what? Aggravated assault? Attempted murder?" He lifted his glass. "Cheers."

"Bullshit," she said.

Shanks opened his little notebook. "Ah," he said, "maybe you think it's bullshit, Maggie, but"—he read from the notebook—"Ronald Stucky of Corpus Christi, Texas, *he* may not think it's bullshit. Mr. Stucky spent four days in a San Antonio hospital after tossing back a couple with you." He raised his head and fixed her with his dark eyes. "You're a dangerous woman."

She tried not to give anything away with her expression, but she didn't hold out much hope of success. This was news to her and it frightened her. The juice wasn't supposed to hurt you, just put you to sleep early.

"Screw you," she said.

"Right. Anyway, I was saying how exposed you are. I pick up the phone, some officers of the law come over, haul you off, take some unflattering pictures with numbers hanging around your neck, send them out all over the country. How many counts you figure they can hit you with, Maggie? Twenty, fifty? A hundred? All of them felonies. Before you know it, you're pushing a laundry cart in a state penitentiary, pulling a forty-year stretch. Another drink?"

An icy wave of fear swept over her.

"Goddamn it, who *are* you?" she said. She was beginning to think he wasn't a cop after all. He talked like a cop, but he was something else, she didn't know what. Whatever it was, it wasn't good for her.

Shanks took another sip and gazed at her, thinking. It seemed like moment-of-truth time.

Finally, he spoke. "I'm a guy who could use a girl like you."

"You may find this hard to believe," said Maggie, "but you're not the first man to tell me that."

"One night's work. Same short con you're running right now. Hotel bar, right down the line. No risk. Straight pay. Ten thousand dollars."

He's got to be kidding.

"Oh, yeah? And what do you get out of it?"

"A man's briefcase."

"What's in it?"

"Let's just say I need a new briefcase," he said.

"Who's the pigeon?"

"I tell you that when I know you're in."

"I don't go along, what happens?"

"I call hotel security and report a heinous crime."

That was it? All this charade because he wanted to hire her to do a job? This last hour, he'd just been checking out her technique, seeing if she was the right girl for him? She thought it over. Ten thousand dollars was a lot of money, no doubt about it. For one night's work. If anything he was saying was true, which she doubted.

Maggie slipped her feet back in her heels and stood. She retrieved the squeeze bottle from the bar, and moved to the door. With her hand on the knob she felt a good deal more secure.

"I don't think you'll call downstairs," she said, opening the door. "You know why? Because I think you're as dirty as I am, Jack Shanks."

He smiled. A relaxed, lizardlike smile.

"Okay," he said. "But before you go, aren't you a little curious how I came to locate a girl like you?"

"Yeah, I was going to ask you about that."

"I mean, you don't just open the Yellow Pages under 'Mickey Finn' and find a listing for a girl with your specialized talents."

Maggie waited for him to get on with it.

Shanks checked his notebook again. He said, "Ever heard of a woman named Jennifer Louise Ostie?"

Maggie shook his head, acting bored.

"You keep up this line of work, you're bound to run into her. She's doing six-to-fourteen at the Northern California Women's Facility in Stockton. Involuntary manslaughter. Same profession as you. Oakland PD made the collar in November 'eighty-seven. She had a partner, a guy named Bernard Lee Landervaal, aka Bernie London, aka . . . Barry Landers?"

There was no hiding her reaction to this bulletin. It hit her like a landslide and he knew it. Who the hell was this guy? How did he know these things?

"Heard of him, huh? Well, Bernard Lee testified against Jennifer Louise and recieved two years suspended. See, *he* didn't actually do anything that bad, jury felt. It was that trashy girl he associated with that caused the orthopedic surgeon to die like he did. She wasn't as careful as you. Bernard Lee, being so cooperative with the prosecutors, helping them bring this murderess to justice, they let him off light."

He closed his notebook.

Throughout his little speech, Maggie had kept the door open, but now she pushed it shut. It didn't lock and she didn't move very far away. She was a woman who was good at making sudden adjustments, good at calculating where the next threat was coming from. But for the moment she wasn't too sure of things and she didn't like the feeling.

"Such easy work," said Shanks. "I figured he'd be back in it again. Figured he'd find some other simple girl to do the dirty work and give him the money."

Bernard Lee Landervaal. That pork-faced pissant son of a bitch.

Shanks stood, looked into the mirror, straightened his tie. "Of course, tracing Bernard was easy, like following the trail of a slug. He's got a brother in Boca Raton he keeps up with. Only his brother's wife, Glenda, she doesn't like Bernard. She was *very* helpful."

Maggie remembered the voice on TV late at night, when the station went off the air. "I have slipped the surly bonds of earth," it said. That was how she felt. Cut loose from her moorings, drifting into space. She wondered if Shanks had spiked her drink.

"Who are you, really?" she asked quietly. "Would you just tell me that?"

"Let's go to dinner," he said. "Someplace nice and quiet, where we can talk."

6

*B*arry Landers had spent seven of his fifty-four years inside various city, county, state, and federal lockups—places where he'd generally found it prudent not to bring up his Jack Ruby stories.

He had been a civilian now since 1982, after completing a twenty-month jolt at the Florida State Penitentiary in Starke, and he did not look to go back to prison again. The joint was becoming a much tougher place to get along in; too many gangs, too many hardasses who didn't play the game by the rules.

That was basically how Barry had settled on his current scam: the risk, all things considered, was pretty minimal. It was kind of like being a pimp, except without the sex.

Which was fine with him, really. Barry was a heavy drinker, and, over the past four or five years, sex had become something of a problem. He liked to kid with Maggie about getting in her pants, making her think he was always rutting after women; but, truthfully, that was one of the reasons he was glad he'd latched on to Maggie: there was no way she was ever going to shine his knob for him. He didn't even have to consider it.

Jennifer, she'd do anything for a buck. They'd always shared motel rooms—something Maggie would never go along with—and she'd give him blowjobs all day long for fifteen bucks a hum. He used to carry a little card in his wallet with her prices on it. She was always thinking up things she could do in bed and then coming up with a price. But she got a little weird toward the end, shooting up in the john when she thought he was asleep. Once he woke up smelling something strange and found her sitting in the dark at the end of the bed, poking herself with a lit cigarette, watching her skin burn, looking all glassy-eyed and dopey.

It got harder and harder to attract the fish with Jennifer as the bait.

Barry was always a little bit afraid that she might get it in her head to sink a shiv in him while he was sleeping. Either that or watch "Opryland USA," it didn't much matter to her. That was Jennifer. Thinking about it sometimes, he wondered if maybe she intended to kill that doctor in Oakland. Barry could picture the guy saying something Jennifer didn't like and her pouring half the bottle of joy juice into his drink, laughing to herself.

Still, he kind of missed her. She had long black hair and big dark eyes and a wild-child look. Sometimes she'd sleep with her head in his lap as he drove along the highway, just like a little kid.

Last October, when he was in California, he'd considered dropping by the pen to see her. He'd never been inside a women's prison. He'd have to write the department of corrections for permission to visit, but they probably wouldn't let him in the gate, not with his record. And she wouldn't want to see him anyway. She'd scream at him is what she'd do. Like she did at the sentencing. He didn't have to show up; he did it to provide moral support. He'd already signed a statement that one of the DA's assistants had handed him, and on the basis of that and all the physical evidence, Jennifer's lawyer plea-bargained her into Stockton. But as soon as Jennifer saw Barry in the court room she went bananas. Jumped right up and started screaming like something from *The Exorcist* until he got the hell out of there.

Like he'd had a fucking choice, for Christ's sake. If he hadn't ratted her out, they'd *both* be doing time, instead of just her. What would be the point of that?

He tried to imagine Jennifer in prison. Someone told him they did upholstering for their vocational trade at Stockton. Barry couldn't picture her cramming stuffing into a couch on a regular basis. He wondered what kinds of tricks she was turning with her bunkies now. No doubt she had a new price sheet listing all the interesting things she'd learned.

What the hell, she'd be up for parole soon.

Maybe he could send her a card, something. She'd always liked M&M's. Maybe he could send her one of those two-pound industrial-size bags of M&M's.

And then he caught himself. I'm going soft in the head, he thought.

Shoulda dumped that crazy girl long before Oakland, long before she checked the good doctor into that big clinic in the sky. Truth was, he was just too goddamn lazy to go out and find another girl.

It was a sign, he felt, that he was losing his touch. In this business, you lose your touch, you can maybe lose your life.

Down to his last two cigarettes, he was wishing he'd bought a pack back at the bar in the Acadian—when he saw Maggie coming out of the arched entranceway. And he knew at once that there was very serious shit heading his way because lagging just behind her was this big guy in a rumpled suit.

A cop, he was sure of it.

Barry started the engine before he realized he didn't have a chance that way. There was a line of cabs waiting to drop off their fares and they were blocking his lane.

The big guy reached under the flap of his jacket and around to the small of his back. There was a flash of metal and Barry saw it was a pair of handcuffs. In one fluid motion the guy snapped the cuffs against Maggie's wrist.

Barry didn't wait to catch the rest of it. With his left hand he opened the car door and with his right—he couldn't resist—he flipped open the glove compartment and snatched Maggie's stash. He hit the street running; he sprinted between two cabs and started down the sidewalk in a sort of half trot, like he was trying to catch a bus. He turned and saw Maggie squirming and kicking at the big guy, who suddenly noticed Barry and began to yell.

"Hey, you! Stop!"

Barry loped down the sidewalk, picking up his pace, thinking it had been ten, fifteen years since he'd tried to run flat out. Already he was straining for each breath. He knew he wasn't going to last long.

Then he heard someone say, "You need help, officer?"

"Get him!" the big guy shouted. "Stop him!"

Barry had to see this. Looking over his shoulder, he spotted a bookish-looking twerp with thinning hair and thick glasses. He was on the same side of the street as Barry, about fifty yards back.

The twerp calmly set down a package of some sort and bolted after Barry. He was wearing big white running shoes and they seemed to move in a blur.

"Get him," shouted the big guy again.

Barry couldn't believe it. As much as he was capable, he kicked up his speed and turned the corner. He thought, What are the odds of this happening? A fucking Good Samaritan helping out the cops, running down the bad guy. This couldn't be happening.

A service alley opened up on Magazine. It angled off to the left and he couldn't see the end of it; it could be boxed off, for all he knew. But he didn't have much in the way of choices. He crashed down the lane, his lungs burning. Soon the guy would be on top of him; he could hear him close behind. There was another turn in the alley and Barry could see people, lots of people in the distance. It was Canal, had to be. If he could make it to Canal, he could lose himself in the crowd, but he'd never make it. He felt like he was going to heave.

Barry grabbed his chest and fell to the pavement. His face hit harder than he would have liked. His glasses came off and there was something wet along his cheek. He was afraid it was piss.

The twerp stopped. Barry could hear him breathing but couldn't see him. Barry's first thought was to pretend he was dead, but there was no way he could control his breathing; his chest sounded like a window air conditioner on the blink.

"Are you okay?" the guy asked.

And Barry thought, What the hell kind of moron have we got here?

Barry said nothing, wasn't sure he could. His eyes were open, he was staring dead ahead at the pebbly asphalt, wheezing for air, but he didn't speak. Let the idiot worry.

"Can you hear me?" the twerp said. He grabbed Barry by the shoulder and turned him over. "Hey, you all right?" he said, leaning down.

Barry stayed where he was, eyes still open, looking stricken.

Then the guy did something that Barry found astonishing. He

bent over and put his lips to Barry's lips, pinched Barry's nostrils, and started trying to blow air into Barry's lungs.

Barry had never had mouth-to-mouth resuscitation performed on him and didn't want to begin now, in an alley in New Orleans, of all places. He bit down hard on the guy's lower lip. He could feel the soft part of the lip and the skin underneath separate like a piece of meat. The guy bellowed and fell over backward.

"You bit me!" he screamed. Only he said it, *You bib me.*

Barry knew he'd taken a good chunk out of him. He struggled to his feet and kicked at the guy, the toe of his shoe just catching the back of his head. That really set him off. He cranked up his decibel count. One hand was grabbing at his bloody mouth and the other was whirling around like a windmill, trying to ward off more blows.

Barry picked up his eyeglasses and staggered off down the alley. A couple of black guys were standing at the end, taking in the spectacle. They watched him closely as he passed by, but didn't make any move toward him. Barry kept walking straight across Canal. At the boulevard he could still hear the guy squawking.

7

To Maggie's surprise, Shanks unlocked the cuffs as soon as Barry was out of sight. He pulled them off and then backed away, like he thought she was going to make a run at him. And she was considering doing exactly that, slapping him or spitting at him, something, but instead she just stood there glaring. She still couldn't figure out his game and it bothered her.

Even so, she decided then and there to get away from him as soon as possible.

Shanks beamed with childlike pleasure as he watched the little pedestrian chase around the corner in hot pursuit of Barry.

"The stuff heroes are made of," he said, going over to the Oldsmobile. "Now we don't have to worry about your associate."

"That hurt," said Maggie, rubbing her wrists where the metal had bit into the skin, still keeping her eye on him.

He offered no apology. "I had to make it look real," he said.

He whistled to a nearby Acadian porter who had been absorbed in the action, then went around to the back of the car. He withdrew a key and opened the trunk.

"What's yours?" he asked her, pointing to the bags.

She didn't really want to turn her luggage over to him, but neither did she want to leave it in the car for Barry. She was beginning to see this as the opportunity she had been looking for to make the break with her partner. Quick and decisive action. There was always a way to work things to your advantage if you thought about it.

Maggie indicated her three paisley-print Diane Von Furstenberg bags to the porter, who pulled them out. She opened the passenger door and reached into the glove compartment. Her $220 was missing, and there was no sign of the traveler's checks or the Rolex. In anger, she banged her hand on the roof of the car.

"Don't tell me he took something that didn't belong to him," said Shanks.

Her can of macadamia nuts lay unmolested on the floormat. She tossed it to the porter, a nervous Latin kid whose eyes flicked back and forth between the two of them, curious what the hell was going on. Shanks took him off to the side and said something to him, then slipped him a bill. The porter nodded and started back to the hotel with her luggage.

Maggie looked around the interior to see if there was anything else she needed from this heap. She couldn't make up her mind about the big bottle of Apivan. On the one hand, if she took it and this guy really was a cop, she might be implicating herself. On the other hand, she didn't want to let go of the bottle. It was hard to come by, particularly in that quantity.

"Better take your firewater," Shanks said. That seemed to decide it for her; she dropped it in her handbag.

He took her by the elbow, signaling it was time to leave. She didn't like men grabbing her by the elbow, steering her around like she was a grocery cart. But she knew it was one of those things that some guys liked to do.

They walked back toward the hotel, down the sidewalk in the opposite direction from where Barry had run.

"How'd you get a key to the trunk?" she asked him.

"It fell out of your purse," he said.

He wasn't a cop, she decided. He was too subtle for a cop.

Following the salad, the waiter placed an ice sculpture in the shape of a swan on Maggie's plate. It was about eight inches high, with a small battery-powered, glass-encased light fitted in the base that caused it to glow. She looked quizzically at the waiter.

He said, "Sorbet," in the manner Mr. Rogers would employ when talking to a five-year-old.

Maggie knew what sorbet was; she had just never seen it inside a swan before. She peered inside and discovered a scoop of orange dessert. Shanks was already biting into his.

They had arrived at the Sazerac just before closing time and were seated at a banquette table in the back of the restaurant. Several other diners were finishing their meals, and a pale young woman was playing the harp softly.

"What's your game?" Maggie asked him once their waiter left them alone.

Shanks took a moment to consider that. He dabbed a slice of butter on a roll. Maggie noticed for the first time that he had a small scar running along his jawline. The white scar tissue stood out against his Marlboro Man tan. Scars, she reflected, were another thing that men liked to embellish. Almost always they got them by falling off a bicycle, but inevitably they turned them into the after-effects of a knife fight or shrapnel wound.

"I'm in the . . . security business," Shanks finally said. "I have a client, a computer software company. My client wants to acquire a sample of some new programming from a competitor. It hasn't been released yet."

"They want you to *steal* it."

"They want me to release it early," he said. "A certain individual has this sample in his possession. This individual is careless. He enjoys the company of women of a special type."

"What type is that?"

"Your type. The kind of woman who makes a man want to drop his pants and charge."

"I don't think I can work with you," said Maggie.

"Why is that?"

"I don't like you."

"Ah, but we know how much you like money."

He reached inside his jacket and withdrew an envelope, then slid it across the tablecloth to her. Inside she found a number of crisp hundred-dollar bills. She started counting them.

"Five thousand dollars," he said.

She continued counting. He was right: five large. She returned the cash to the envelope and set it back on the table between them.

"The other half comes when you knock the guy out. I cover all expenses."

He flashed his high-wattage smile. He was surprisingly smooth, Maggie thought. Looking at him, with his lean, sharp-featured face, you wouldn't think he'd be so smooth. But he had a sly, laid-back charm that seemed to come out of nowhere, rising to the surface at unpredictable moments. She knew enough about men like him to suspect it was a ploy, a trick he used to draw his victims closer.

"How much is it worth, this sample?" she asked.

"To you, ten thousand dollars."

"But more to you, huh?"

He looked at her very hard, with black, piercing eyes. "There are only a half dozen people in the world who would know what to do with it. Even if you were able to figure out who they were and approached them, most of them would puddle in their pants and call the cops. You're being well paid for a half hour's work."

Maggie surveyed the restaurant. Everything was quite plush. By now, only one other table was occupied. Two older couples, dining out on a weeknight, rich ladies and gentlemen serenely enjoying the pleasures money can buy. The harpist smiled placidly at her.

Maggie picked up the envelope. At the very least, she told herself, she would be taking him for five thousand dollars.

She couldn't tell if he was pleased with her acceptance. There was no smile for her this time.

"When?" she asked.

"Tomorrow night," he said.

"You're kidding. Where?"

"Out of town. You'll find out when we board the plane."

"But what if this guy doesn't fall for me? Hard to believe, I know, but some marks *are* immune to my charms. I can't guarantee anything."

"He'll go for you." He said it like there was no doubt on that score. How could he know for sure?

Maggie sipped her wine. "I think I liked you better as a mortician," she said.

"You thought I was a sucker then."

"No more?" she teased.

"You screw with me," he said very evenly, "I'll come down on you like a hammer. I found you once, I can find you again."

"I still think you're a cop."

He shook his head. "I'm just like you, Maggie. A cheat."

Maggie's face betrayed a small but distinct measure of pain.

*   *   *

Barry walked the streets a long while. He needed to light some-where but he was afraid word might already have filtered out to some of the hotels. He kept himself downriver, pounding the Vieux Carré grid and the wharf area, retracing the same grimy streets over and over. Once, at the corner of North Rampart and St. Louis, on the edge of the Quarter, he looked up to find himself in front of a police station. He spun around and hiked back a couple of blocks to Louis Armstrong Park, where he took a seat on a bench, then remembered that he had more than twenty-five hundred dollars, including traveler's checks, riding on his hip. Plus two Rolexes, a Jean Lassale, three wedding bands, and his own eighteen-karat-gold diamond pinkie ring. Glancing about, he realized that an empty park on the rough side of town wasn't the best place to hang around at night, particularly when he looked like a lost Shriner with his HI! I'M DON D. DONALDSON name tag on. All he lacked was a fez. He tramped off, but kept having the same problem, turning the corner into third-world battle zones, then immediately doubling back to where the people were.

He was a mess. In Jackson Square he'd washed his chin in a water fountain, to clean off the guy's blood from when Barry bit away his lip. But there were still traces of it on his shirt collar and lapel. Besides that, the front of his jacket was stained from whatever the hell he fell into back in the alley.

What upset him most was the car. It wasn't that great a car, sure, and he could easily get another, but the car had all his stuff. His Dopp kit, his clothes, his highway maps, just about everything he owned. The only things he didn't keep in the trunk were his memen-tos, like the World War II Japanese ceremonial sword he owned and his collection of Kennedy assassination material, which he kept with his brother in Boca Raton.

Right now he figured the cops were winching up his car, hauling it off to impound it. Either that or they'd locked the back wheel with a Denver boot and would come back and pick it up in the morning. But if that was the case, then he might be able to sneak into the trunk sometime during the night. It was possible they didn't remove everything. It was possible they just immobilized it and forgot about the crap in the back.

Not likely, but possible.

So he started winding his way back toward the Acadian.

Barry's thoughts centered on Maggie. This was the end of his little blond meal ticket, and he wasn't sure how to set about locating another one. New Orleans was as good a town as any for locating a cute little con artist, of course, but he didn't have any contacts here, and besides, he couldn't afford to hang around. By tomorrow morning they'd have a warrant out for his arrest and cops would be looking for him for a couple of days at least. Then they'd forget all about it. It wasn't like he was Dillinger.

A cop turned the corner, right on top of him. Young black guy with a goatee and a big nightstick in his hand. His eyes focused on Barry for an instant, then slipped over to a group of drunk college kids yelling and screaming outside a skin bar. He sidled past Barry, then on past the kids, who didn't pay him any mind.

Barry's stomach turned over. He knew he should cut out of town right away, but where could he go? Florida, maybe. Visit his brother for a week or two. Think things over. He needed a vacation. Then he could set about finding another girl. Miami would be a prime place to start; he knew Miami pretty good. He could fly out there tonight, even charge the ticket on one of Bob Sarcominia's cards.

He considered hiring a lawyer to make bail for Maggie; he wasn't about to go to a bondsman himself. But he figured she didn't need his help, not really. She could get her own lawyer. And she'd probably get off, if she found a good one. First offense under this statute. She wouldn't have any trouble affording a lawyer, that's for sure. She sent most of her money home to that aunt who was supposed to be banking it for her. And of course she was holding back on him, he knew that. He wasn't born yesterday.

No, Maggie could make do for herself.

As for him, what he needed more than anything was a cigarette. That was what would set the world right.

8

*M*aggie didn't much care for books, but she loved magazines, any magazines. She would buy anything: *U.S. News and World Report*, *Variety*, *Muscle and Fitness*, *Forbes*, *Unique Homes*, *Buzzworm*, *Yachting World* and, without fail, *People*—whatever looked good.

But when she told Shanks she didn't want to go straight back to the hotel after dinner, that she wanted to get some magazines first, he had a problem accepting it. He seemed to think she was planning to skip out on him.

So he went along to protect his five-thousand-dollar investment.

They found a newsstand on Royal that was open. The narrow sidewalks were still teeming with marks and grifters and lost souls. Somewhere in the distance a saxophone wailed.

In Maggie's opinion, New Orleans was one of the sleaziest places on the planet, and that was probably why she enjoyed it so much. It reminded her of some huge carny theme park. The way Disneyland might have turned out if Walt had started life as a sideshow geek. If he had enjoyed biting off the heads of mice instead of drawing pictures of them.

She bought eighty dollars' worth of magazines and newspapers. Coming out of the newsstand, she noticed an antique set of scales just inside the awning. *MacReedy Emporium Sets the Standard*, it said in elaborate, gilt-leaf lettering. It brought back old memories. Her uncle, a route salesman for a vending machine company, had once kept an identical machine in his garage. It told your weight and your fortune. She could remember the crisp, solid look of the block type on the big green tickets it dispensed.

A street hustler came up to Shanks—a wiry, hyped-up young black man. There were dozens working the streets.

He said, "Say, my man, want a shine?" He was holding a dirty rag. "Bet I can guess where you got those shoes, Jack."

Maggie smiled at his accidental use of Shanks's first name, and the hustler picked up on it instantly.

"Jack your name? See, I know your name, Jack, and I know where you got them shoes. Bet me five dollars, Jack, huh? You win, I shine 'em free, okay?"

Shanks pushed ahead, obviously not a customer.

The guy had dancing eyes and kept rubbing at his jeans with his hands. Maggie wondered what he had in his system. An autopsy probably wouldn't reveal everything. How long had he worked these streets? How long had he plied his peculiar craft?

"I'm telling you," he said, "I can tell you *exactly* where you got them shoes."

Maggie said, "Got them on his feet, right?"

The hustler grinned. "Lady, you wise to my scam!"

His wild eyes bounced all over Maggie and Shanks, cutting from their faces to their jewelry, then back to their faces, then to their clothes and back again to their faces, always back to the faces, taking the measure of his marks eye to eye because the eyes told him everything he really needed to know. The rest was random information, facts that might or might not be useful in a clinch. All the while, his brain was cooking up schemes, sizing them up, reviewing his options. What will work with these two? How much can I take them for? His problem, Maggie reflected, was that he didn't know how to put any English on the ball, he had no depth of experience in this line of work. He wasn't committed to the profession; he was committed to making it through the night.

Maggie decided to rewire a few of his circuits.

"Tell you what," she said. "I bet you five dollars I can guess your weight according to those scales over there—within five pounds. What d'ya say?"

The hustler was still grinning, but you could see his mind seizing up. He glanced at Shanks, but he was finding, as Maggie had, that Shanks didn't hand out many answers.

And then Maggie had a thought: Was Shanks a con man? He sure didn't have the look. A grifter was always out there hanging on the edge, hurtling toward earth at Mach 2 but supremely confident of making a pinpoint landing. The best couldn't help themselves, it was second nature with them. Shanks seemed too removed from life; he appeared to see things from on high. Still, she knew he was running some kind of game on her.

The essence of the successful scam, Maggie felt, was found in a quotation she had seen on a poster in a head shop when she was a kid: *Everything should be made as simple as possible but not simpler.* The picture on the poster was of Albert Einstein with his tongue sticking out at the photographer. The quote was his, too. She didn't know physics but she figured Einstein probably had the soul of a con artist. Probably he made it up as he went along. That's what you had to do. Extemporize, her mother used to tell her.

"Five dollars," said the hustler, "and you guess my weight?"

"That's it."

"With my shoes on?"

"You've got a shoe fix. Yeah, just like you're standing there."

She could see the distress in his face. He was violating the first rule of the con man and he knew it. Don't get yourself conned. But she was betting he would pay five dollars to learn a new trick.

They moved over to the scales, Shanks scowling at her. He wanted to get out of here and back to the hotel. This wasn't in his plans. Maggie was thinking that over the next few hours she might show him a few other developments that he hadn't counted on.

Maggie stood on the scales and dropped a dime into the machine. The big red needle arced sharply, then swung back again. It quivered awhile, then eventually settled on 114. Four pounds light. That's all she needed to know.

A card popped out but Maggie ignored it. She was disappointed that it wasn't big and green, like those in her uncle's machine.

"So," she said, "we got a deal?"

A few other shoe scammers had drifted over, and this seemed to agitate the hustler. He wanted to consider the matter some more, but he also wanted out of this situation with a minimum of harassment.

He stepped up to the scales.

"Go ahead on, lady," he said. "Five bucks."

Maggie looked him over. He was tall and skinny. He had black cowboy boots on, with silver caps on the toes and horseshoe taps on the heels.

"Remember," she said, "all I have to do is get within five pounds either way of whatever it says on this scale, right?"

"Yeah, yeah," he said. A condemned man on the gallows. He knew this was a mistake.

"I say you weight one-forty—no, one-thirty-five. Shoes and all."

His face fell. She knew she had him.

"I'm right, huh?"

"See what the machine say."

Maggie slipped a dime in the slot. The needle flew back around, hovered, then came to rest on 132.

"Hot damn!" hooted a wizened little man. "She skinned you, man!"

"Dumb shit," said another, poking him in the side.

"Five bucks," said Maggie.

He reached deep into a front pocket of his tight jeans and withdrew a surprisingly large wad of bills, peeling off a five.

"I give you another five, you tell me the trick."

"No trick," she said. "It's a skill. Just something you get good at, like picking pockets."

Involuntarily, he slipped his hand back to check his wallet, then caught himself. Apparently he kept money all over his body. Laughing with the others, Maggie turned to catch Shanks's reaction. No smiles from him. What does it take, she wondered, to crack his safe?

He grabbed her elbow to steer her out of the crowd. She let him, but she was thinking this would be the last time. This elbow shit had to stop.

As they moved away, heading back toward the hotel, the hustler ran up to them.

"Hey, lady!" he said, handing her the two tickets from the machine. "Must be your fortune 'cause it sure don't sound like mine."

The first one read: *You will go far in this world.* The second: *Success is in your own backyard.*

"Right," she said, tosssing them in a trash can. Sounded like her kind of fortune, all right. Wealth and fame in front of her face, so she goes traveling.

*   *   *

Barry found a package store on Iberville and picked up a pint of Early Times and two packs of generic cigarettes. Turning the corner onto Royal, he uncapped the bottle and took a snort and felt immediately better; felt like a new man, in fact. He took another swig. It was wonderful. He thought about going back and buying a fifth, to make sure he had enough for the night, but, hell, this was New Orleans. The bars were open all night.

There was a little crowd gathered around a newsstand, and Barry was afraid it might be a fight or something, so he crossed over to the other side of the street. Above him someone shouted, "I love you, baby! I love your pants, baby!" It was a guy hanging over a cantilevered balcony. He was wearing panties and a bra and looked about seventy years old. At first Barry thought he was yelling at him, but then he saw it was someone just behind him, a flabby young guy wearing leopard-print leotards and three-inch heels. He stomped forward, flipping off the old guy.

Ahead, by the newsstand, Barry saw a woman that looked like Maggie, a little blonde in a black dress like she wore, and then he realized it *was* Maggie. It stopped him cold, and the guy with the leopard-print leotards and heels bumped into his back. Barry ducked into the nearest door, a bar. A fat man with a red beard said, "How'ya doing? How'ya doing?" and clapped him on the back.

Barry moved to a window. The big cop had hold of Maggie's elbow. They were walking back down to Canal. They didn't seem all that friendly but they didn't seem like cop and jailbird, either. And he noticed the cuffs were definitely off.

What the hell was going on here?

The guy with the red beard was trying to hustle him for a beer, so Barry slipped back outside. He dropped back aways, following them.

He wondered if maybe the cop was taking her around the streets, trying to get her to tag Barry, but that wasn't it. Neither of them was paying attention to the crowd.

He kept behind them all the way until they turned into the front entrance of the Acadian. It was the damnedest thing. They looked like they were calling it a night and going up to bed.

9

*A*s Shanks inserted his key card in the lock of the door to room 2250, Maggie stood beside him, wondering what he thought he was going to do next with her. All evening long, he'd behaved like she was little better than a whore. Now he would be acting on that assumption, expecting a pull on his chain as one of the services she provided for his ten thousand dollars. He would have a surprise coming.

But once he opened the door, he slipped the key card back in his jacket pocket and pulled out another, which he handed to her.

"You're next door," he said flatly.

"I am?"

Shanks entered his room and let the door swing shut—leaving Maggie alone in the corridor.

It took her a moment to consider what had just happened. At first she felt insulted somehow. Undesirable. But then she figured he was playing with her. He was the kind of guy who liked to give you little spins every once in a while, keep you on edge. Lots of guys were like that.

Mostly, though, she felt cheated out of her fun. There was nothing like pouring cold water on a guy with a hard-on. That would have been a kick. But she knew guys. Shanks would be scratching at her door before this was over.

She moved to her own room—2252—and opened the door.

It was a nice suite, just like Shanks's. Her luggage was out, the bed turned down, the same little mint on the sheets. There was a connecting door across from the bed and, as she noticed it, it opened.

And there was Shanks. His jacket off, his tie still on. He already had a drink in his hand.

Men. They were perfect.

"So," he said, "we have a deal?"

"Do you trust me?"

His black eyes raked her over.

"See you in the morning," he said. "Early."

And he shut his door. She heard the click of the lock from his side.

He's worried about *me* trying to get in?

Barry sat in the shadows of a doorway near the corner of Common and Carondelet, taking an occasional nip from his bottle of Early Times. Now he was wishing he had gone back and bought some more.

He could see his car. It was still parked right where it had been, halfway down the block from the hotel. It was just sitting there, a parking citation sticking between the wiper and the windshield. No Denver boot, no nothing.

He watched the cabs and limos pull in and out of the Acadian. It was well after midnight, so the flow had slowed down considerably. But there were still some high rollers coming and going. One couple looked like they'd just gotten back from a ball; the woman had one of those hooped skirts like Scarlett O'Hara wore. Except she was sixty years old and looked ridiculous.

Mainly, Barry looked for signs of the presence of cops. He didn't see anybody lurking around. After he saw Maggie and Shanks go inside the hotel, he went the long way around to the other corner at Baronne and staked out the Olds from that angle. There hadn't been anything going on that he could tell.

He was thinking it was time to go over to his car, see if he could just hop in and drive it away. But he was scared. He was afraid he'd be walking into a trap, that the whole fucking world would fall down on his head with flashing lights and sirens and police dogs.

He knew the odds against that were large, but he couldn't bring himself to make a move just yet.

Soon he'd have to do something, though. It was early April and the weather was still too cold at night. Besides that, he was running out of hooch. He couldn't see dawdling on this doorstep the whole night.

It struck him that anyone walking by would think he was a bum. At first he thought that was funny, then he didn't think it was so funny after all. He could picture a stranger tossing him two bits. Him with his dirty clothes, swigging from a bottle in a paper sack, huddled against a door. Hell of a way to end up. He wished he'd set aside some money, owned some property, something. He sure as hell wouldn't be getting no Social Security. He couldn't see his brother taking care of him. Not unless Barry popped Glenda for him, which he would gladly do in a New York minute.

But shit, he might have one more big score in him. Who could tell?

All it'd take would be a nice piece of change, then he could move out to Mexico, to Baja. There were a lot of military retirees living real cheap down along the ocean. He could supplement his income by running the occasional quack quickie on the widows, hustle them lifetime supplies of Wrinkle Remover or Immune Milk or Colono-Clenz or Cancer Salve; he'd done all that before, years ago. He could do it again. For that matter, he could marry one of them, some rich rear admiral's widow, if he had to.

Life still offered some possibilities; no sense blubbering in your bourbon.

He drained the last of the Early Times and raised himself up. It was hard work. His bones and joints ached after charging down the street and flopping around in the alley the way he had, and he was afraid something might be wrong with his knee. It was sore as hell. He stood in the doorway another couple of minutes, studying the Olds.

He didn't want to do this.

Increasingly, though, he was certain this wasn't a cop thing at all. As a general rule, cops don't cuff you, then take you out for a stroll in the French Quarter and up to a room in a fancy hotel before they book you. And he couldn't see the Acadian offering an hourly rate.

But if the guy wasn't a cop, what was he? How come Maggie

was diddling him? Had she worked all this out in advance, trying to get rid of him? She sure as hell wasn't the sort of girl to fall for a mark. Besides, coming to the Acadian was *his* idea, not hers.

He stepped out onto the sidewalk. There were no cars coming from either direction. The doorman at the Acadian was inside, leaning against the concierge counter.

Now or never.

Barry shuffled across the street to his car. Cautiously, he nosed around it, not knowing what he expected to find, a bomb maybe. He pulled the ticket off the windshield and tossed it to the pavement. Then he opened the driver's door and climbed inside. He depressed the accelerator, held it a beat, then slowly let up. It was the only way you could start the damn thing once it'd been sitting for a while.

He twisted the key and the engine turned over like magic. Barry backed up the Olds, cut the wheels, and got the hell out of there. No lights, no sirens, no dogs.

On Metairie Road, Barry spotted a bank with a drive-in ATM machine and a big AVAIL logo out front. He couldn't see any video camera so he pulled in and withdrew five hundred dollars of Bob Sarcominia's money using the access code Mrs. Sarcominia had helpfully provided.

Ten minutes later he stopped at a fleabag motel with a blinking VACANCY sign. He was at the front counter, scribbling his all-purpose Don D. Donaldson signature on the registration card, when he realized he had to go back to the Acadian. He wadded up the card and put it in his pocket. The clerk was absorbed in "The Patty Duke Show" and didn't even turn around to watch him leave. A hand-lettered sign above the TV said neither firearms nor cooking was allowed in the rooms.

Barry had to find out what Maggie was up to.

So he returned to the Acadian and found another parking space at the other end of the block. He hoofed it over to the Quarter to an all-night package store and bought a quart of Early Times, a carton of Winstons, a butane lighter, and a jumbo bag of Hot'n'-Spicy fried pork skins.

NINE

Back in the Olds, he settled into the front seat and tried to develop some theories on what was going down with Maggie, but his brain was fuzzy and he soon gave it up. Best approach, he felt, was to stay close and poke around when openings presented themselves. Either that or blindside Maggie, but until he had some facts, that wouldn't be too smart.

He got to wondering about big Jim Garrison, the ex–New Orleans DA who'd charged Clay Shaw with conspiring to assassinate the president. Barry had paid to see the movie they did about him; it was the first Hollywood movie he'd been to since *Rio Lobo*. He'd liked it well enough, but they missed so much of the big picture. They didn't say anything about the Masons, for example. Or Marilyn Monroe, who was in it up to her tits before they knocked her off for talking too much at the early stages. At one time Barry had kept a list of everyone connected with the assassination who had died of unnatural causes or in mysterious ways, but he'd lost it several years back. It was interesting, though. It was impossible to see that list and not believe there was a conspiracy.

Barry had an urge to look up Garrison's name in the phone book, maybe give him a call while he was in town. Barry had some interesting theories on the assassination that no one else had ever written about, to his knowledge. It would be great to talk to someone like Garrison about his ideas.

Suddenly there was a terrific thump on the roof of his car, like a brick falling on top of it.

Barry whirled around and saw a face pressed against the glass, inches away. It was an old guy, a bum. With his features mashed down, he looked like a carnival freak.

It scared the hell out of him.

The bum pulled back, leaving a greasy imprint on the glass.

He said, "Hey, buddy, help a fellow out?" The window was down about an inch, to keep the air circulating, and the old man's voice sounded raspy, like he hadn't talked out loud for a time.

"Get out of my face," said Barry.

The old man craned his neck back down, peering inside at Barry.

He said, "Hey, you know what's green and yellow and goes backwards?"

"Get the fuck outta here."

The bum answered his own riddle. He made a ghastly sound, as though sucking back snot.

Barry's adrenaline was pumping. "Jesus," he said, rolling up the window the rest of the way, "get away from me."

The old man cackled. He went around to the front of the Olds and banged on the hood with the palms of his hands, like he was playing bongos. Then he lumbered off into the night.

Inside Maggie's room there was only the glow of the TV, from which a stream of groaning and giggling emanated. She had finally pushed aside her magazines and macadamia nuts and turned out the lights and was tuning in on each of the pay movie channels. She knew they wouldn't charge you if you switched off before five minutes, but she didn't care, she wasn't paying. So she'd watch a movie for ten or fifteen minutes, then switch back to another one.

At two-fifteen a porno movie called *Spanked by Satan's Slaves* came on. As near as she could tell, it was about a cult of horny satanists loose in L.A. Actually, there wasn't much plot to speak of.

She knew this wasn't a bright thing for her to be doing because, despite the mechanical, loveless nature of the proceedings, watching it was beginning to make her horny. She had not been with a man in over a year. And that experience had been a mistake.

Maggie had been visiting her aunt in North Little Rock. A friend of her cousin's had dropped by, a spot welder, a good-looking young guy who sat at the kitchen table and sucked down beers. They got to talking about one thing or another, and the next day he called her for a real live date. Maggie didn't have anything better to do, so they went to a movie and then out for pizza. They ended up at his place and eventually in his bed. He had a Samantha Fox poster on the wall and he kept popping up and changing tapes like he was afraid she'd disappear if there was a lull in the New Age music. Maggie kept thinking he was going to play "Bolero." Afterward, he fell asleep and she lay there looking at him, thinking about marriage and what that kind of life must be like. Calling up Sears to come out and repair the garage-door opener, crap like that. She couldn't see it. The spot welder was smitten, though, and kept hounding her the next couple of days, eager for another bang, until she finally left town.

"Oh yes, yes!" said the actress on the screen. She played a convenience store clerk being ravished by one of the satanists, who sprouted little red horns and a tail during the sex act. The clerk was a tall, plain-faced young woman with enormous breasts and suck marks all over her neck, which the moviemakers hadn't attempted to cover up. "That's it!" the actress said. "That's it!" She looked like she was about to laugh and ruin the take.

Maggie wondered how much she had been paid to appear in this piece of shit. Whatever it was, it hadn't been enough. She felt like finding out who she was and calling her up and telling her there were better ways to earn a living.

She turned off the TV and watched the cathode ray tube flare out.

The thing to do, she told herself, is to get out now. Grab her bags and hit the door. That way she would be five thousand dollars ahead and Smiling Jack would be left holding his little leather-bound notebook and scratching his ass over the sudden drop in his bank account. She wasn't that worried about his threat to find her. Without Barry dragging her down, she could float away without a trace.

So why wasn't she taking off?

Same reason she would never commit suicide, she mused. She was too curious to learn how it all ended. Besides, she could jump off his train anytime. Might as well hang around for a few more stops.

Maggie looked at the inset passageway between the two rooms. Her door remained open, his shut. She swung out of bed and crept over to his door. She dropped to her knees and peeked underneath.

No light, no sound, nothing.

She stood and paced restlessly around the room, finally halting in front of the mini-bar. Sighing, she squatted down, opened it, and began picking through the goodies inside.

Only a few feet away, Shanks reclined on the chaise in the dark. The curtains were pulled back and a three-quarter moon beamed high above the river. He was still in his dress pants and shirt, with the sleeves rolled up and the tie loosened.

He was sipping from a glass of chilled vodka that he had placed in the refrigerator chest of the mini-bar some hours earlier. Next to him, on the glass tabletop, lay his notebook. He'd been over it page by page, made all the phone calls, figured it from every angle he could think of.

But he was losing faith in the plan. It was a little too complicated, he knew. At best, he estimated it had a fifty-fifty chance of working. It would either go off without a hitch or blow up in his face. He would end up either dead or alive—that's what it came down to.

A big problem, of course, was that success depended far too much on the abilities of the girl in the next room. And wasn't she a piece of work? A born hustler. But seeing her in the flesh, she wasn't exactly what he'd imagined. Not as brassy. She had a quality about her, a vulnerability he was sure she could manufacture at will, that had undoubtedly served her well throughout her career.

Maggie. Her name is Maggie. He realized he had a hard time thinking of her by her name. He supposed that was because if he thought about her as a person, he might not be able to do what he was about to do to her.

10

*F*ive hundred miles away, at a sprawling office complex in Norcross, Georgia, a bedroom community north of Atlanta, a man named Gordon Wexler sat at his computer. But his mind wasn't on the spreadsheet glowing on the screen in front of him.

He was thinking how, in two weeks' time, he was going to disappear. It was something he had been looking forward to for almost a year.

Gordon Wexler was a bright, obsessive accountant in his early thirties who had given his disappearance considerable thought. At home he had more than two dozen books, several stolen from the main library on Margaret Mitchell Square, on the subject of establishing a new identity. Over the past months he had managed, by the careful application of layer upon layer of paperwork, to slowly, painstakingly give birth to a new being—Max A. Zerle. A regeneration, actually, since the original Max checked out in 1960 at the age of ten days. Gordon's Max was a piece of refined work, a citizen of independent means. Unlike Gordon, with his bushy black hair and smooth face and thick glasses and perpetually knitted brow, his Max's passport and driver's license pictured a blond with close-cropped hair, dashing mustache, ready smile, and contact lenses. His creation now possessed a Social Security card, birth certificate, checking and money market accounts, library card, even a Gold Card. He leased a small riverfront home in Astoria, Oregon, with a new Chrysler LeBaron convertible sitting in its two-car garage. He was already receiving mail from Ed McMahon.

Once he transformed completely into Max, he would indulge in a round or two of plastic surgery, finally ridding himself forever of Gordon's longish nose and baggy eyes. Then, he felt, he would be finally and irrevocably Max.

Wexler was beginning to feel a little schizophrenic. Sometimes, in his dreams, he had already shed his old persona and become the snub-nosed, clear-eyed Max. Max was a tough, outdoorsy kind of guy, a man at home in the wild. He wore plaid shirts and fishing vests fitted with lots of small pockets; he always had a pipe clenched between his teeth. Women were attracted by his blunt manner, his air of mystery. Max could have all the women he wanted, in fact, and never have to pay.

Should the federal government ever elect to seize his property, Gordon Wexler kept Max's identity papers inside a ten-by-ten safe deposit box in the National Royale Bank of Montego Bay, Jamaica. And within forty-eight hours he would be retrieving them once and for all.

That action was one of only a half dozen remaining on his four-page disappearance checklist. The last was to destroy all his books and articles on changing identities.

His plan was this: On or about the first of May, he would vanish. He would ransack his place in north Atlanta, making it appear there had been a violent robbery. His empty wallet would be discovered in the bed sheets. However, he would leave more than two thousand dollars inside his wall safe, so that the police would figure the robber was dumb, a crackhead. Wexler would spill a small portion of his blood on the carpet near the front door, and sometime during the night he would walk out the door, leaving the radio alarm clock set for his usual six o'clock wake-up. He would start his unregistered garage-sale Moped and drive to the MARTA station at Chamblee, parking the bike near a housing project a few blocks away, the key hanging in the switch. Next, he would board a train that would take him, in forty minutes, to Hartsfield, where he would later board a Delta jet to Chicago. He would pay cash for his ticket, using an assumed name. At O'Hare he would take a room in the Quality Inn International Airport, bleach and trim his hair, then depart early in the morning, under still another phony name, for

Portland. And there, as Max A. Zerle, he would rent a car and drive to his new home and begin his new life as a multimillionaire. No one knew. Not his mother or brother, no one.

Fireworks were bursting on the monitor of his Macintosh SE. After two minutes of disuse, a special utility was programmed to automatically take effect. It produced pyrotechnic displays in order to prevent screen burn-in. Wexler watched the explosions for a moment, then popped open a plastic vial of white capsules. He dropped two in his mouth and washed them down with the remains of a Diet Dr Pepper.

It wouldn't take long for the uppers to kick in, and it wouldn't matter when they did. His main work for the night was accomplished. He just needed to make a couple of backup disks. He wasn't planning on sleeping tonight.

Gordon Wexler managed a small money-laundering operation for a hood named Albert Magliocco. Primarily, they washed mob cash from a pair of families who controlled the southeastern seaboard down to Miami. The income derived from traditional sources, loan-sharking and prostitution and numbers and the proceeds from hijacking.

Wexler and Magliocco didn't handle much drug money. Partly, that was because their clients didn't happen to have a piece of that action. And partly because drug money was growing progressively difficult to sanitize without drawing a lot of attention.

Magliocco, who first made his name hustling stolen gas-rationing stamps in Newark during World War II with Settemo Accardi's outfit, was under indictment by the United States Department of Justice for violation of the RICO statutes and had found it expedient to reside outside the country. Nobody within the gang knew exactly where he was at any given moment, not even Wexler. Mainly, he kept to a boat he owned in the Caribbean, shuttling between the Caymans and Curaçao and Jamaica and, some said, Haiti—places known to be a little lax on extradition procedures. Magliocco no longer took much interest in his criminal activities and preferred fishing for marlin and albacore.

Originally, the laundry business had been just a sideline, but in

Gordon's skillful hands, it had prospered. Last year it had earned Magliocco just under eight million dollars, and was now the principal source of his revenues. Wexler received a small percentage of the net after payoffs; not bad, but not enough, he felt, since he did all the work.

It was a complicated enterprise. It involved a number of rinse cycles including shell corporations set up in places like Panama and Luxembourg, and dozens of wire transfers that took place every day, switching money back and forth from front company to foreign bank. Currency fluctuations alone produced thousands of dollars a month. Wexler was the only one who knew what was going on; Magliocco accepted that fact, but he didn't like it.

Twice, Magliocco had brought in examiners to check the books. The first time it had been a nephew of another capo, a pimply-faced little college accounting major whose face went slack half an hour into the audit. He never understood what Wexler was explaining but he said that he did, and things went along swimmingly for a couple of years after that.

The next guy had a different style. An establishment type with silver-gray hair and designer suspenders, he uncapped his Montblanc pen filled with red ink and spent four days inside Wexler's office drinking mineral water and munching fruit and poring over everything. But in the end, he didn't comprehend stash accounting any better than the kid did, really. To earn his pay, he made a few suggestions to Magliocco, which the mobster didn't understand. Wexler genially agreed to put them into practice.

Basically, what Magliocco wanted to know was whether Wexler was skimming money or keeping two sets of books. And the silver-gray–haired guy said, no, he didn't find any evidence of that.

It was shortly after that experience that Wexler came up with his scheme. It, too, was complicated, but essentially it involved a bogus surcharge applied to wire transfers in and out of certain European countries. Wexler notified Magliocco of the "new regulations" but also told him it was too minuscule to worry about, just one of the problems of doing business in strange lands. Besides, the expense would be passed on to his clients. Magliocco, who had spent a lifetime greasing palms, had no problem.

What Wexler didn't mention was that frequently the same cash traversed the same country two or three times. So the surcharges, which ranged from .0065 percent to .0125 percent, started adding up. Wexler was now twenty-two months into the scam and had collected $3.28 million. He couldn't believe how effortless it was.

In the beginning, Wexler told himself that when he reached $3 million, he would split. Max could be reasonably happy with $3 million, he assured himself. And he knew he could hang around for another year—or until the silver-gray–haired man returned—and build the kitty up to twice that sum. Easily. In fact, if he had the balls, he could wipe out most of Magliocco's standing funds, amounting sometimes to as much as $40 million.

But there were some difficulties with that scenario.

The primary one was that Wexler was terrified of Albert Magliocco and his brother, Arthur. Albert had the street name of Headache, and Wexler had heard a dozen stories about how the name came about. All of them involved decapitation. Arthur had the nickname of Maytag because he was the brother who founded the laundry and ran it until he went to jail. At this moment he was languishing a few miles downtown in a cell inside Atlanta Federal Penitentiary, where, if there was a God, he would remain for at least the next six years for RICO convictions. Then he was supposed to be transferred to the state penitentiary for a two-to-seven-year hitch on aggravated sodomy. A prince of a guy.

So Wexler figured it would be best for all concerned if the Magliocco brothers retained what they believed to be all of their money. As long as they felt reasonably confident that Wexler hadn't skimmed off any of it, they probably wouldn't come looking for him. Although Wexler felt the mob was overestimated when it came to tracking people down, he didn't want to put his theory to a test.

However, Wexler's biggest fear was the United States government. In their pursuit of drug heavies, the feds were now knocking over dirty-money laundries every couple of days. In 1989 the DEA busted La Mina, the General Motors of washaterias, an outfit that had moved over $1.2 billion in greasy twenties and fifties in three years. With their high-speed money-counting machines clicking along twenty-four hours a day in tiny, airless L.A. hovels, the Colombians were literally getting sick on the fumes from all that cash.

More than $400 million had rotted away in a basement because they couldn't get it out of the country fast enough. The government documented the operation like a NASA moon launch, with thousands of feet of audio- and videotape detailing every step, and returned more than 120 indictments. Since then, they'd developed dozens of fresh ways to trap money movers—information-exchange treaties, a new division inside the Treasury Department, tougher enforcement of currency transaction reports from banks, lots of scary things.

Wexler felt his little world was imploding. His dreams were haunted by the image of men in FBI windbreakers crashing through the door and yelling at him to freeze. And if the government did manage to pick him up, he wasn't sure he would be able to rat out Magliocco. Not that he wouldn't try. In order to enter the witness protection program and avoid prison, he'd spill his guts to the first stenographer he saw, but the plain truth was that they might not be all that interested in what Wexler had to confess. They already had a case on Headache; they just couldn't find him. And Maytag was already in jail. So who did they really have to burn? Just Wexler.

The idea of twenty years in a federal pen, playing canasta with Maytag, spreading his cheeks for the Aryan Brotherhood, didn't appeal to Wexler. Even if he made it into the witness program, what kind of life would that be? Selling small appliances in Amarillo?

No, the time had come to get out of the business. And Max was the only safe way to pull it off.

Tomorrow he was leaving for Jamaica. He would arrive in the afternoon, snort some coke, sniff some pussy. Next morning Headache's boys would pick him up. He'd take a run on the boat, go over the books, chew the fat. He could already see Headache's bored look, the old man just going through the motions, basically just sizing Wexler up, making sure he could still trust him. Then they'd say so long, and Wexler would drop by the bank, pick up his papers, and fly back to Atlanta that afternoon.

And that would be the last he'd ever see of Albert fucking Magliocco.

Around three o'clock in the morning he heard something outside his office. An Anita Baker CD was playing, and between cuts there was a distant sound, like a cough. Wexler turned down the volume and listened.

The silence seemed absolute.

He tried to think of what else it could be. A passing car, the heating unit switching on, a radio somewhere—but nothing else made sense. It had sounded exactly like a human cough.

It bothered him. He knew he was the only person in the building, probably in the whole complex. On his wing he shared a reception area with an insurance appraiser and a utility consultant, but they were never around at this hour. The cleaning people had left hours ago.

And there it came again: a cough.

Then a throat clearing.

Since whoever it was wasn't making any attempt to muffle the sound, it was probably some office worker who had arrived either very late or very early. There was a small advertising agency located on the floor; they sometimes worked all weekend on a presentation.

Still, it put him on edge.

From his desk drawer he removed a Charter Arms .38 Special. Wexler loved guns and owned fifty or more, but he hadn't fired a round since the summer. He stood and walked to the door and listened again.

Nothing.

Slowly, he opened the door to the reception area. Sitting on a molded plastic chair, leafing through a *National Geographic* with the floor lamp turned on, was a man named Artie De Sola.

"Shit," said Wexler.

Artie put down his magazine but stayed where he was. He grinned when he saw the gun.

"You gonna draw down on me, computer man?"

Artie was a flunkie for a man named Tony Musta, an accomplice of Magliocco's. Wexler had seen him around and didn't care for him. He was a rock-and-roll wiseguy, with a little ponytail and a silver earring, and somehow he always managed to keep a two- or three-day growth of beard on his narrow, pasty face. He was hot-tempered and stupid and had ambitions of becoming a made man, but his connections apparently weren't that good. Tony once called him "Candy Ass," and that was the name people used when he wasn't around.

"Hey, if I'da known you was packing," he said to Wexler, "I'da brought along my own piece. Then we coulda showed each other our pieces, you know? I coulda felt your piece, you coulda felt my piece? That woulda been fun, huh?" As he was talking, he glanced around Wexler, who turned and saw another man standing behind him, someone he didn't know. The guy had been flat against the wall, shielded by the open door. Wexler, after seeing Artie, hadn't thought to check it.

"But I ain't packing," said Artie to his friend, smiling. "You packing, George?"

George was a big, blockish man, probably around fifty-five. He wore a threadbare sharkskin jacket, diamond pinkie rings, shiny polyester pants, and grimy two-tone loafers—a run-down Classic Mobster. A full mane of white hair swept around his skull and up into a spray-cast pompadour. Wexler noticed there was some kind of growth on his neck, just above the collar.

George didn't say anything. He was holding a big scuffed leather catalog case, the kind salesmen carried their samples in.

Wexler had the sinking feeling that he was going to be put away right then and there. Even though he was the only one holding a gun, he felt things still wouldn't be going his way. They were going to kill him and cut him up and pack him in the suitcase. He moved to his right, away from George, but still keeping his distance from Artie.

Wexler said, "What the fuck do you want?" He believed it was best to get your bluff in early with these schmucks.

"Got a little present for you," Artie said, still smiling. Artie liked scaring people; he was getting off on this. "George?"

The other guy made a move forward and Wexler raised his gun slightly. He felt a little dumb doing it. No one had threatened him yet. But George stopped, then slowly extended the suitcase toward Wexler.

Wexler didn't take it.

"What is it?" he asked.

"It's for your boss," said Artie. "For Headache, from Tony. Some laundry Tony wants cleaned and pressed. He cleared it with Headache."

"I can't do that, for Christ's sake. Taking cash out of the country is a fucking felony, he knows that."

"Tony says you do it right, they don't check you. Tony says you got a man on the line in Jamaica, he won't check you."

Dumb guineas.

Wexler slipped the revolver inside his waistband, feeling good about the way he did it but also half afraid he would shoot his nuts off. "Yeah, right. That's the way it's *supposed* to work. But what if Headache's man wakes up with a chest cold or a brain tumor tomorrow, huh? Decides he's not going in, wants to lay around and watch Vanna White change the fucking letters around. And I'm standing in line at customs with seventy pounds of dirty money, thinking, Oh, shit, this ain't the guy who's supposed to be there, supposed to be some other guy." He shook his head, walking back into his office. "I'm not doing it, no way. I'm not going down cause Tony Musta got a sudden itch to make a deposit, you can tell him that. We don't do that grab-and-carry shit anymore."

"That right?" said Artie, following him in. "You want me to tell Tony them exact words?"

Wexler dropped into his leather desk chair, wishing now he hadn't popped the Benzedrine. You didn't need to be that sharp talking with Artie, but he was nervous that he might miss a nuance, an exchange of glances between the two hoods. He wasn't out of the woods yet.

"Maybe we should go over there now," said Artie, "so's you can tell Tony to his face, just those words, how you don't do that grab-and-carry shit. Tony, he'd like to hear that, I bet, from a broke-dick computer hack. What'd you think, Georgie, think Tony'd get a rise outta that?"

Artie made a gun with his hand and pulled the imaginary trigger, smiling as the fireworks burst across Wexler's computer monitor.

Wexler felt the blood drain from his face. He didn't want any one-to-ones with Tony Musta. He rubbed his cheeks, acting like he was chasing away sleep.

Then Artie said, "Lucky for you, buttfucker, nobody wants you taking it down in the first place. George here is gonna take it. He's flying down with you."

"Him?" said Wexler. George didn't seem involved in the conversation. He loomed in the doorway, his expression blank, as though Artie and Wexler were speaking a foreign language.

"That's right," said Artie, still staring at the screen, grinning at the little explosions flashing everywhere. "Georgie's gonna mule it down. Gets to go to Jamaica, have his banana peeled by one of them beach niggers."

Wexler didn't like it. It complicated things. He never liked last-minute changes, but there wasn't much he could do about it.

Artie pulled himself away from the screen and strolled back toward the reception area. "You don't mind," he said, "George is going to keep you company, go down with you tomorrow to the airport."

Wexler glanced from George to Artie, then back to George. The thing on George's neck seemed like a boil or something. It was big and raw, with the skin peeling off around it. George smiled at him, showing the white, even teeth of dentures, smiling like he was looking forward to a trip on an airplane.

11

*T*he next morning at seven o'clock Shanks banged on the connecting door and informed Maggie that they would be going down for breakfast in one hour. She ignored him and fell back asleep. But fifteen minutes later he knocked again and insisted, drillmaster style, that she get up and get going.

He told her they had "an appointment" at nine-thirty.

They ate inside the hotel at a restaurant that fronted Canal. It was fashioned after a French brasserie, airy and elegant with dark beveled mirrors and mosaic tile flooring. Shanks seemed taken aback by Maggie's outfit: pleated linen shorts, espadrilles, and a burnt orange T-shirt with a bold-type message: DIE YUPPIE SCUM.

Maggie swooped down on the breakfast buffet like a greedy child, piling her plate high with scrambled eggs and croissants and fried bacon and melon slices and hash browns. Shanks sipped black coffee and watched her gorge.

Today, she noticed, he was wearing a standard-issue Seiko.

"What happened to your Rolex?" she asked.

"I sent it back."

Maggie looked at him curiously.

"It did what it was supposed to do," he said.

"You bought it just for our date, huh?" she said, amused.

"Tell me, you ever roll a guy wearing a Timex?"

She laughed. "I figure a guy's dumb enough to have five, ten thousand dollars hanging from his wrist, he deserves to wake up with a headache once in a while."

They left a little before nine. Outside, the world seemed bright and fresh, a dazzling spring morning. You could almost believe the sun had burned away the haze of scum that cloaked the city during the night.

They took a cab from the Acadian, heading up Common, then turning south on Baronne. That was when Barry lost sight of them. He was sitting at the counter of a coffee shop across from the hotel, watching them through the greasy plate-glass window. He noted the time on the Dixie beer clock above the grill, then dunked his last jelly doughnut into his coffee and gobbled it down.

Since they didn't bring out any luggage, Barry wasn't concerned they were leaving town. Taking a cab only meant they were going someplace that wasn't within walking distance, and then they would be coming back. He judged he had thirty minutes to an hour, minimum.

Barry picked up his check and moved toward the register. There were already two people ahead of him, waiting to pay their bills. The cashier, a heavyset black woman wearing a shower cap, was also doubling as the counter waitress and she was distracted by the chattering of the short-order cook. Barry slipped the check into his pocket and walked out the door. A bell jingled as he left but he didn't look back and nobody said anything or came running out after him, so he figured he was okay.

Since around six-thirty he'd been making passes through the Acadian's lobby and shopping arcade, looking for signs of Maggie and her boyfriend. He had even called the hotel, asking for Maggie, but they didn't have her registered. Finally, around eight-thirty, he'd glimpsed them eating breakfast inside the hotel. He watched them awhile from a window off the arcade, trying to read something in their actions, their body language. They could have been an old married couple for all he could tell. Afraid of being spotted, he returned to his station at the coffee shop, where he could observe both exits, and waited.

Now he hustled into the hotel restaurant and found the waitress he'd seen serving them.

"Excuse me, miss?"

Her name tag said LOUISE. She noted that his said DON. Louise and Don, having a conversation.

"Yes?"

"You were just waiting on a couple at that table over there, by the window? A tall gentleman with a blond lady?"

"Yes?" Louise was now staring at the bloodstains on his lapel.

"The blond lady is an associate of mine and I was supposed to join her and our new business prospect for breakfast, but, as you can see"—he pointed at his blood-smeared jacket—"I've had a terrible car accident."

Louise flinched.

"My problem is, *I* was supposed to pick up the tab for breakfast. It was supposed to be my company's treat, you see? I really can't let him pay for it; my boss would never forgive me. So what I'm asking is for you to just tear up his ticket, and charge it to my credit card. I know it's inconvenient for you, and I'm really sorry for the trouble, but I think I can make it worth your while with the new tip. Okay?"

"Put the whole thing on your card?" she said.

"That's right—and just tear his ticket up and throw it away. Can you do that for me?"

It took her a minute to retrieve the charge receipt, but she wouldn't let Barry examine it. Apparently she had been cautioned against giving out credit card numbers.

"I just want to verify it's the right ticket," said Barry. Actually, he had been hoping that the breakfast had been charged to the man's room, so he'd also have a number with the name. But he'd settle for the name.

"Mr. Shanks?" she said, reading off the yellow carbon. "John D. Shanks?"

"Spell it."

"Spell it? S-h-a-n-k-s?"

"Nah," he said. "That's not it." He turned and left the restaurant.

At around the same time that Bob Sarcominia was returning to consciousness inside his ransacked room in the Warwick Hotel, the woman of his dreams was getting her hair done in a small salon on Rampart called the Rape of the Lock.

Shanks had ushered her inside, saying only, "We have to do something about your hair." They were expecting "Mrs. Shanks" and escorted her to a private parlor in the back.

The hairdresser was a brassy-looking old crone with absurdly long silver-colored nails. She handed Shanks an auburn-hued paint chip, the type you would expect to see at Sherwin-Williams.

She said, "Is this the tint you prefer for your wife, Mr. Shanks?" Her voice was rather deep. Maggie began to suspect she might not have begun life as a female.

"Redder," said Mr. Shanks.

"Would you leave us alone for a minute," said Mrs. Shanks to the hairdresser.

When she closed the door, Maggie said, "What the hell is this all about?"

"I need you to be a redhead for a couple of days."

"Screw you. I don't want to be a redhead."

"It's part of how you earn your money. Day after tomorrow, you don't want to be a redhead anymore, you peroxide your hair back again."

Asshole.

"Why red? My skin doesn't look like a redhead's skin."

"Our boy isn't going to be looking at your skin. It'll be dark."

"Why not a wig? We could buy a wig."

"It'd look like a wig. It needs to look real. Don't worry about it."

Actually she didn't mind all that much. In fact, she'd always wondered how she would look as a redhead. Now she was being paid ten thousand dollars to find out, so she guessed she could go along with it.

What she objected to was the way this clown was treating her. It was like she was a hot car he was taking to Earl Scheib's for a ninety-nine-dollar one-coat special. No question that she would go along with the deal; he didn't even bother to ask.

He was so cocksure of himself. That was what ticked her off. He never doubted things would go his way.

But soon, very soon, she knew she was going to get to him. Crack open his plastic shell, see all the messy wiring below the surface. And then she was going to shut him down.

So she haggled some more with him, pushing for the fun of it. But he just sat there, smiling patiently at her, never raising his voice, in command for now.

Forty-five minutes later Maggie was a flaming redhead.

*　　*　　*

Barry felt the Acadian's registration area was too confining, with a fancy brass-and-glass waterfall taking up all the space. It was like working in an elevator. There were two marble counters at a right angle, one for checking in and one for checking out. Each was manned by a couple of young, sharply uniformed women.

Off to the right, beyond the waterfall, was another restaurant, this one a very ritzy establishment called Evangeline's. It was closed at this time of day, but just the other side of its entrance Barry spied a single, unused wall telephone.

From there he called the hotel and watched the smaller of the two women behind the check-in counter pick up the phone. She thanked him for calling the hotel and asked how she might assist him.

"Connect me with John Shanks, please."

"Would that be *Jack* Shanks, sir?"

"That's him."

After four rings, she came back on the line and told him what he knew: Jack Shanks wasn't answering.

"What room is he in?" asked Barry. "I forget."

"I'm sorry, sir, but we're unable to give out that information."

"I understand perfectly. And I appreciate the fact that your hotel practices that policy, I really do. It's very wise, these days. Could I perhaps leave a message for Jack?"

"Certainly."

He watched her pick up a pen.

"Tell Jack to call his mother."

"His mother?"

"Yeah, that's it. Have him call his mother."

"And your name, sir?"

Barry had already broken the connection. He was sprinting across the reception area to the registration desks. He arrived in time to see the little clerk tear the note from the pad and place it in one of the message slots on the top row. He wasn't close enough to read the numbers yet.

What was interesting to him, though, was that the slot already had something in it, an envelope of some kind.

His problem was that, at the moment, the place was deserted.

Nobody checking in or out. The two women behind the arrivals desk were just standing there clicking away at their keyboards. It looked like busy work to him.

So Barry went outside. He paced on the sidewalk a few minutes, thinking. He'd already allowed fifteen minutes to pass. He knew he had to make his move fairly soon.

Ten minutes later, standing inside by the phone and pretending to make another call, he got the opportunity he needed.

A stretch limo dumped a gaggle of Japanese tourists. Both clerks suddenly had their hands full.

Barry went up to the counter, pushing past the Japanese. He rapped on the counter as he read the number on the message slot.

"Jack Shanks. Room twenty-two-fifty. You got any messages for me?"

"Pardon me?" said the clerk.

"Shanks, twenty-two-fifty. I'm in a hurry, between meetings. You have any messages for me or don't you?" He drummed his fingers on the marble.

She handed him the contents of slot 2250.

Barry found a sofa by the concierge desk, hidden from the registration clerk but with a good view of the entrance. He wadded up the message to call Mom and shoved it in his side pocket.

The envelope held a pair of airline tickets for a Mr. and Mrs. Jack Shanks. The reservations were for this afternoon, a 3:15 departure on American flight 276A from New Orleans International Airport, bound for Sir Donald Sangster International Airport in Montego Bay, Jamaica.

Jamaica. Barry let out a low whistle.

He thumped the tickets against the palm of his hand, mulling it over, before finally replacing them in the envelope. Presently, when the front desk was again crowded and the clerk as harried as before, Barry reappeared. He slid the envelope across the countertop so that it fell to the floor behind the desk near one of the clerks. The clerk did not seem to notice, but he knew eventually she would come upon it. And then she would return it to slot 2250.

He moved on.

*   *   *

Gaping into the rearview mirror of the cab that was taking them someplace in the Garden District, Maggie wasn't pleased with the vision that confronted her.

"I look like a forest fire," she said.

Shanks didn't respond.

She kept staring at herself in the mirror until she noticed the Arab driver was also staring at her. She leaned back in the seat.

Shanks was making an entry in his ever-present leather notebook.

"You're not a bookmaker, are you, Jack?"

Again, nothing.

"Want me to check your spelling for you?"

He wasn't paying the slightest attention to her. She craned her neck a bit, to see what he was jotting down. Numbers, a series of numbers. He seemed to be adding up times. He was down to "7:30."

"Want me to take off my clothes and clog dance for you?" she asked.

He turned sheepishly to her, only half-aware she had been talking. There was a boyish quality about him, she decided. Maybe he was a kid hiding behind this tough-guy pose. Or maybe that was just wishful thinking. Maybe he was a psycho killer hiding behind this tough-guy pose. In America in the 1990s, there was no way to tell.

He finished whatever the hell he was doing and put away the notebook.

She said, "When do we have to leave town, mind if I ask?"

"Three o'clock."

"Ah. And where are we going now?"

"Need to buy you some equipment," he said distractedly.

"What kind of equipment is that?"

She'd lost him again. His eyes were focused on the dome light of the cab, but his mind was miles away.

The cab dropped them in front of a tiny shop sheathed in wrought iron. An elaborately painted sign with ornate, curlicue lettering read: *SECRET CURVES—Ladies' Foundations & Nocturnal Wear.*

As Shanks paid the driver, Maggie went over to the display window. On a background of crushed velvet lay an arrangement of vintage lingerie, the kind she imagined the old Storyville whores used to wear.

Most of the case, though, was taken up with a selection of foam rubber falsies.

"Nobody's ever criticized my equipment before," she said to Shanks.

He sighed wearily. "Look, our pigeon likes babes, you under-stand? Big-breasted redheaded babes are what makes his saliva drip. That's what we're trying to do here: make him lose his good sense and start scratching himself and rutting around after you so it never crosses his mind that his gin and tonic all of a sudden tastes a little funny. Your look is too classy for this guy—you have to drop down to his level for a day, okay?"

"You really think I have a classy look?" she said, and then regret-ted it.

Shanks opened the door.

"Think *babe*."

Maggie did an exaggerated sexpot wiggle into the shop. She couldn't tell whether he was amused or not. And she wondered why she cared.

Barry was looking down the hallway at a cleaning cart parked outside the open door of room 2240. He'd had his eye on it for some time now. Whenever any doors opened or people appeared, he would launch down the corridor, striding purposefully like he had some legitimate business being there, always returning to the cart.

At first, he'd hoped to boost a set of passkeys, but he didn't see any hanging on the cart. Then he noticed it was all done with plastic. The maid apparently kept her card on her person.

Timing the maid, he discovered it was taking her anywhere from eight to twenty-two minutes to clean a room. The corner suites didn't seem to take any longer than the regular rooms.

This maid was five doors down from Shanks's suite, 2250. Barry calculated he had at least forty minutes to go before she made it there, then he'd want to give her another eight minutes or so tidying up in the room. He hoped Shanks was neat. He fantasized about the two of them, Shanks and Maggie, tearing up the place with their lovemaking. Collapsing the bed and knocking down lamps, with big bottles of baby oil leaking into the carpet, and the manager having to come up and write out a report on the damage.

Get a handle on it, he told himself. Still, he couldn't imagine what was going on here. Did she latch on to a rich john, one she couldn't let go of? Was the guy a cop or not? If not, what was he doing with a set of bracelets? Was she being held against her will? No way—he saw how they were acting at breakfast. She wasn't worried about anything except whether she could go back for seconds.

He couldn't shake the feeling that it was a setup, Maggie looking to cut him out of the action, but he kept butting up against the fact that he was the one pushing the Acadian. She had wanted to call it quits for the night. It just didn't add up.

Someone came out of a room, right in front of him. A little girl about eight or nine, looking like a miniature Madonna with ruby red, bee-stung lips. Barry bolted down the hallway, feeling dumb. He realized he couldn't keep doing this. Someone would report him for a short eyes. Better to go back down to the lobby, look around the shops, kill some time, then come back in half an hour.

There was a serious problem with his plan, though. By then it would be almost an hour and a half since Shanks and Maggie had left the hotel. A long time, way over the thirty to forty minutes he'd allowed for this. And even if they were still away when he came back upstairs, the two of them could pop in at any minute. There he'd be, old Barry, checking under the bed, his butt in the air.

They'd have a lot to talk about then, wouldn't they?

Maggie said she was hungry again. After his purchase of a set of 36D polyurethane falsies, Shanks wanted to return to the hotel but she wouldn't give in. "I'm hypoglycemic," she told him. "I gotta have food all the time." But she wasn't hypoglycemic; she wasn't even that hungry.

Stopping to eat wasn't part of his plan, and she liked that. She felt it was important to force him off his agenda whenever she could; it gave her a shot at tripping him up. Maggie suspected Shanks was pretty good at thinking on his feet, but she believed she was better.

After all, she didn't have to check a notebook to figure out what to do next.

So she told him she wanted to go to Audubon Park, just down the block, and find something to eat there, maybe inside the zoo. A hot dog, maybe.

"We don't need to go to a park to eat," he said. "There's lots of places on the street here."

"I'm eating in the park," she said, and sashayed across St. Charles, right in front of a streetcar packed with tourists. She didn't even need to look back to see if he was following after her. What else could he do?

It was a good feeling, she decided. Putting the spin on him.

Each town Maggie visited, she liked to see the sights. During the day she would grab a cab or a bus and tour the planetariums and aquariums, the cycloramas and the out-of-the-way museums. In the last month alone she'd seen Mud Island in Memphis and Twitty City outside Nashville. She'd never been to the zoo in New Orleans, but today was as good as any.

"We don't have time for this," he said, catching up. He had the large pink Secret Curves sack in his hands and you could tell he felt a little silly holding it.

"You said we didn't leave till three. We can make it." Did he think she was going to beg him to go to the zoo, like some kid? What he didn't understand was, she was a twenty-five-year-old independent woman with more than seventeen thousand dollars saved up and no debts. She was a woman of substance. She didn't have to put up with shit. She didn't have to put up with anything she didn't want to.

12

*I*nside Shanks's room the maid was humming and moving around. She'd been in 2250 almost six minutes, the door wide open. Barry had walked past the room once and glanced inside; the bed looked like it hadn't even been slept in. The maid was emptying a wastebasket, her back to him. She would be finished soon.

He took a deep breath and marched past the laundry cart and into the room.

"Hi ya," he said to the maid.

"I be out in a minute, sir," she said apologetically. She was Hispanic, built like a small tractor.

"Take your time, take your time. I forgot some stuff. Had to come back."

He was all smiles, striding through the room like it was his ancestral home. He removed his jacket and draped it over a chair by the writing desk. There was a briefcase on the desk and he tried the catches. It opened nicely. He sat down in the chaise, plopped the briefcase in his lap, and began rummaging inside.

The cuffs were there, inside a black leather pouch. Barry had a certain familiarity with handcuffs, but when they're locked behind you, you don't get too good a view of them. In any event, these didn't look like any he'd ever encountered before. They were stiff-hinged, not the traditional chain-link kind he was accustomed to. They bore the manufacturer's mark—HIATTS OF ENGLAND—and folded flat in the pouch.

A plain white envelope contained the reservation receipt for a double room at the Lucinda Resort Hotel in Montego Bay, Jamaica, in the name of Jack Shanks.

For one night only—tonight.

That either meant the score was going down tonight, which was unlikely, or that they needed to move someplace else on the next night. But there weren't any other hotel reservation slips in the briefcase.

There were several ballpoint pens, a yellow highlighter, a blank legal pad, and a Shell Oil map of the southeastern United States. He opened the map and found something interesting: each of the cities he and Maggie had hit in the last two weeks was circled, with the route they'd taken highlighted: Raleigh, Charlotte, Knoxville, Nashville, Memphis, Jackson, New Orleans.

He refolded the map, after a couple of tries. He hated folding maps.

Wint-O-Green Lifesavers. A pad of checks for a bank in Virginia, with no name or address, and no register.

And that was it.

"Thank you, sir," said the maid.

"No, no, thank you. You do good work."

She shut the door and he checked his watch. 11:45. He was already way, way over his time limit. He had to work fast.

Maggie found she was more interested in Shanks than in any of the other animals at the zoo, except maybe the rhinoceros. At her suggestion, Shanks bought her a banana-coconut snowball after she ate her two corn dogs. When he admitted he'd never had a New Orleans snowball, she insisted he try one, which he did grudgingly. She kept trying to draw him out in conversation, get him to reveal something, but he never took the bait.

Now they were strolling past the primates, about to leave. She could tell he was edgy, ready to get on with it. She was afraid he was bored with her. Not many men had found her boring.

She said, "You know, I'm beginning to think this is all just some kind of sicko perversion of yours. You abduct young women and trick them into changing their hair color and wearing false body parts. It's how you get off."

Shank smiled, but said nothing.

"How *do* you get off, Shanks? What is it? Women? Money? Professional football? Cross dressing?"

"How'd you hook up with Bernie?" he asked.

So maybe he was a little interested.

"Him? I was running an airport scam in Orlando. The catsup scam, you know it? I'd come up behind a businessman, splat him on the jacket with catsup, from one of those squeeze packs, you know? Then, friendly me, I'd point out to him that he had some sort of stain on his jacket, help him take it off, tell him some cute little 'Hints from Heloise' tip on how to clean it—"

"While you lifted his wallet?"

"That's it."

"So picking pockets is one of your skills?"

"It's no big deal," she said. She thought then of a man she'd known as a child, an elderly dwarf known as the Goat Man because his head was shaped roughly like that of a goat, with big floppy ears. To accentuate the resemblance, he also wore a long white goatee. The Goat Man had spent countless hours with Maggie inside his old Airstream trailer, training her on a department store mannequin, instructing her in the art and science of picking pockets—the coat lift, fanning the inside pockets, razor slitting, everything. After each session, he would make her a glass of chocolate milk and climb into his Barcalounger and tell her the stories of his travels.

Shanks actually smiled at her then. Maggie noticed for the first time that little dimples formed when he smiled. She would have to discuss them with him when an opportune moment arrived.

"Anyway," she said, "Barry, or Bernie, whatever you want to call him, he was running the same scam, same airport. I saw him pull a job, walked up to him, told him I was airport security. I have a badge, did I show you my badge? I found it on a guy who owned a private investigating agency, guy I picked up in . . . Kansas City, I think it was. I flashed my badge at Barry and I really thought he was going to cry. I made him hand over the wallet and told him to sit right there, I'd be back for him. Soon as I turn the corner, of course, he's gone. Hour later, he's halfway to Tampa and he finally figures it out, comes back looking for me. He didn't think it was as funny as I did, but he had a proposition for me. He tells me how a smart girl like me can make five hundred, a thousand bucks a night, without half trying. He was right."

"But what do you need him for?"

"Lately, I've been wondering about that myself," she said. In fact, she'd given it a lot of thought. Barry wasn't good company, but he *was* company. He didn't paw at her and he was somebody to talk to. He had a lot of interesting stories about old-time scams, when you could get him off that Kennedy assassination crap. But what it really came down to was that sometimes you just needed to latch on to a person, go a few miles with them, pretend you were part of the species. Otherwise you'd go crazy.

"I guess I felt I owed him something," she said lamely, "for teaching me the trick. I don't know."

"What is he, good in bed or something?"

Maggie pulled up.

"I wondered when that was coming," she said. "You've been panting to ask that since last night, haven't you? Guy like you, you had to know. Well, just so you'll be able to sleep nights, I'll tell you: Barry and me, we have a strictly professional relationship. Besides, you wouldn't believe how bad his breath can get." She could read the doubt in his face. "And I don't care if you believe me or not. You have a problem, don't you? What is it with you?"

Shanks made a "let it pass" gesture and continued walking. Out on their little island sanctuary, the monkeys chattered away.

"You think you're too good for me, Jack? Is that it? You afraid you might soil your uptown hands, you associate with me?"

"We're different people, Maggie. Not better or worse, just different. Let it go at that."

"I don't know what kind of world you live in, Jack, but it's not the one I'm swimming in. In my world, guys are always trying to hustle me. *Always.* They want something for nothing, you know? My money, my body, my love, whatever I've got, they want it. But they don't think they have to give me anything back. It's a hustle. So I hustle them right back. I'm just better at it."

"Except it's illegal, the way you do it."

"Laws are made by men for men. What do they know?"

She couldn't tell, but she thought he might be feeling it was a mistake bringing up Barry. What is it with me? she wondered. I try to get him to talk and when he does, I jump all over him.

"You never answered my question," she said, trying another tack. "What turns on an Ivory Snow kind of guy like you?"

"I like to pick up felons in bars."

"See, that's how come I'm worried you're a cop. Regular guy, he'd say *crooks*. *Felons* is cop talk. If you're a cop, by law you gotta tell me that's what you are. Making me do this, it's illegal, if you're a cop."

"It's illegal even if you're not a cop."

"You know what I mean. It's . . ."

"Entrapment?"

"Yeah. I bet you say things like *alleged perpetrator*, too, don't you?"

"Let's go."

Maggie stopped again, looked up at him.

"Tell me you're not a cop," she said.

"I'm not a cop."

"Mean it."

"I'm *not* a cop, okay?" he said, looking her straight in the eye. "You can get that out of your head."

She didn't really think he was a cop. It was just that she couldn't figure out what else he could be.

A forlorn-looking female gorilla sat behind the bars of her cage. Her disposition seemed to match Maggie's at the moment.

"I identify with her," she said.

"You don't change your ways, you'll end up just like her."

"Getting screwed by big apes?"

"Behind bars."

Barry was more than a little embarrassed when it finally dawned on him that none of Maggie's things were in Shanks's room. Last night, in the parking lot of that crummy motel he'd almost stayed in, he had checked the trunk of the car and discovered all her luggage was gone. That meant, of course, that she had another room in the hotel. Looking over at the connecting door, he had a good idea where it was.

So he tossed her room, too, not sure what he'd find. Tucked away among the lingerie still inside her suitcase he found close to eight hundred dollars in tens, fives, and singles—and that caused him to sit down for a second and rethink the situation. He could cash out now and be eight bills ahead, risk free. And that would be a good, solid plan. It'd serve that little bitch right. Problem was, that way he couldn't horn in on the big guy's scam—*if* he had a fucking scam. By swiping the money now, Maggie would know it was him; from then on, they'd be looking over their shoulders for him. That'd be the end of it.

He was forced to make a decision. Looking at the digital clock on the phone console, he sat on the bed, transfixed, not knowing what to do. Common sense told him to take the money and run. That's what common sense had always told him to do.

But, somehow, he felt big bucks were just around the corner. In Jamaica. He didn't know why, but he had one of those feelings you get, just before a top-of-the-mark score. There was something big going down and he wanted to be in on it. Who knew, there might be enough money to retire on. You couldn't tell. After all, he had a big advantage here, if he played it right: surprise. They didn't know he was still hanging around.

Worst thing that could happen, he'd be out a couple hundred bucks and a few days in the sun. Might come back with a sunburn and a dose of the clap.

He put the money back inside the suitcase.

And immediately, he knew he'd done the right thing.

Because when he walked back into the other room he was overwhelmed with the suspicion that Jack Shanks had a secret and it was hidden somewhere in his room. Everybody had their secrets, didn't they? There was something clearly missing in the briefcase and the furniture drawers and the clothes pockets, something glaring in its absence. There was nothing whatsoever that told who the son of a bitch was. No business card or appointment calendar or address book, nothing.

But it had to be there.

Six minutes later, running his hand along the underside of the center drawer of the writing desk, he found it. A manila envelope taped along the bottom.

"Bingo!"

It was thick and heavy, secured only by a single brad. The flap hadn't been sealed. He spilled the contents on the bed.

There was an apparatus with wires and a small microphone. He held it up, dangled it, set it down. It looked to him like a wire, some kind of body mike. He didn't know what to make of it.

The next item, though, held significantly more interest. It was a black leather ID case. A single-fold, like police detectives carry. Barry flipped it open and saw a red-white-and-blue government seal that read DEPARTMENT OF JUSTICE and FEDERAL BUREAU OF INVESTIGATION. It had stars and stripes and a set of scales and stalks of wheat and more words written underneath a wavy banner: FIDELITY, BRAVERY, INTEGRITY.

In the lower half of the case was a laminated plastic ID card and a bronze badge. He read the name JOHN DENNIS SHANKS and saw the words SPECIAL AGENT. There was a color photo. He looked about five, ten years younger, but it was the same guy. It was Shanks, all right.

On the way back to the Acadian they stopped at a bank so that Maggie could purchase a money order. With the down payment from Shanks and the other cash she had been carrying around, she had a tidy sum to send to her aunt.

In the hotel corridor, Shanks told her, "The bellman will be up in thirty minutes. You need to be ready to go."

Maggie followed him into his room. She didn't want to bother with the rigamarole of unlocking her own door. She could go through the connecting doors. Also, she wanted to get a look at his room, see if there was anything interesting lying about.

"You going to tell me where we're going?" she asked.

"Jamaica," he said, watching her face.

"The Jamaica in New York or the Jamaica in the Caribbean?"

"The one in the Caribbean."

She didn't know what to think about that. She acted calm, though, turned her back to him and strolled around his room. Neat as a pin. An orderly room for an orderly man.

Jamaica.

She hadn't counted on anything like that. Was that good or bad?

She had never been out of the country before, except for a weekend escapade in Nuevo Laredo when she was in her teens, but she liked to travel. Jamaica sounded like an interesting place. But the rules weren't the same there, were they?

"Don't get excited," he said. "We blow in, we blow out. We don't futz around on beaches or lap up rum punch."

"Who's excited?"

Maybe you're not going to futz around on beaches, Jack Shanks.

He opened the connecting door, ushering her out of his room. A most peculiar man, she thought. He turned it on and off. Last night, smiling and intimate. Today, after he'd signed her up, he was all cool and businesslike. He wanted to get on with it, get it over with. Get rid of her.

She passed through the passageway, closing her own door behind her.

Maggie flopped on her bed. She caught a whiff of something— alcohol? Cleaning compound, no doubt. Or maybe the maids were hitting the miniatures in the mini-bar.

Shanks was getting under her skin and she wondered why. She wanted him to like her—that was it. Men always liked her, that was how she made her living. Shanks wasn't behaving like a mark and he wasn't behaving like a partner. And if he wasn't a mark or a partner, what the hell was he?

She realized what she wanted was another goddamn smile. He had a killer smile, it transformed his face. When he smiled he looked human. When he didn't smile, he scared her a little.

She sensed that the more he smiled at her, the better her chances were in this little scheme of his.

Or was it his approval she wanted? Why? Who was he that she should worry whether he liked her or not? Who gave a rat's ass?

And suddenly she feared she was going to cry. She would rather cut her throat with nail clippers than cry.

She was acting like a goddamn kid.

She pushed open the connecting door.

Shanks was in his underwear, sitting in a chair by the writing desk. His hand was under the desk, as though he was dropping some trash in the wastebasket. When he heard her enter, he jerked around, surprised, and she saw it wasn't trash in his other hand, it was something else. A manila envelope.

"Relax," she said. "I won't hurt you."

You could tell he felt a little silly. She had caught him off guard. For a moment, he kept the envelope half-hidden under the desk, like he didn't want her to see it, but then he went ahead and pulled it out, trying to act natural. She saw it had tape all over it.

His stash. She laughed aloud.

"What do you want?" he said, recovering. He dropped the envelope in his suitcase, now making no attempt to conceal it.

But there he was, the great man, standing in his ribbed, white cotton Fruit of the Loom briefs, a little embarrassed.

Maggie figured she was one up on him. It was a nice feeling.

She said, "Guy I used to know, he was, what d'ya' call it—a sociopath. He lived to lie. You could ask him what day it was and he'd say Monday even though he knew it was Tuesday, just to see if you'd believe him."

Shanks walked over to the closet and picked out a pair of pants. He was surprisingly muscular. She liked the way the muscles moved along the lower part of his back. It was obvious he worked out, and that was something she wouldn't have guessed about him.

"One time," she said, "we're sitting around his apartment and this guy, he's bored, you know, so he picks up the phone and calls information and gets the number for a hair salon, okay? He tells the owner he's with the government and convinces the man to give him the names and telephone numbers of the women that came in that morning. Then he calls up these women and tells them he's with the United States Department of Health, Education, and Welfare, whatever, and there's a serious problem with the hair rinse this place used on them and now they are highly contagious and subject to a potentially fatal brain disease. An inspector is coming over to quarantine their houses, okay? Then he tells the women the only way to save themselves is to immediately shave off *all* their body hair and put it in a sealed paper sack and set it outside their front door for the inspector to pick up so he can take it to the lab and run some tests, okay?"

Shank had his pants on now and there was an air of concern in his eyes.

"So this guy," she continues, "my boyfriend at the time, he does this to six women until he gets bored with it. Then we hop in the

car and drive by all six houses. Five out of the six have paper bags
sitting outside the front door. Next day it made the front page of
the newspaper. They interviewed one of them, this little yuppie
woman, on TV. Real pissed off, she was, bald as a wall."

Shanks said, "Is there a point to this story?"

"Yeah. See, at the time I thought it was the greatest thing that
ever happened. I thought my boyfriend was a genius. I was seventeen, you understand. The idea that you could just pick up the
phone and get people to do *anything*—it was incredible. Then I
started to think about it and saw how stupid it was. He didn't get
anything out of it—no money or anything. Just the pleasure of being
. . . cruel. And that's when I knew I had to leave him. I knew I'd
never, ever be able to trust him. I knew he was the kind of guy
would lie to me same as to the marks. He'd lie to *anyone*, no distinc-
tion. And the point is, I'm beginning to think you're the same kind
of guy. I don't trust you."

There, she'd gotten it out.

"Are you setting me up for something, Jack? Huh?" She moved
closer to him and realized she wanted him to kiss her. It shocked
her. "Lie to me, make me believe you."

But he started bringing over some shirts and things on hangers
and setting them on the bed next to his open suitcase.

"We don't need to trust each other," he said, not looking at her,
packing the clothes in the suitcase. "We can still do business. It's
the American way."

"Do you trust me, Jack?"

He stopped his packing.

"Maggie," he said coldly, "I think you run scams in your head
from the moment you get up until the moment you go to sleep.
And when you sleep, you dream about new ways to con old ladies
out of their life savings. That's your profession, tricking people into
trusting you. I can say I trust you but I don't, so why should I say
it? You want something to trust, trust the five thousand dollars I
gave you."

"You're no better than I am," she said.

He returned to his packing, his face a blank. He *did* think he was
better. That arrogant asshole.

She didn't know what to say. She burst out of his room.

TWELVE

In her own room she paced the floor, furious, wanting to destroy the Acadian's posh little suite. To absolutely trash it, to claw the wallpaper and set fire to the bed.

But instead she returned to Shanks's room.

"I want you to know something," she said to him. "I never stole anybody's life savings, ever."

"Okay."

"I wouldn't do that."

Once upon a time, Maggie dated a cop who had arrested her on a theft-of-property warrant. On the stand he stated he had failed to read her her Miranda rights, even though he had, and the case was dismissed. In the hall outside the courtroom he asked her out. One night, he told her that what he hated most about his job was dealing with an EDP, an emotionally disturbed person. Their brains just weren't wired the same way ours were, he said, and you felt sorry for them because they weren't crackheads or criminals, they were just screwy. But they could end up killing you just the same, if you weren't careful.

That was the way Shanks was looking at her now, she thought. Like she was a goddamn EDP and he had to be careful around her because there was no telling what she might do.

Maybe that was good.

She made a point of slamming both the connecting doors this time, but it didn't really work. The doors were so close together that the suction destroyed the effect she was going for. It came off a little feeble.

She couldn't even slam a door, for Christ's sake.

13

*M*aggie had once read an article in *Reader's Digest* about a flight attendant who was sucked out of a jet. The cabin door came loose or something and out she went. It took her forever to hit the ground. Maggie couldn't recall the point of the story, though. No one saved the woman, she just fell to earth and died.

Anyway, leaning back in her window seat, Eddie Van Halen booming in her earphones, she considered what that particular sensation might be like. What would go through your mind, she wondered, during the half hour or so it took you to reach the ground? Would you think about your life and the different ways you'd screwed up, or would you just pee all over yourself and scream the whole way down?

You never knew what you'd do, of course, but Maggie couldn't see herself just screaming and peeing. She liked to think she'd try to get something out of it once she accepted the inevitable, maybe skydive a little, do some figure eights, anything, before she went splat.

Next to her, Shanks was resting. He'd lifted the armrest between the aisle and center seats, and drifted off to sleep. His forehead was pressed against the edge of Maggie's seat and his lips were parted, moving slightly as he breathed. She studied the sharp planes of his face, the light sprinkling of gray around his temples, the tiny scar on his chin. It was an interesting face. Maggie couldn't imagine Shanks screaming and peeing on himself either.

Probably, if she asked him what he'd do in a situation like that, he'd frown and tell her that a person would just turn blue and die

from the lack of oxygen or the air pressure or the freezing tempera-
tures, or whatever the hell caused people to turn blue when they
fell out of airplanes. He'd know things like that.

Maggie adjusted the volume of the music and thought what a
nice-looking couple they made. That was what her aunt would say
if she saw them. Watching him sleep, Maggie wondered what it
would be like to lie beside him in bed, to wrap herself around his
body and rub against the muscles of his back.

Jesus Christ. Get a grip.

Then she noticed his leather notepad protruding from his inside
jacket pocket. The way Shanks was turned, half on his side, the
jacket bulged open around the chest. The weight of the notepad
caused it to spill forward a bit. Just enough.

Maggie had always had a hard time with temptation and this was
more than she could comfortably cope with. This was what the
Goat Man would call a cream puff. She eased her hand into the
fold of his jacket and, without any difficulty at all, sprang the notepad. The two-finger snag. She held it in the air a moment, watching
his eyes, then set it in her lap.

Dropping her earphones down to her shoulders, she opened the
notepad. Tucked under the inside-cover flap were some pieces of
folded paper. She pulled them out and opened them and saw the
first one was an arrest sheet for Barry. It was a fax, printed on that
slimy, coated paper they used. At the bottom of the page she could
read the date it had been faxed—three months before.

She read the top paragraph:

*LANDERVAAL, Bernard L., AKA Bernard (Bernie) London, Barry
Landers.*
DOB 12-14-35, MW 5-8, 210#, brn Newark, NJ
No out wrnts. Photo at CAS.

There followed a lengthy arrest record in small, almost illegible
computer type. The first entry was for theft by shoplifting, June
14, 1951, Jersey City, New Jersey. She scanned the others: forgery
in the first degree, credit card theft, credit card fraud, making a
false statement as a telephone solicitor, theft by deception, theft by

receiving stolen property, uttering, entering an automobile with intent to commit theft, dumping.

Dumping? *Dumping of litter on public property, 9/12/78, Norwalk, Connecticut. Suspect fined $50, no jail sentence.*

It went on: Felony burglary, fraud, fraud, etcetera. Twenty, twenty-five convictions in all. It listed the sentences and dispositions. Barry had served time in places all over the country, from Soledad in California to Angola in Louisiana. Definitely a career criminal.

The next sheet took her breath away: it was *her* arrest record.

ROHRER, Margaret Cummings
DOB 1-13-66, FW 5-8, 118#, brn Denton, TX
No out wrnts. Photo at CAS.

Her sheet was considerably shorter than Barry's, but then she was younger. Four arrests, two convictions.

Theft by shoplifting, 9/1/82, North Little Rock, AR. Instantly, the whole episode opened before her like rotten flooring giving way. She could remember the stifling, windowless office in the back of the Woolco store as they waited for the police to arrive, and the sign tacked to the unpainted dryboard wall: SHOPLIFTING IS *NOT* A PRANK! SHOPLIFTING IS *NOT* A THRILL! SHOPLIFTING IS A *CRIME*!! The assistant manager wore a clip-on Razorback tie and smelled of English Leather. Maggie and a girl named Janice Culpepper used to hit the store every afternoon after school, when they bothered to go to school. They usually nicked makeup or costume jewelry but this time Maggie had reached behind a display case and snatched a Seiko watch. A cashier chased her down in the parking lot.

Her bewildered aunt and uncle were forced to come down to the station house and post bail. Maggie had been living with them for two years. Before then, she had knocked about on the carny circuit with her mother, Eloise, who ran low-end grab joints. They lived out of a trailer with a man named Earl Dodd, a patchman who greased the sheriff's hands and settled disputes on the midway. He was a smooth-talking, back-slapping man who turned mean when he went on a binge, which was every six to eight months. Around the time Maggie turned fourteen, he began to find opportunities to feel her up, and her mother, a simple, sad-eyed lush, packed Maggie off to visit her sister. Maggie never saw Eloise again. In 1984 she gouged her wrists with a potato peeler and lay down in a tub of water and never got up again. She was thirty-six. Her only legacy to her daughter was a deep-rooted horror of abandonment, a failing that had driven Maggie into a series of disastrous romantic entanglements.

Maggie didn't know who her father was, and was never really sure her mother did, either. Eloise had always kept her maiden name, Rohrer.

Maggie's aunt and uncle were decent, churchgoing people but, after the Life, she found day-to-day existence with them intolerable. She ran away several times, eventually succeeding after her return from the Arkansas Girls' School, where she spent nine months following the Woolco incident.

She had been on her own now for eight years.

Her aunt Nancy and cousin Susan were now the only relatives she knew about, Uncle John having died of a stroke. Once a year Maggie made a point of going to see her aunt. They went shopping at McCain Mall, or sometimes drove out to a commercial catfish pond; her aunt loved to fish when she knew she was going to catch something. After partnering with Barry, Maggie had started sending money for Aunt Nancy to set aside. It was now starting to add up.

Looking at the arrest sheet, it occurred to Maggie that she had started out just like Barry, on a shoplifting charge. At the same age, too. Sixteen. It was a depressing thought.

Issuance of bad checks, 12/22/86, Tulsa, OK. That put her into McAlester for six months, then out for two months on parole, then back in for four months for violation of parole because she consorted with a known criminal. That was when she was living with Jimmy, a thirty-eight-year-old hot-check artist who snatched Maggie out of the Trade Mart in Dallas, Texas, and taught her the art of kiting. It took her a couple of weeks to realize he was a psychopath and then another year to dump him. A bad time.

Theft of property, 10/10/88, Shreveport, LA. That was the cop who decided he cared more about making it with Maggie than about making his case. Ralph was his name, a property crimes officer. She wondered what he was doing now, if he was still a cop.

Theft by deception, 5/8/89, Kansas City, MO. Arrested by the head of the bunko squad himself, but they didn't nab her partner, a girl named Allison Delillo. They were running a distraction scam but the victim, an advertising account executive named Teddy something, refused to prosecute. She never knew what happened to Allison.

And there it was, her life as computer printout. This is what the world knew of her. Shoplifting, bad checks, theft.

She looked over at Shanks, breathing as gently as a baby. This sheet of paper, she thought, was what Shanks thought of her. A tramp.

She liked to kid herself that she was an independent woman, making her way in life on her own terms. Nobody's fool.

Suddenly she felt small and nasty and miserable.

Idly, she flipped through the pages of Shanks's little book, not really paying any attention. One page had a listing of times on it, just times, with various markings for "arr" and "dep."

At the top of another were the initials *GW* and a listing of what looked like travel entries. *8/18/89-AT to JA, Saf; 8/20/89-JA to AT.* All of them one- or two-day trips, maybe twenty altogether, stretching out for two years.

On another page, the word *HEAD.* With dozens of entries she couldn't make any sense of.

Another page—

Shanks seized the notepad, tearing it from her hands.

"And you're the girl I'm supposed to trust?" he said, spitting it out.

Instantly her eyes glistened with tears at the injustice of it all. She had just confirmed his worst opinion of her. "I want to know what's going on," she said. "You're not telling me everything."

He sat up in his seat, shaking the sleep from his face.

"I'm not as tough as you think I am," she said. She had no idea why she said it.

"Yes, you are."

"You don't know anything about me. About who I am. Not really."

"I know enough," he said, retrieving the arrest sheets that had fallen into her lap. "I know you're a carny girl. I know the world divides right down the middle for you: Maggie Rohrer on one side, the marks on the other. You see me like you see everyone else on the planet, someone to use. That's what I *know* about you. I wouldn't tell you what I *suspect* about you."

She could feel the blood rushing to her head, pounding in her ears. Her skull was erupting in pain.

"I'm not that," she said, looking at the notepad. "You're wrong. I . . ." But the words choked in her throat.

He regarded her for a long, melancholy moment.

"This is business between us, Maggie. A 'professional relationship,' just like with you and Bernie, remember?"

"Right," she said, tears starting to streak down her cheeks.

She stood suddenly, causing the earphones to yank loose from her neck, and pushed herself past him, breaking into a run once she got into the aisle.

In the restroom she sat on the toilet and bawled. It took the incessant tap-tap-tapping of the flight attendant to rouse her. Maggie was told she needed to return to her seat; they were making their descent.

Washing her face, she stared at the redheaded stranger in the mirror. What was wrong with her? Why was this getting to her?

Slouched across the front seat of the little Civic he'd rented at the Sir Donald Sangster International Airport, which he thought resembled a bus station more than an airport, Barry Landers looked up at the wisps of clouds floating in the deep blue Caribbean sky and waited.

Soon, in about ten minutes, from the direction those clouds were drifting, he expected a big American Super 80 to swoop down carrying Jack Shanks and Maggie Rohrer.

That's what he hoped, at least.

But what, he wondered, if they aren't on the plane? Then what? He'd be shit out of luck then, is what. And what if the tickets were phonies, just lying around to throw him off their real destination? Wouldn't that be a kick in the pants? He'd have come fifteen hundred miles for nothing.

He shifted in the seat, his skin sticking to the vinyl upholstery. He was parked along the side of the road on a hill overlooking the airport, in the shade of some bizarre tree dripping with huge, mustard-colored seed pods. Even so, the heat was broiling him. Big blue flies buzzed lazily in and out of the open windows like miniature flying fortresses. In a minute, once he saw the plane coming in, he would crank up the air conditioning again.

Somehow, some way, he was going to find time to take a bath today. In close quarters, like this, his smell was beginning to grow unpleasant.

He already had a room at a nice little place called the Sunsplash Inn, right on the first floor. It had a mini-bar just like Maggie was so fond of, and paintings of stick-figure black guys chopping sugarcane and old women balancing baskets of fruit on their heads. The room had a sliding glass door and a small patio with steps leading down the hill to the beach. Standing there, watching the surf hit the rocks, he felt just like a fucking tourist.

The hotel was a half mile down from the Lucinda Resort Hotel, where Shanks and Maggie were supposed to be bedding down for the night. Only their place was considerably jazzier than his. Since he'd had almost two hours to kill between his flight and theirs, he dropped by for a look-see. A uniformed Jamaican was stationed inside a guardhouse at the front gate. Barry waved to him as he drove past and the guy smiled back at him, showing lots of teeth.

Maggie would love it when she discovered she had her own private cottage, bungalow 5. It was tucked away in a regular tropical jungle, backed off from a narrow, winding macadam lane. Barry didn't get out of the car, just stopped and took it all in and filed it away. Sitting there in the Civic, listening to the *thunk* of tennis balls somewhere in the distance, he calculated that busting into bungalow 5 would be as easy as opening a milk carton, if it came to that. All those banana trees and thick hedges and hanging plants and crap, it made for a perfect screen.

The heat was getting to him. He'd sweated so much the last fifteen minutes, he was worrying about heat prostration. He turned on the ignition and the air conditioner started blowing, and he began rolling up all the windows. A kid who was coming up to him for a handout veered off, probably thinking Barry was leaving. Or maybe he thought Barry looked like a child molester. Since he'd been parked here, maybe a dozen little kids and even an old woman had come up to him, begging.

Barry was beginning to have second thoughts about this trip. At first, back at the Acadian, it seemed like a great idea, one of those bold, devil-may-care moves he always pictured himself taking. And everything had gone so smooth since then, like it was destiny or something. He'd called the airport and they'd had two flights out that very afternoon. From the tickets, he knew Maggie and her boyfriend were supposed to be on the second one, so he hustled over to the airport and barely made it to the gate. And he didn't need any shots or a passport, only a driver's license. He figured he'd show them Bob Sarcominia's, since Barry looked a little like the picture on the license, especially if he wet his hair down before they arrived. How close would they check? He'd already taken a big chance and charged the ticket to old Bob, and there hadn't been any problem with them accepting the card. So things were definitely going okay.

Still . . . he wasn't sure how he was going to handle the next couple of days, and it worried him. He'd spent fifty years thinking on his feet, sure, but he was always running a scam he knew dead solid. It was different when you knew what you were doing. He was like a salesman with a sample case full of tricks; if the mark bought into just one of them, he was in business. But this—here he was swimming in the same pond with the fucking Fibbies and they swallowed tadpoles like him without a burp.

Panic suddenly shook his insides around, like he was having an ice-water colonic. For a second he thought he'd have to find a john somewhere but he calmed himself with another shot of Jack Daniel's. On the plane he'd lifted three of the miniatures off the cart when they came by.

Droplets of condensation were sliding down the inside of the windshield. Stay on top of it, he told himself. Just play it by ear, hang around on the fringe, be alert and ready. Somehow, though he was going to have to get to Maggie, before or during the score, let her know what she was up against. If the guy was taping his credentials under a desk drawer, it was a safe bet he hadn't told her the facts.

Wouldn't she be surprised?

Flight 276A was twelve minutes late arriving in Montego Bay. Twenty more minutes passed before Barry saw Jack Shanks emerge from the terminal and walk across to the taxi stand. It took another minute for Barry to realize the red-haired woman standing behind him was Maggie. He wondered if it was a wig.

There was something else that was different. To Barry the couple did not seem nearly as chummy as they had the night before. It was obvious Maggie was keeping her distance.

Following them, he held back a long way, since he was pretty certain they'd head directly to the Lucinda. At the resort, he made a U-turn past the entrance and pulled over until he saw their cab leave the gate a few minutes later. Then he swung into the driveway, waved again at the same, grinning guard, and drove past bungalow 5.

Earlier, he'd found a good spot to settle into. It was in the shade beside a little shop that rented beach towels and floats. The place closed down at three o'clock, so there was nobody to bother him.

Fifteen minutes later, Shanks came out of the bungalow. He had changed into khaki trousers and a yellow polo shirt. He strolled down the lane to the main office and went inside. When he reappeared—now wearing aviator shades—he walked over to a silver Honda Accord. Barry could make out a rental company decal on the back bumper. Shanks climbed inside and drove out toward the main gate.

Barry couldn't think of anything better to do, so he followed him.

This time it was a little trickier. He had to keep closer and was afraid Shanks might make the tail. But the trip was a short one: they returned to the airport.

Barry found his old spot under the weird seedpod tree and watched Shanks circle the airport parking lot below, finally backing into a space at the rear of the lot.

Together, they waited.

For Barry the problem was that the shadow of the tree had shifted and now only shaded the back half of the Civic. Soon he was burning from the heat, even with the air-conditioning on. Sweat sluiced down his neck and the small of his back and even the Jack Daniels didn't help. Besides that, the jungle tree with its big seedpods made him a little nervous. He kept looking back at the thing, couldn't help himself, like he thought it was going to attack or something.

Barry leaned against the door panel and caught his reflection in the outside mirror, saw the broken blood vessels in his nose and cheeks, and thought of how many hours he seemed to spend sitting in cars waiting for something to happen.

14

*O*ut of Miami, Gordon Wexler was able to move into first class. He ordered a gin and tonic and kicked back, feeling pretty good. He was wearing his double-breasted silk sport coat and a cinnamon chamois shirt buttoned at the neck, with pleated silk trousers and his leather Gianni Versace driving shoes, looking like a powerful guy with a lot of loose money, like the millionaire he was. He was stretched out in the soft leather seat, making eyes at the flight attendant, who definitely seemed interested. She wasn't really his type; she didn't seem to have any tits to speak of, and he was unequivocally a tit man. He'd been married twice—that was enough—and both women had big tits and red hair.

It was better to buy it than marry it, though. That was one thing he'd learned in life.

The flight attendant bent over and asked him if he wanted a magazine and he said, no, what he'd really like was for her to sit on his face.

Which was probably the wrong thing to say because she pulled back as though he'd slapped her.

What the fuck. She'd calm down and he'd hit on her later.

He popped a handful of whites, washing it down with the dregs of his gin. Then thought about his new pal, George, and what exactly he was going to do with him.

Last night it had taken him another half hour to clear the deck after Artie finally left. Artie had some "periodicals" in the trunk of his car that he wanted to show Wexler. His uncle was a porn distributor who ran a string of skin shops in south Atlanta, so

Artie was able to pick up a lot of interesting material. Wexler had bought a dozen magazines, mostly European and Scandinavian. All the text was foreign language; but he hadn't bought them for reading.

George just hung back, watching them exchange magazines and money. He didn't say anything much, didn't express any interest in looking at the rags. When Artie was gone, Wexler suggested to George that he go on to the airport, where he'd meet him later, but George said, no, he'd just as soon go home with Wexler, wait in his house, so they could go to the airport together.

Normally, Wexler wouldn't put up with shit like that. But he noticed George could get a funny look on his face. He'd keep smiling at you, keep showing you those dental school teeth, but his eyes would narrow down on you. The pupils actually seemed to constrict as you watched, and it was a little eerie to see. A little scary.

That and the fact that the guy had been a mob goon for forty years or more, fetching coffee and fitting corpses for oil drums, convinced Wexler to let it ride. Let him come home and watch TV in the living room if that's what George wanted to do.

Wexler was experiencing a nice little buzz from the uppers. He withdrew a magazine from his carry-on, one with a German name. On the cover was a strange-looking naked girl strapped in chains. Her hair was cut short like a boy's and she had a nice set on her, but her snatch was a kid's snatch. She didn't resemble any kid Wexler had ever seen, though. Her eye sockets were dark and hollow and her eyes looked like little black seeds, and her mouth was stretched ear to ear like a Halloween pumpkin. It was kind of interesting, like she might be already dead.

He opened the magazine and a second later noticed the flight attentant was staring at the cover, her mouth forming a little *o*. Their eyes met and Wexler could tell he wasn't going to get anywhere with her, not this trip or ever. She looked like she was going to run and tell the captain about him.

Back in steerage, George was gazing out the porthole at a field of puffy, white clouds below. It was the first time he had ever been outside the United States and he was enjoying the trip. They gave him little bags of peanuts and a hot meal and they only hit him up a buck for the beer.

His feet were perched on the catalog case. When he boarded, they tried to store it in the overhead compartment, but George wasn't having any of that. He wanted it close to him, where he could keep his eyes on it. It didn't quite fit under the seat in front of him, but that was all right. The flight attendant had been a little prissy about it but he gave her a look and she left him alone after that.

They'd have to kill him to take it away from him.

A little bell sounded and the captain came on and said they were approaching Jamaica. George buckled his seat belt and looked back outside, watching the descent. Off on the horizon the sun flared, the pink and yellow rays bouncing off the clouds and the dark water below.

He hoped Jamaica was on his side of the plane.

They had a little trouble at customs, but the funny thing was it wasn't George who had the trouble. It was Wexler.

There were three black guys checking the bags and it was obvious which of them was Headache's man. He was the thin, twitchy one who looked like he was having a breakdown. He kept glancing down the line of tourists, then across at his supervisor, then over at the other inspectors, all the time grabbing at his collar and jerking his neck like Rodney Dangerfield on speed. He spotted George right away, though. A blind man would have spotted George.

Wexler made a point of getting in another line. He was behind a little Puerto Rican woman with two kids. One of them, a little girl about five, kept rubbing her hands on Wexler's pants, like she'd never felt silk before. The mother seemed to find it amusing. Wexler's attention was on George and the wild-eyed customs inspector. George didn't bat an eye the whole time, looked like he was waiting in line to see a movie. The customs guy couldn't get him out of there fast enough.

George looked back at Wexler and actually smiled.

Then Wexler's inspector told him to open his carry-on and Wexler said, "If it'll make you happy," and unzipped it for the guy. And the guy reached in and pulled out Artie's magazines and flopped them on the counter. His hands flew back like he'd touched a flame.

"What is this?" said the inspector.

Wexler didn't understand at first. "Magazines," he said. "What d'ya think?"

The man opened one of them, not the one with the girl in chains but another, with Asian twins on the cover. They were both naked and completely shaved and had identical pornographic tattoos covering virtually every inch of their bodies, including their faces. The inspector flipped through the magazine for a moment, then set it down and called another guy in. Together, they spent a few minutes going through them; then the Rodney Dangerfield inspector edged over to see what the problem was.

Spread out on the counter, the magazines did look a little weird, Wexler had to admit. It was beginning to make him nervous. There were maybe two hundred passengers in the inspection area and they were all craning their necks and nudging each other, curious what was happening. Finally, a horse-faced, steely-eyed supervisor marched over. He picked up the magazine with the girl in chains.

"Hey, boys," said Wexler. "You think maybe you could beat your meat on somebody else's time?" It was the Benzedrine talking; he knew it, but he couldn't do anything about it.

The supervisor did not smile. "Come with me," he said. He snatched the magazines out of the hands of the other inspectors, pivoted, and headed for a room with a sign that read OFFICIAL GOVERNMENT BUSINESS ONLY! Wexler grabbed his carry-on and the rest of his luggage and followed.

It took two hours to clear up the matter. During that time dozens of officials entered and left and reentered the room. Wexler was made to sit in a folding metal chair while the others lounged about on tables or stood with their backs to the wall, thumbing through the magazines and pointing out pages of special interest to their associates. Once Wexler jumped up and demanded to see the American consulate, which provoked general laughter. A dapper little man in a pith helmet and a crisp blue-and-white dress uniform stepped forward and identified himself as a member of the Jamaica Constabulary Force and cited specific statutes in the Suppression of Crimes Act forbidding the trafficking of obscene materials into Jamaica. The notion of passing any time at all inside a Jamaican prison completely cowed Wexler and he slumped back down. Finally, after every uniformed male in the immediate vicinity had pawed through every magazine, Wexler's name and hotel address were taken down and he was told he could leave, but that his "printed materials" would be confiscated.

Wexler drifted through the terminal in a fog of fatigue. At the taxi stand, he felt a tap on his shoulder. Turning around, he was presented with the catalog case and a small, tarnished key by George.

"You take care of that," said George, "you understand?" He waited for an answer.

"Yeah, right," said Wexler.

George saw something in Wexler's eyes that he didn't like. "You're a fuckup," he said. "You know that?" He moved in closer and thumped Wexler on the chest with his forefinger. "And don't you go saying you didn't get the goods delivered to you, or nothin' like that, 'cause I'm giving it to you right now, and now it's yours to take care of, like Tony said."

Wexler nodded. The boil on George's neck was roughly the shape of the top of his head; it was like there was a tiny George pushing his way out.

"You lose it or somethin'," said George, narrowing his eyes, "you'll see me again—and you don't want to see me again, you understand what I'm saying?"

Wexler knew.

George shook his shoulders like a dog shaking off water, then smiled his white, even smile. He turned and went back inside the airport, his vacation over.

Wexler breathed in the hot, heavy air of the late Jamaica afternoon. The suitcase was much heavier than he'd imagined. He wondered exactly how much money was inside and wished he could think of a way to take it with him when he departed his old life. But that wasn't likely. George was right: Wexler didn't want to see him again, ever.

15

hen Shanks returned to the bungalow, Maggie was reclining on a wicker recamier on the terrace in her shorts and a tube top, drinking a Ladystinger she had ordered from room service. It was her second. Earlier, when he'd gone out, Shanks asked her—*asked* her, not told her—to have her work outfit on by the time he got back. She hoped he'd make something of it. She wanted to get into a fight with the son of a bitch.

But he didn't say anything, just went into the bedroom. They only had the one bedroom this time. He said they wouldn't be staying the night.

A moment later he came outside and pulled a chair up to the wrought iron patio table.

"We need to go over some things," he said, setting down a manila envelope.

"Like what?"

"Like who you'll be putting to sleep tonight."

"Oh, that."

He handed her a five-by-seven color print of a youngish man with black curly hair and thick tortoiseshell glasses. The picture was a little blurred, as though it had been enlarged and cropped. The subject seemed to be looking right at the camera but not seeing it.

"Gordon Wexler," said Shanks.

"Our computer programmer," said Maggie.

She caught him looking at the cocktail glass. He was trying to determine if she was looped or not. She wasn't going to help him.

"He's thirty-two," said Shanks. "Sharp dresser. Expensive clothes."

She flipped the photo back on the table.

"It's important you follow your usual MO. Take his cash and plastic, the standard stuff, so maybe he'll think it was just a robbery. But the thing we're after is a set of floppy disks that he keeps in a nylon travel pack. Looks like this."

He handed her a sheet torn from a catalog. A gray disk carrier was circled in yellow highlighter. It had Velcro straps and was lightweight and came in six designer colors and cost $4.95 but was available three for $12. Maggie tossed the sheet toward the table but didn't quite make it; she watched it float down and land on the tile.

Shanks picked up the sheet and set it on the table. While he was at it, he rearranged the photo so Gordon Wexler faced her.

"Get the disks and get out quick," he said. "I'll be in the lobby. Any problems, we meet up at the airport, okay? We have a midnight flight to Miami."

Maybe we do, thought Maggie, and maybe we don't.

He pointed to the photo. "You sure you can recognize him?"

"I always get my man, Jack." She crushed out her cigarette in a large terra cotta ashtray.

"We need to go," he said. He was acting like a man handling a highly volatile explosive. It occurred to her that maybe he just didn't know how to act around women.

The sooner she got dressed and out of here, she told herself, the sooner it would all be over. She stood and looked over the edge of the terrace. Below, a steep hillside of banana trees and red dracaena bushes pitched into the dark, foaming sea. Gulls soared overhead. Soon it would all be over. And then where would she be?

"Okay," she said. "I'll get in my costume."

When Shanks finally made his move on her, Maggie was genuinely startled. She was accustomed to men lurching at her, pawing her; she knew all the signals. But this was a complete surprise. She didn't have time to comprehend what was happening, or how she felt about it.

It happened in the bedroom, as she dressed by the fading light from a high, louvered window. She hadn't bothered to turn the lamp on. An overhead fan turned the hot air. Maggie was barefoot, with her slip and padded bra on.

FIFTEEN

Shanks just appeared in the doorway. She hadn't heard him in the living room.

Instinctively, she raised her hands to cover herself, then lowered them disdainfully.

"What is it?" she said. "You want a look at your merchandise?"

But there was something wrong. Something odd in his eyes. She had the ominous feeling that he'd been shot or stabbed, that he was going to fall forward with blood all over his back.

Shanks moved quickly toward her and embraced her, kissing her hard on the lips. It was what Maggie called a black-and-white kiss— like an old movie, no tongue. When he finally released her, he seemed unsteady.

He started to speak but Maggie touched his lips with a finger.

"Don't say anything," she said. "With us, words are for lying."

They kissed again, a colorized version, and the passion heated up until she felt they would tumble onto the bed—and then, inexplicably, it faded. They both felt it. Maggie pulled away.

Shanks looked down at his hands, suddenly embarrassed. This hadn't been part of the master plan. Something else that wasn't in his notebook.

"What I told you on the plane," he said, "I don't really believe it. I wish I did, it'd make things easier. Real grifters, they feel good about what they do. Fucking people over makes them feel great. You're good at your work, Maggie, but you feel bad about it. You need another line of work."

"Sure," said Maggie. "I'll sell yogurt in the mall."

She pecked him on the lips, then turned her back to him.

"You know, Jack, if I wasn't such a trusting girl, I might think you're sweet-talking me because you're sweating the scam. I might think you're afraid I'm too emotional and generally pissed off to bring it off in a professional, businesslike manner because you didn't do such a great job of getting your horse to the post—or is it *whore?*"

She reached into her suitcase for a new package of stockings, then sat on the bed, looking Shanks in the eyes.

"But don't worry your cold little heart, Jack. I'll put your guy to sleep for you and get you your goodies and then you won't have to see me again."

She began slipping on her hose, not at all concerned with whether he looked or didn't look. She felt she got the knife in him pretty good, but it wasn't all that pleasurable, not like she thought it would be.

Night was falling on Montego Bay. Rolling through the crowded downtown streets, heading toward a hotel this side of Negril, the car shuddered with every bump. Maggie chewed the inside of her mouth and tapped on the armrest.

"When do I get my other five grand?" asked Maggie.

"At the airport."

"Mind if I see it first? Make sure you have it?"

He smiled. "You don't trust me, Maggie?"

"Spare me the Vaseline rub, Jack. All this is, is money."

He reached into his pocket and withdrew an envelope. The guy was a magician, she thought, only he pulled out envelopes instead of rabbits. Inside this one she found another stack of hundred-dollar bills. This time she didn't count it.

She handed back the envelope.

"Keep it," he said. "It'll be yours in a couple hours anyway."

Was he kidding? "No," she said. "You hang on to it until we're done."

She peered out the window. Less than twenty-four hours ago she had been looking out of another car window at the dark streets of New Orleans, going off to do violence to another stranger in a hotel. Here the streets were much the same, with the same people and sounds and the same desperate search for pleasure, but tonight the landscape somehow seemed more perverse. Occasionally she would catch gimpses in the alleyways of different lives: gaunt beggars, haunted children, sullen policemen. Maggie shuddered, suddenly filled with dread.

16

Gordon Wexler had fallen asleep on the sofa, fantasizing about his new life in Oregon. When he was eight, his parents had one of their first big blowouts and the old man snatched Gordon and his brother, Bobby, and hauled them off to what he kept calling "the Great Northwest" for a fishing expedition. It took four days of driving. The afternoon they arrived, the old man bought bait and tackle and waders, and shoved the boys into the first river he found, while he sat in a lounge chair on the bank and drank beer out of a cooler and called out instructions until he finally fell asleep. They didn't catch any trout but it was the most fun Wexler could remember having as a kid. The next day, the old man met up with a cocktail waitress and the day after that, he drove them into the city of Astoria and put the boys on a bus back home. But ever since that experience, Oregon had held a special allure for Wexler. Now, dreaming, he was Max Zerle, decked out in all his L. L. Bean finery, with his willow creel and trout net and pipe, standing in a stream and casting his line perfectly across the clear, running water, flyfishing forever.

Soon. Very soon.

When he finally awoke, he was still in his silk jacket, slumped on the sofa. His drink had turned over and spilled on the carpet. He rubbed his face and saw the time on the television clock: seven-twenty.

Wexler hadn't planned on sleeping but it didn't matter. There was nothing to do until tomorrow morning, when he'd head over to the bank and remove his IDs from the safe deposit box. Then he'd hang around the pool, waiting for Headache's goons to come pick him up.

On the coffee table was a large envelope stamped with the Safari Hotel and Golf Club insignia. Moments after checking in, a bellman had brought it to him. Although he knew its contents, he ripped open the envelope for the sheer pleasure of touching what was inside: a nine-millimeter American Derringer Model 1. Two-shot, over-and-under, neoprene grips. Holstered in a lightweight plastic ankle rig. Nothing special, really; not an expensive piece. It just felt very solid and comfortable in his hand. At fifteen ounces, it had more heft than other derringers he'd owned. Wexler never liked to go anywhere unarmed, and since the airlines frowned on passengers transporting weapons, he had gotten in the practice of storing it in the hotel safe. He had purchased the derringer a couple of years before, from Headache's main man, a Rastafarian named Daniel Poole. Wexler sighted, checked the action, and dry-fired it, aiming at an engraving on the wall that showed the cultivation of sugar cane. Perfect.

It took him a second to stand up. His head was a little dizzy. He went to his carry-on and found his Bennies. In the bathroom he swallowed an assortment, cupping his hand under the faucet.

What he'd do, he decided, was take a cold shower, put on some fresh clothes, then go downstairs and check things out. That was his normal routine. You never knew what you'd find in the bar. The Safari was too upscale for the secretaries and schoolteachers who flew down on the discount packages, but they liked to drop by and rubberneck. They'd flop in the lounge and tank up, waiting for some rich, good-looking guy like himself to come sweep them away for the night. Wexler was always agreeable to that.

When he came out of the shower, his message light was blinking. He rang the hotel clerk, who gave him the cryptic communication: *Will arrive tonight. Stay at hotel.* No name, of course.

Wexler didn't know what to make of that exactly. Headache was coming ashore, something he rarely did. That was okay because it meant Wexler didn't have to pitch and roll on his goddamn smelly boat, going over the numbers with the old guy. But what did he want? With Headache, you never knew. It could have something to do with the money in the suitcase, or he might be buying a new piece of rigging.

No matter. Wexler could still drift down to the lounge. Headache wouldn't show up until well after dark. Who knew what could happen in an hour or two?

Before going up to the registration desk at the Safari Hotel, Barry Landers stopped to pin on his HI! I'M DON D. DONALDSON name tag, hoping it might help. He needn't have worried. Here the clerk wasn't nearly as fastidious about giving out information as the one at the Acadian. When Barry asked who the curly-haired guy was that just checked in, the woman nonchalantly ran her finger down the registry and produced the name for him.

"Gordon Wexler," she said, smiling. "Room twenty-three-oh-two."

Barry went back to the car and thought a while. Earlier, Shanks had followed Wexler from the airport all the way to the Safari, watched him register, then drove on off. Since Barry figured Shanks was returning to his own place, he didn't see any hurry about going back there.

In fact, he was fairly certain the action had just shifted over here to Mr. Gordon Wexler's place. Wexler was the mark.

So who the fuck was Gordon Wexler?

Itchy to do something, anything, other than sit in the car some more, Barry went back inside the hotel, took the elevator up to the twenty-third floor, and strolled around until he came upon room 2302. It wasn't hard to find; it was the penthouse level and there were only three suites on the whole floor.

He put his ear to the door and listened intently. Nothing. No music or TV, nothing. He put his hand on the doorknob and twisted it. Locked. But he was glad to see it was a regular key-lock door, not one of those credit card jobs. Easier to open.

So what was going on? Either they planned to knock over Wexler, or else Wexler was going to lead them to someone else. He'd bet the house it was Wexler. Wexler had sucker written all over him: fancy clothes, staying in a fancy hotel, in the best suite.

A juicy thought hit Barry: Maybe he could bypass Maggie altogether. Wait until Wexler went downstairs, then take a peek at suite 2302.

But he didn't get very far with the idea. Sensing a movement, a presence, he turned and saw a hulking figure at the farthest reach of the hall. The corridor light was out at that end and the man was standing in front of the door to the stairwell. Barry could just make out some of his features by the red light of the exit sign. A black guy, enormous, wearing a white guayabera shirt. He started moving Barry's way, like a forklift coming at him.

Barry whirled and hurried back to the elevator, slapping the down button, watching the corner behind him with gathering apprehension. If the guy came after him, Barry was trapped. But the elevator arrived in short order.

Riding downstairs, he mulled it over. It had the strangeness of a dream, the big guy coming at him out of the shadows. Maybe he was a security guard or something. Barry felt like Mickey Mouse racing down the overgrown beanstalk through the clouds, with the big giant about to tumble after him. Except Barry didn't have the golden goose, not yet. Hell, he didn't even have the beans yet.

He didn't feel safe until he was back inside the car, pulling out of the parking lot. What he'd do, he decided, was head back to Maggie's place and wait for them. First he had to take a dump, though. He felt like he had a live squid loose in his guts. And he might find a place to buy himself some new clothes, look a little more sporting. If he couldn't have a bath, a new shirt and some Bermuda shorts would be nice.

And maybe he could pick up a bottle. That would be even nicer.

Entering the hotel lobby, Maggie felt like a female impersonator. Jutting, car-bumper breasts, a short red skirt with a slit halfway up the thigh, three-inch heels.

A cartoon floozie.

Shanks had let her out in the parking lot, just down from the entrance to Gordon Wexler's garish, Vegas-style high-rise hotel. He didn't want anyone to see the two of them together.

Maggie spotted the lounge immediately, a shadowy Banana Republic–like affair set off by a pair of huge, crossed fiberglass tusks. She went *clack-clack-clacking* across the marble lobby, feeling every male eye on her.

The room was jammed with dark rattan furniture and palm trees in copper pots and walls festooned with antelope skulls and synthetic zebra hides—but no patrons. There was only one guy at the bar, a big black man sitting at the end. She hadn't expected this.

Robbed of her audience, Maggie hesitated a moment, then strutted over to a table near the center of the room. She could see the bartender and waitress exchange glances. Obviously, it had been a while since they had seen anything quite this outrageous.

Behind her stood a floor-to-ceiling wicker bird cage housing a cockatoo. Maggie and the bird scrutinized each other. Two exotic, kindred spirits.

The waitress, a tiny woman dressed in a dashiki, remained at the bar watching her.

Maggie said to her: "So what does a girl have to do to get a drink around here?"

The woman snapped to, and hurried over.

Shanks stationed himself outside on the nearly deserted hotel terrace, with a view of the colonnaded lobby and the entrance to the cocktail lounge. He reclined on a chaise and ordered a light beer.

In the pool a doughy old woman swam laps, while off to the side, workers were setting up for some hotel function. One of them was pouring coals into a grill fashioned from an old oil drum. Another was unfolding the legs of a buffet table.

After a while, a group of calypso musicians arrived and began positioning their steel drums nearby. One of them, a teenager, pounded out a reggae riff—then smiled brightly at Shanks.

"Dead Mon Bop," he said.

"What?"

"Name of de song, mon. 'Dead Mon Bop.' "

Shanks nodded, then watched the waiter bring his beer.

* * *

Maggie was afraid the guy at the bar—a huge, surly-looking Jamaican in a guayabera shirt—was going to come over and annoy her. When she walked in, he had twisted completely around on his barstool to get a better view, and so far hadn't taken his eyes off her. Once or twice, without thinking, she had glanced his way, and the scowling intensity of his expression disturbed her.

Outside by the pool, where Shanks was supposed to be, Maggie could hear calypso music cranking up. Through the tinted, mullioned windows, she saw people milling about. That's where everyone was, she realized. There was sure nothing going on inside the lounge. Only one other table was occupied.

And of course, there was the big Jamaican. He was still there, still glowering at her. He was gripping a bottle of Red Stripe in his outsized hands, like a little bird he'd captured, whose neck he was slowly twisting. Maggie swallowed, feeling her own neck constrict.

She gave him her best drop-dead look, then turned away. Screw him.

All around Shanks were sun-baked bodies jerking to the music. He didn't like it. The pool party was throwing everything off. Wexler might decide to check out the action here rather than in the lounge. Without working very hard, he was sure to find something to his taste.

Now they were doing the limbo.

A very fat, very tanned, very bald European gentleman adorned in gold chains and a pair of iridescent briefs led the way, trying to squeeze his bulk under the limbo bar. Surprisingly, he made it. Apparently, he'd had a lot of practice.

He was followed by an even more burned middle-aged blonde in a thong bikini. Shanks's line of vision was right at crotch level, straight across the pool. She, too, was practiced at the art. Her legs were spread very wide apart and her arms were extended and steady. Their eyes met and she gave him a big grin.

If and when the mark finally made his entrance, Maggie didn't want him to spot her watching his arrival, so she positioned herself to catch the entrance reflection in a nearby window. Also, it was a way to avoid eye contact with the big geek at the bar.

So it was at that angle that she caught Barry Landers swaggering into the room. She turned around to verify what she hoped she wasn't seeing. He hustled over, breaking into a smile.

"Maggo," he said.

He had on fuchsia-colored shorts, a Hawaiian shirt, and a straw touring cap. And, of course, his nametag.

"Get out of here," she said.

"Hey, that's no way to act," he said sitting down.

"How did you get here?"

"Same as you, on a plane. I came down a little before you did, though. Getting the lay of the land." He was enjoying himself.

"You have to leave, Barry."

"Afraid I'll spook your pigeon? Baby, I ain't going nowhere. You think I'm down here for my health, just happened to run into you?" He leaned back and took her in with his eyes, licking his lips. "Jeez, you really filled out since I seen you last." Then, bending forward, he said: "What's the setup?"

"If you don't leave now, I'll have the bartender throw you out."

"I don't think so, Maggo. I think he'd like my story more than yours, tell the truth. I know a little bit about the score, you know? I might even know more than you, I bet. Let's see, your boyfriend's outside, waiting for you to spread some joy juice around, right?"

Maggie stood up. Behind her, the cockatoo fluttered in its cage.

Barry grabbed at her arm but she pulled away. The bartender was drawing a beer and he stopped and looked over at them.

"Relax, relax, Maggo. I ain't gonna piss on your parade. I just want to ride on one of the floats. That's fair, ain't it? You ran out on me, no two-weeks' notice, left me cold."

"Look," said Maggie. "I've got nothing for you. You queer this deal, Jack will overhaul your internal organs. He told me about you, *Bernard*. He told me your whole stinking story. I know how you ratted out your last partner."

"Yeah. He tell you about hisself?"

"I know all I want to know."

"You don't know shit, Maggo. You know he's a government man, a fed? You know that?"

There was a sudden, whispery intake of breath from Maggie. Barry smiled, getting a kick out of her reaction.

"I tossed his room," he said. "I seen his ID. He's with the FBI, sweetheart. What d'ya think of that, huh?"

The blonde in the thong bikini cut loose from the crowd and sauntered over to Shanks. She stood in front of him, blocking his view, moving her head up and down slowly, as though confirming something to herself. Shanks figured she was half in the bag.

"Are you a consenting adult?" she said, smiling brightly.

"Depends on what you want me to consent to."

"*I'm* a consenting adult."

Shanks said nothing.

"You know what that means, don't you?" she giggled. "Two consenting adults, we can do any fucking thing we want to do!"

This didn't get quite the reaction she was hoping for. She adjusted the top of her bikini. Shanks noticed she had a ring on each of her fingers.

"So what do you want to do?" she asked.

"Right now I just want to sit here."

"Okie dokie." She flopped down on the chaise with him, forcing him to move his legs out of the way.

"You like lawyer jokes? I know a lawyer joke. My ex-husband was a goddamn lawyer. He's like the original lawyer joke, you know?" Her face bunched up as she sifted through her memory. "Uh, you know why scientists want to use lawyers instead of rats in their experiments?"

Looking beyond her to the lobby, Shanks shook his head no. Gordon Wexler was moving around under the trellised walkway that connected the hotel to the terrace. Dressed in a floral print shirt, linen trousers, and loafers without socks, he shifted back and forth on the balls of his feet, hyped up, surveying the party crowd. Shanks watched him walk over to a table holding several galvanized tubs of rum punch. He inclined forward in his seat, to put the blonde between him and Wexler.

She took this as encouragement. "Let's see . . . 'cause there are more lawyers than rats . . . and 'cause you can get lawyers to do things you can't get rats to do. And . . . 'cause it's possible to get attached to a rat." After each line she beamed with the pleasure of getting the words out in the right order.

Wexler was conferring with the bartender manning the rum punch. He gestured angrily at a trash bag filled with paper cups. Apparently there were no fresh cups. Eventually, he turned and threaded his way through the crowd and back into the lobby.

"My husband," said the woman, "the goddamn lawyer? I found a bigger rat than him for the divorce. Now he lives in a little bitty garage apartment, a rat hole. Teach him to fuck with me."

With that, she burrowed into his shoulder, a serene expression on her tanned face.

Maggie hadn't heard much of what Barry said after he dropped his little bomb. She was trying to absorb it, assess the damage. All along, she'd known better than to trust Shanks. She'd suspected he was playing his own game, not telling her everything. So now she knew it for a fact. Her instincts had been right on the money. But that didn't keep her stomach from knotting up. That didn't prevent her from feeling betrayed.

She didn't question that Barry was telling her the truth. He was too pleased with himself.

"Don't you see it, Maggo?" he said. "Your boy's running a trap on this pigeon—and *you*."

"What do you want?"

"Hey, I'm here to help you, Maggo." If he called her Maggo one more time, just one, she was going to grab a swizzle stick and plunge it into his eye. "There's only one thing to do, that's go ahead and make the score. Only you keep the goods. You and me, we split it down the middle. We drive over to Kingston tonight, hop a plane— we're back in business, same as before. Right?"

Wrong. She couldn't see letting Barry Landers back into her life. In her pursuit of a partner, she'd gone through girlfriends and psycho boyfriends, and now she'd tried a smelly old fart. She didn't need anyone anymore; she'd go it alone.

Nothing made any sense to her. There wasn't a jury in the world that would convict her of anything, not with the FBI pushing her along at every step. This little affair went way beyond entrapment. They weren't aiding and abetting her crime; she was aiding and abetting *theirs*. They had solicited her for a criminal activity they'd devised. Any case they built would get thrown out. Hell, it'd make Peter Jennings.

Unless, of course, they didn't plan on any of this ever getting out. There was a thought that put her spine on ice.

Barry passed her a slip of paper. "Look here," he said. "Here's where I'm staying. Sunsplash Inn, back the other side of Mo Bay? On your right. You do the thing, meet me back there, okay? Room four-eleven." He smiled. "Even got a mini-bar, the way you like it."

Anything to get rid of him, she thought. The limbo crowd was now spilling into the lounge. It was evident that Maggie was badly overdressed for the occasion. Everyone else was arrayed in island garb—T-shirts, shorts, and rubber flip-flops.

"Okay," she said.

Gordon Wexler arrived. He didn't enter the room so much as reel into it, bumping into an old woman with tight, sun-leathered skin. He sailed on past her, oblivious, heading to the bar. Maggie had no doubt he was the mark; Shanks's photo could have been taken yesterday.

"Only problem I got," said Barry, his back to the bar, "what's the goods, huh? What's your boyfriend after?"

"He says it's computer programming."

Barry's face fell. "Computer programming?"

"He says he has a buyer for some programming he wants me to appropriate for him."

"Oh, yeah?" His eyes grew dull, like the eyes of a dead fish floating in the water. Then they brightened. "Well, we can find a buyer, too, same as him. Maybe sell it back to the guy we take it from, huh?"

"The pigeon's here," said Maggie.

"He is? Now?" He stood. "Hey," he said, raising his voice theatrically. "Been great seeing you again." Then, a whisper: "You know where to find me, right?"

Maggie held up the piece of paper. "Sunsplash Inn," she said. "Room four-eleven. Go away."

"Don't cut me out, baby."

With any luck, thought Maggie, I'll never see him again. As Barry left the lounge, she felt a rage welling up inside her. That was good. Maybe that could get her through this.

17

*G*ordon Wexler was wondering how young is too young.

He was at the bar, waiting for his drink before going back outside to the pool party, forming an attachment for a girl in a Spandex bandeau and acid-washed cutoffs. She was sitting at a table not ten feet away, both legs propped up in her chair, giving the world a nice crotch shot. She was sucking a Coke out of a plastic straw, one hand playing in her long blond hair. She was covered with freckles. Her little brother was next to her, fidgeting with a Magna-Doodle drawing board.

Wexler seemed to recall that if you screwed around with a girl under sixteen, it was carnal abuse. Under fourteen, it was rape. That was Georgia, though. In Jamaica they probably didn't have any laws on that sort of thing.

This one looked around fifteen or sixteen, but thirteen or fourteen was probably more like it. She could even go as low as ten or eleven for all he knew. You couldn't tell with girls today.

She smiled at him and ran her tongue along her upper lip. Jesus, he thought, she's actually missing her fucking two front teeth.

Wexler grinned back. He wanted to go over and say something funny to her, check her out, but he wasn't sure how you go about making time with a preteen American girl nowadays. While he was pondering that dilemma, he noticed the man at the table next to her. Dad. Dad sitting with the grown-ups. A redneck with a St. Louis Cardinals ball cap and *Semper Fidelis* tattooed on his meaty forearm. Dad was looking at Wexler very, very hard.

Wexler turned around so fast he spilled his drink.

That was when he finally caught Big Red's act. The sight hit him like a speedball. And for an instant he thought it might be something like that, maybe the drugs and the gin and the lack of sleep causing some kind of weird chemical reaction you get just before you convulse. If that was it, it was worth it; he'd fucking increase his dosage.

Hair the color of a firetruck, a major league set of funbags, the eyes of an angel, the lips of a whore—his wet dream materialized. There even seemed to be a soft, fuzzy halo around her, like in a movie, when they smear Vaseline on the lens.

Without a second thought, Wexler started her way. It would require every ounce of control he possessed to refrain from dragging her off behind the bar and having at her right then and there. But he knew ultimately he would pay her any amount of money, tell her any lie, even have her abducted if that's what it took. One way or another, he was going to get in this woman's pants tonight.

As he glided toward her though, Wexler could spot there was something wrong. She had an odd, immobilized look, like she'd just had the breath knocked out of her, or like the doctor just told her she had cancer.

Well, baby, he thought, what you need is a new doctor. And here I am. Dr. W. will fix you right up.

When Wexler loomed before her, Maggie couldn't help thinking how well Shanks seemed to know his man.

"Tell me you're not married," was his opening. Some day, thought Maggie, she was going to compile a book of pickup lines.

"I'm not married," she said. And then she licked the rim of her glass and smiled. She wasn't sure how she wanted to play this—or *if* she wanted to play it at all—but for the moment she thought it best to get him excited.

"Tell me I can sit down and buy you a drink."

She smiled again.

"Now tell me you'll bear my children," he said, taking up Barry's old chair. "Ha, ha. What are you drinking, Red?"

Up close, Gordon Wexler had the look of a yuppie under extreme stress, like maybe the monthly time-share payment was pushing him to the edge. Now his dancing eyes had found a new toy.

"Tell me something," said Maggie. "You a computer programmer?"

"Me?" He looked nonplussed. "Do I look like a computer programmer?"

"Yeah. You do."

"I'm retired. I mainly trout fish now."

"So you're a rich guy, huh?"

"Money to burn, Red. Money to burn."

He looks *exactly* like a computer programmer, she thought. Like a computer programmer who had gotten hold of a *GQ*.

Shanks thought he'd give it another minute, then take up a position in the gift shop, so he could better observe the two of them leaving the lounge. Next to him the blonde was snoring softly against his shoulder. He found himself contemplating her stretch marks and the nice way she was slipping out of her bikini.

The jerk pork grill was smoking copiously. Now and then, a gust of wind would blow smoke in his direction, burning his eyes and obscuring his view of the lobby.

On one of these occasions, a lean, dark Jamaican with thick, coiling dreadlocks appeared on the terrace and paused. He wore a wool cap, cutoffs, tire-tread sandals, and a Lakers T-shirt. His cheeks were hollow and drawn, and the skin very tight, giving his face the appearance of a skull on a pirate's flag. His name was Daniel Poole and Shanks was not pleased to see him.

Poole took in the scene but did not appear to see Shanks. He then reentered the lobby and strode toward the lounge.

Quickly, Shanks extricated himself from his companion, who rolled over on the chaise, the pattern of the plastic webbing embedded in her skin. He weaved past the crowd, which was now roaring drunk, and edgily peered through a window into the lounge.

Concentrating on her mark, Maggie failed to notice that the big Jamaican at the bar had acquired a friend, or that the two of them had taken a great interest in her table.

Wexler didn't pick up on it, either.

"You look like a girl likes to have fun," Wexler told her.

"Funny how everyone can spot that."

"How much you going for, a girl like you?"

"Pardon me?"

"Your price. For the night."

In this getup, what could she expect? But what did he think, that she was down here for the North American Whores Convention, doing a seminar on fast bar pickups?

"One thousand dollars," she said.

It was a nice round figure and Wexler seemed to appreciate the sound of it. "No shit?" he said. Then made up his mind: "Okay. I think we can do business."

A money guy, she thought. With guys like this, around women, money was never a problem. They couldn't allow it to be; they'd lose too much face. Later, they might take out a second mortgage to settle accounts, but for now, money was like water to the ocean.

"So let's see it," said Maggie.

"Now? Right now?"

"Yep."

"You got a business sense. I can appreciate that."

As he dug into his wallet, Maggie finally sensed the attentions of the Jamaicans at the bar. When he had finally caught her eye, the one with the dreadlocks smiled at her; but it wasn't a smile exactly, it was more like he was showing her his teeth. Like a dog might bare its fangs before ripping into flesh.

Wexler, cash in hand, noticed the problem.

"Jesus fucking Christ," he said. "Wonderful. This is fucking great."

"They seem to know you."

"My fucking bodyguards is what they are."

"Bodyguards?"

"They're supposed to keep me out of trouble," he said, winking. "But I don't think they're up to the job." He stood up, his movements suddenly twitchy. "I gotta do something about this. Be right back."

He lurched toward the two men as the waitress brought their drinks. It was now or never, thought Maggie. She unsnapped her handbag and withdrew the squeeze bottle, but then heard shouting from the bar. Wexler was yelling at Dreadlocks. She watched him raise his hand as though about to strike. In a blur of motion, Dreadlocks bobbed to one side and seized Wexler's arm, twisting it and forcing him to the floor. Wexler shrieked like a child. Just as quickly, Dreadlocks let him go. He smiled down at Wexler, then turned and smiled again at Maggie. She was taken aback by the speed of the whole episode. It scared her.

The lounge came to a stop. Red-faced and seething, Wexler struggled to lift himself up. Keeping his distance, he spat an unintelligible insult to Dreadlocks, who continued to smile venomously. Maggie watched the bartender signal the waitress to go find somebody.

Maggie tore herself from the scene to squeeze the Apivan into Wexler's gin and tonic. She watched the yellow liquid dissipate into the alcohol. When she looked up, Guayabera was staring straight at her.

Retracting the bottle, she bumped the rim of her own glass. Trying to prevent a spill, she ended up dropping the Apivan. In horror she watched it fall to the carpet—and then saw that Wexler, who was starting back to the table from the bar, had spotted it too. Desperately, she clawed under the table for the lost bottle. Wexler bent down and snatched it—then handed it over without a second thought.

He picked up his glass and drained the gin with one long swallow.

Looking around for the missing waitress, he shouted across the room to the bartender: "Hey! Gimme two more here!" All eyes were on him and he knew it. A fist clenched the tablecloth in anger.

Maggie noticed Guayabera whispering to Dreadlocks. Another viper smile. She forced herself to look away, thinking maybe she should scoot out the door and never look back. She couldn't really tell if she'd been made or not.

"They don't know it yet," said Wexler, "but this time tomorrow, they'll be back in the fields cutting sugarcane."

A gawky, hook-nosed hotel manager stepped into the lounge and huddled with the bartender, who set a pair of drinks on a tray and shoved it at the waitress. The manager glanced nervously back and forth between Wexler and the Jamaicans, then retreated.

As the waitress set down their glasses, Maggie caught Shanks's face through a window giving on to the terrace. Her expression hardened; she wanted to make him sweat. With her eyes still on him, she leaned across the table to Wexler and whispered: "Let's you and me go up to your room. Would you like that?"

He would. He gulped down his gin and tossed some bills carelessly on the table. But as they moved toward the front, the two Jamaicans fell in behind them.

Wexler turned and snarled: "You keep your fucking distance."

Another jagged smile flickered across Dreadlocks. Maggie wished she were far, far away, back in a place like Fort Worth, hustling some regional sales manager.

"Really—who are these guys?" she said to Wexler.

"An associate of mine, they're his monkeys. But I fucking won't stand for this shit. Won't stand for it."

Wexler lost his balance momentarily, lurching forward as though about to fall, but quickly recovering. A very bad sign, thought Maggie. She didn't want him collapsing before they got to the room. The juice shouldn't be kicking in this fast.

"What's wrong?" she asked.

"Nothing," said Wexler, shaking it off. "Felt kinda dizzy for a second."

Together, they crossed to the bank of elevators, the goons trailing closely behind. Word had spread throughout the hotel, it seemed, because all eyes in the lobby were on their merry little band. The hotel manager stood next to the registration desk, observing them apprehensively.

As they entered the elevator car, Maggie's gaze moved to the gift shop. Shanks stood behind a rack of cards, his expression easy to read: *What's going on?* She stared stonily at him as the door slid shut.

"It's fucking hot in here," mumbled Wexler. Sweat glistened on his forehead and there was a spooky white light shining in his eyes. Maggie was familiar with the signs. He was starting to fade.

Wexler brought out an unlabeled vial of white capsules and shook a half dozen into his hand.

"What are you doing?" said Maggie.

"These fucking Jamaican elevators, make you want to throw up," he said, blowing out air.

He put the pills to his mouth, preparing to gulp them down. Maggie bumped his hand, scattering the pills on the floor.

"What the fuck?"

"I'm sorry," she said.

He opened his mouth and she thought he was going to say something else, but he tottered backward, grabbing at the handrail and bracing himself against the wall of the elevator. Maggie was aware of something brushing against her lower back, then felt the steely grip of Dreadlocks on her ass.

"Get your hands off me," she said, slapping at his hand. But he'd already retracted it. He had very sudden moves. Once Maggie had gone to a boxing match between a pair of light middleweights and she had been surprised at the whirling speed of their punches. That was what Dreadlocks reminded her of.

He made a kissy-kissy motion with his lips. Absorbed with the effects of his sudden illness, Wexler wasn't aware of anything.

The floor number kept climbing digitally—eight, nine, ten—then the elevator stopped.

Wexler sagged noticeably as the door opened. A little boy about twelve years old, dressed in a swimsuit and holding oversized flippers, boarded the car and pressed the button for the first floor.

"I gotta lie down or something," said Wexler, as the elevator resumed its movement.

The little boy screwed up his face. "It's going up," he said to Maggie.

"Yes."

"Shit."

Wexler's face was waxen. Maggie knew it couldn't be long. She felt the taste of blood and realized she was chewing the inside of her mouth.

"You don't look so good, mon," said Dreadlocks. "I think maybe you gonna crap out wit' de Red Hot Mama here."

"Fuck you," said Wexler. He was looking at the diamond-shaped pattern on the carpet, working to manage his breathing.

"You don't talk to me like that, remember what I say?"

"Fuck you."

Dreadlocks cocked his head to one side, as though considering the matter. To crack Wexler's head or not. He looked over at the little boy, whose eyes were extra wide. Before Dreadlocks could make up his mind, though, they'd reached their destination—the top floor. The door slid open and the group spilled out, leaving the kid with a new perspective on adult life.

Maggie propped up Wexler, struggling hard to get them to the door. Behind them she heard Dreadlocks whisper something. Guayabera laughed.

"Give me your keys, honey," she said.

Wexler pulled a key from his pocket. She read the number but couldn't see any room directions on the walls.

"Which one?" she asked.

Wexler gestured down the nearest hall. As Maggie fumbled with Wexler and the key, she saw Guayabera drag a chair over from the foyer, positioning it in the corridor to face Wexler's suite. Dreadlocks pressed against her.

"I be next door, sweet meat," he said. "You want de real thing, you come on over."

Again, he placed his hand on her ass.

Maggie slapped him hard across the cheek as Wexler pitched forward into the room.

"I told you to get your fucking hands off me, hairball."

She slammed the door on him and immediately felt it shudder, kicked from the other side. She jerked the dead bolt in place and backed away. From the corridor she heard Dreadlocks screaming at her.

Then she heard a crash, like a wrecker ball had broken through the side of the hotel . . . but realized it was coming from inside the room. Wexler had gone down, knocking over a lamp. She went to him and he grabbed wildly at her, snagging the top of her dress and ripping it down the middle.

And then his head fell to one side and he was out.

Maggie dropped beside him, taking his carotid pulse. Feeling woozy herself, she counted down for fifteen seconds, then multiplied by four. Seventy-six. High, but within the range.

Satisfied she was not sharing the room with a corpse, she went back to the door and peered out the peephole. Guayabera was still there, sprawled in the chair across the hall.

Sagging against the door, Maggie inhaled a deep, deep breath of air. One of her falsies slipped and she laughed aloud. She yanked them both out of her torn dress and hurled them across the room, then kicked off her stiletto heels and sank down to the carpet.

"You're right about one thing, Jack," she said. "I gotta get in another line of work."

18

*I*n ten minutes, Maggie had searched the suite twice. Gordon Wexler's bed was filled with a score of credit cards, a gold money clip, a diamond-and-onyx ring, a Swiss Army knife, a nifty little Gianfranco Ferré chronometer, a pair of Leica Trinovid high-power binoculars, a Braun travel clock, a Montblanc fountain pen, $942 in cash, $2,000 in traveler's checks, a Nintendo Game Boy—everything but the disks.

She went into the bathroom and splashed her face with cold water and sat on the rim of the tub, and found she couldn't govern her trembling. Nearby on a plaster pedestal stood a crystal vase of fresh oleander; the heavy, sweetish odor was oppressive. Maggie lit a cigarette, sucked in a deep, corrosive breath of tobacco, and struggled to get herself under control.

But try as she did, she couldn't find a comfortable slant on her situation. Outside a massive thug guarded the door. Downstairs an FBI man lay in wait. A berserk Rastafarian roamed the halls. On top of all this, the plastic treasure she had been hired to steal—the disks with which she was planning to buy her safety—was nowhere to be found. Maggie had been in many tight spots before, but the downside was only a stretch in jail. This time, she couldn't shake the fear that she might actually die. The Jamaicans were killers; she could read it in their eyes, the way they handled themselves. She had disturbed their nest and soon they would swarm her.

And she didn't even know what the hell was really going on. That's what galled her more than anything. If she was going to die

. . . *No*—no, she wasn't going to die. She couldn't start thinking that way. She wouldn't.

She had to get out of this room, this hotel, this goddamn country, fast—but how?

Maggie stared at the sky blue terrazzo tile, the marble lavatory, the peach-colored wall telephone. Her gaze shifted to the back of the bathroom door where a laminated plastic sheet was posted. She read the headline but it took a moment to comprehend.

FOR THE SAFETY OF YOUR VALUABLE POSSESSIONS.

She stood and examined it more closely. A paragraph of copy, repeated in French and Spanish, provided information about a room safe "available in penthouse suites as a special courtesy extended to the hotel's valued patrons." Childlike diagrams described its usage and location.

Under the carpet in the bedroom closet.

Disbelieving, Maggie jerked the poster off the door. In the bedroom the louvered folding doors of the closet stood open from her previous exploration of its shelves and clothing, including even the insides of Wexler's bucks and fancy spectator oxfords. Bending over, she lifted the corner of the carpet. And there it was—the door of a safe embedded in the concrete flooring. She tried the recessed handle, but it was locked.

Amazed, she let the carpet fall back in place and remained there, on her knees. Then she scuttled across to Wexler, whom she had pushed over on his side so that he wouldn't swallow his tongue. His pockets were turned inside out; flung about his splayed body were the rejects of her search. She sifted through the loose change and ballpoint pens and bottles of white capsules until she found his key ring. It held two keys from the Safari.

The smaller one fit the lock. It was awkward lifting the door while holding back the carpet flap, but it took her no time at all. Wedged inside the flimsy safe was a scuffed brown leather catalog case. On top of the case was a gray nylon diskette carrier.

The phone rang. It jangled in three locations, the bathroom, the bed table, and the sitting room. The reverberations cut into the air like a razor.

Riiiiiiiiinnnnng. It wouldn't stop. It must have rung twenty times by now. She stood before the phone by the bed, pressing the diskette case against her chest, holding up the loose top of her ripped dress. *Riiiiiiiiinnnnng.*

She lifted the receiver. It was very cold to the touch.

"Yes," she said.

"Are you all right?" said Shanks.

She put the receiver against her forehead. It felt like an ice cube. She wondered if she had a fever. Then she brought it back down to her lips.

"You have the wrong number," she finally said.

She hung up. Then took the receiver off the hook.

Then she had an idea.

Mrs. Marguerite Alt, the night clerk at the registration desk of the Safari Hotel and Golf Club, was disturbed by the manner of the American gentleman. For the past quarter of an hour he had been pacing the lobby, his eye always going back to the elevator. It was this that caught her attention: the fierceness of his black eyes, the brooding intensity. He had the look of a violent man, barely held in check.

She thought about paging the manager, Mr. Orsini, but after the earlier problem in the bar he had wandered off, probably to have a drink in his office, and it was never wise to trouble him without good cause. Besides, the American wasn't actually *doing* anything, just moving back and forth, back and forth, like a large predator in a small and brittle cage.

Finally, the man went to a courtesy phone beside the concierge desk and punched in a number. The phone was a dedicated line reserved for hotel use; it was obvious he was waiting for a hotel guest who was extremely late. Mrs. Alt would not want to be that person. But if he was in such a hurry, why didn't he simply go upstairs and rouse the party?

She glanced at the clock. Ten-fourteen. In less than two hours her shift would be over and she could go home.

There was a sharp crack from the American's direction. He had kicked the wall. Mrs. Alt saw a chunk of plaster fall to the floor and explode in a spray of dust. The American stared at the phone in his hand for a moment, then carefully set it down in its cradle as though handling a live bomb. Through great force of will he had regained his composure. She did not want to be present when he lost it again; next time the damage would surely be greater than a few particles of falling plaster.

She opened the door to the staff offices, hoping to find Mr. Orsini quickly.

Through the fisheye of the peephole the big Jamaican appeared even larger to Maggie. His huge girth swamped the fragile armchair. He was tilting back against the wall, trying to balance the chair on its back legs.

She turned and rested her back against the door, facing the sitting room. It was now very tidy. She had cleaned everything off the floors and shoved it into the desk drawers. She had done the same in the bedroom.

Now it was time to tidy up the body of Gordon Wexler.

She returned to the bedroom and grabbed Wexler by the arms, dragging him flush against the bed, then forcing him roughly into a sitting position. The next part would be the roughest. She figured he weighed 160, 165, and wasn't at all sure she could manage him. She straddled his legs and clasped his torso under the arms, took a breath, then heaved. It worked. She got enough of him onto the bed so that she could hold him there, take another breath, and finish the job. One titanic push and he was on top of the covers.

She wanted another cigarette but there was no time. She'd wasted far too much time already. Shanks might well do something stupid and come up to the room, or else the Jamaicans might investigate. She had to rush.

Maggie removed Wexler's flowered shirt; if she'd had any scissors, she would have snipped it off like an emergency room nurse. She loosened the belt to his oyster linen trousers, then slipped off his Bally loafers. She grasped the cuffs of his pants and tugged them off in jerks—and discovered Gordon Wexler had a little surprise.

Strapped around his ankle was a cheap-looking plastic holster with a strapped-in pistol that looked like a toy. She snapped the strap and pulled out the little gun. A derringer, of all things. A real one. Why did he pack a gun? There was no time to waste thought on it now; she tossed it on the keeper pile.

In another minute Gordon Wexler lay naked on the sheets, the covers pulled back to the foot of the bed, the loot packed inside a pillowcase Maggie was holding in her hand. The caseless pillow lay hidden underneath the bed.

Now it was her time. She undressed in the bathroom. She wasn't sure about whether to leave her panties on or not, finally deciding against it. A terry cloth hotel robe hung inside a closet just off the bathroom; it was too big for her, coming down to her ankles, but it would have to do.

She grabbed up her clothes and Wexler's and arranged them on the floor from the door to the bed, straining to make it appear entirely random. Careless, bodice-ripping passion was the effect she was aiming for.

She placed the pillowcase under a small table just inside the entrance door. Checking the peephole once more, she found Guayabera cleaning his ear.

She returned the receiver to the phone, then called the front desk.

Then quickly hung up—she'd forgotten something. It was incredible to her that she could have forgotten the safe. The suitcase in the safe.

She opened the doors and pulled back the flap of carpet. The keys were still in the lock. It was a tight fit but she was able to get a hand around the handle of the suitcase and hoist it out. It was very heavy. She lugged it over to the coffee table. She hadn't seen a suitcase like this in years, one of those things that salesmen used to carry around. It opened from the top and you had to dig into it. It was locked.

Maggie tried all the keys on Wexler's ring, but none of them fit. Undoubtedly, he'd hidden it somewhere in the room, but she didn't have time to look. She found a metal letter opener in the writing desk and tried to force the lock but the blade snapped off.

Should she take it or not? It was really too heavy to cart around, not with what she was planning. Still, it wouldn't be tucked away in a room safe unless Gordon Wexler attached some value to it. She pulled off another pillowcase and tried to slip it over the valise, but it wouldn't fit. So she carried the bag over and sat it down next to her other stash. If it got too heavy, she thought, if things didn't work out, she'd simply jettison the damn thing. The diskette carrier—that was the keeper.

Now she was ready. She picked up the phone and called the front desk again. A woman answered.

"This is room twenty-three-oh-two," Maggie said. "Help me—a man's just had a heart attack! *Hurry!*"

She hung up. She was pleased. She felt she had incorporated just the right touch of hysteria.

Then she screamed. A hell of a scream, a raving, gasping-for-air, slasher-movie screech. Then, still shrieking, she ran for the door, on which Guayabera was already pounding.

She made a show of fumbling with the locks, even banging on the door in desperation. Then she loosened the belt to her robe, parting it just enough.

Finally, she opened the door.

"He's dead," she screamed, *"I think he's dead!"*

The Jamaican's eyes widened at the sight of what was under the robe. Cinching her belt, she grabbed him by the frilly front of his shirt and pulled him toward the body on the bed.

"My God—," she said. "He was okay and then—I think he had a heart attack. *Jesus!* He just . . . *stopped* moving—"

Guayabera looked dumbly at Wexler's nude body, then back at Maggie, then past her to the doorway. Dreadlocks had arrived. Maggie could not fail to notice that he had a knife in his hand. It was an unusual knife; she'd never seen anything like it before. It had a mother-of-pearl handle with a long, curved, serrated blade. It scared the hell out of her.

"Do *something!* Is he okay?"

She made no attempt to pull Dreadlocks over to the body. She didn't want any part of him. Very deliberately, his eyes combing the suite, he moved forward toward the bedroom. Maggie began to sob hysterically; it was not a difficult performance.

Dreadlocks folded the knife back into the handle, slipping it under his Lakers T-shirt. He went over the bed and looked down at Wexler. It was clear he suspected some kind of trick and didn't want to be made a fool. Then, with a speed and fluidity of motion that shocked Maggie, he slapped Wexler's face, like a snake striking its prey. Wexler's face jerked sideways. There was no other reaction. Dreadlocks turned to face Maggie. He wanted an explanation. She felt the remains of her confidence crumbling into dust; she couldn't fake it with him.

Edging backward, Maggie peered into the sitting area toward the open door, praying for someone, anyone, to make an appearance. When she glanced back she saw Guayabera reaching under the dust ruffle of the bed, picking up something. Her heart slammed wildly.

It was one of her foam rubber falsies. He looked bewilderedly at Maggie.

There was a light tapping on the door. An elderly Japanese gentleman and his tiny wife stood at the threshold, gaping inside, inquiring visitors at the gates of hell. Maggie sprang forward at them, seizing the old fellow's hand to drag him into the fray.

"Help him, please! Somebody help him!"

The Japanese gentleman eased into the group, bent over, and listened to Wexler's heartbeat, then felt tentatively for a pulse. Gently, he set down the hand, glancing between his wife and the two Jamaicans. Plainly, they made him nervous. Then, seeking to shield his wife from embarrassment, he delicately spread a corner of the bed sheet across Gordon Wexler's exposed genitalia.

By then, Maggie had edged out of the bedroom and through the sitting room and into the corridor. She had her stash in hand and had made it as far as the stairwell door before she heard Dreadlocks snarling behind her.

19

*F*or most of Jack Shanks's fourteen years with the Federal Bureau of Investigation, he had been a brick agent attached to resident offices throughout the Northeast. Before his career turned to shit, he had arrested more than five hundred fugitives and earned more than twenty-five commendations. His performance ratings ranked consistently at the exceptional level. Once, for a fourteen-month period, he had gone deep undercover in Philadelphia, setting up a sting operation on the South Side that netted eighty-five arrests and a 90 percent conviction rate and even drew two columns in the *New York Times*. He had survived all this because he was street-smart and had steady nerves, but mostly because he had a little bell inside his head that rang when things began to fall apart. He knew when to pull in—or thought he did.

For the past forty-five minutes the bell inside Jack Shanks's head had been clanging like a ship going down at sea.

Field agents had an expression—*when the situation goes fluid*. It was the moment when all your training and your instincts and your guts merged, when the adrenaline surge swept you into action. It was the moment when you couldn't afford to screw up.

Tonight the situation had gone fluid when Daniel Poole, the man with the dreadlocks, appeared on the terrace of the Safari Hotel and Golf Club. Shanks knew then and there that he should go inside the cocktail lounge and drag Maggie out to safety. But he hadn't. He'd ignored the bell in his head, and waited.

Now he couldn't get an accurate read on the situation. Was it going down or not? Was Maggie in danger—or setting up shop on her own? All along, he'd worried that Maggie might pull a double-cross. He'd taken precautions against the possibility.

The indecision gnawed at him until finally he didn't care. He had to act. He would go upstairs and deal with the situation. Anything to quiet the goddamn bell in his head.

Both elevator cars opened their doors simultaneously. Shanks let a young couple, honeymooners, he presumed, enter one. Then he took the other.

On the twenty-third floor Shanks started out the door, then saw the big Jamaican charging toward him. He stepped back inside the car. The Jamaican paid no attention to him. Frazzled, he banged away with his beefy hand at the "L" button. Finally, the door closed.

Shanks knew the Jamaican, but the Jamaican didn't know him. Back in his hotel room, in fact, he had a JCF arrest sheet on him. His name was Ernest Hopper, he was thirty-two, six feet six, 250 pounds, a native of Port Antonio. As a teenager he had clubbed his grandfather to death with a washing machine agitator. Some time after his release from the St. Catherine District Prison he fell into the employ of Albert Magliocco.

Hopper was in a rush about something. Shanks felt certain the object of his attention must be Maggie. Hopper thumped his hand nervously on the double door, watching the numbers count down. Aware that a stranger's eyes were upon him, he glanced over.

Shanks pointed at the floor.

Confused, Hopper looked down. When he raised his head again, he got an elbow in his face. It was well timed, a hard smash into the eye socket, and Hopper screamed. Shanks grabbed him by the hair and, pulling his head down, kneed him sharply in the face. He could distinctly hear the sound of Hopper's nose cartilage breaking apart. The big Jamaican slumped against the wall of the elevator and Shanks kicked at his groin, instead catching his massive thigh as Hopper turned instinctively to his side. Still, he was going down. His big hands were at his face and he was gagging as though about to vomit. Blood had sprayed all over the lower wall and floor.

Shanks pressed the button for the next floor, taking his eyes off Hopper for an instant—but it was long enough. The big man came at him like an underground missile, propelled by fear as much as anger. He slammed Shanks into the back wall with enough force to knock loose a plastic overhead light cover. Shanks felt an excruciating, piercing sensation in his side and knew something bad had happened to a rib. Hopper brought his head up suddenly, catching Shanks's jaw by accident. It loosened a tooth and brought blood to his mouth; light-headed, he was afraid he might actually pass out.

The Jamaican pushed away then, to get a better look at the damage he'd inflicted. Shanks gripped the rail with both hands and rammed his feet into Hopper's chest. As he did, pain shot through him from the rib.

Hopper's back hit the door and he stumbled forward, toward Shanks. Again, Shanks lifted up—again felt the jolt in his side— and planted both feet squarely in Hopper's chest.

The elevator door opened at that instant and Hopper pitched backward, into the hall and past a waiting family. The father grabbed for his child, who stood transfixed, watching the man-mountain sweep past him like a landslide. Hopper's momentum carried him into the opposite wall, where he collapsed against a floor-to-ceiling mirror. Shanks caught a transient image of himself, his hand and the front of his shirt glistening with blood.

Hopper, dazed, looked up at him, and Shanks lashed out with his leg, the toe of his shoe snapping back the Jamaican's head.

Shanks bolted down the corridor toward the exit stairwell.

Behind him, the door to the elevator began to close and the father reached out to block it. Quickly, he shepherded his little family into the elevator and passed an agonizing few seconds until the door finally closed.

Maggie knew there was no point in running. Soon Dreadlocks would sweep down upon her. Even if she wasn't lugging all this crap with her, she'd never have a chance against his speed.

She was on the half landing, two floors down, when she heard the stairwell door above her crash open. She almost shouted in fear. Now was the time to drop the catalog case, she told herself, but she couldn't. Something inside forced her to hang on to it until the last possible second.

She raced down the last few steps, the concrete cold and damp on her bare feet, the terry cloth robe flapping against her ankles. Above, she could hear Dreadlocks charging after her; the stairwell reverberated with the sound of him. But at the door, with *20* stenciled in large numbers, she changed her mind. She pushed it open wide, then slipped down the steps, hoping to trick him into thinking she'd tried to escape down the corridor.

But as Maggie turned the corner on the next half-landing, the pillowcase snagged on a jagged newel cap. The fabric ripped open and, as the door fell shut with an echoing boom, credit cards and cash and jewelry cascaded down the steps and through the balusters and into the stairwell. She saw the diskette case fall. Over it went, slapping against a passing handrail as it tumbled end over end, eventually skidding to rest on a step a few flights down.

It was too far; she could never retrieve it.

She clutched at the tear in the pillowcase, trying to prevent more loss, wanting to save the few items still inside. Her right arm felt like it was about to snap from the strain of lugging the suitcase, but she couldn't let go, not now, now that this was all she had.

She became aware that the stairwell had fallen silent. *Had that stupid son of a bitch taken off down the corridor on twenty?*

She looked up—and there he was, leaning over the railing, grinning at her. He was on the next landing.

Maggie ran.

When he first hit the stairwell, Shanks didn't know for certain what floor he was on. But he knew he was close, he could hear the echo of footsteps above him. Taking the steps two and three at a time, he leapt up the darkened well. Each step sent a shiver of pain lancing through his side.

On the next landing he saw the painted number: *16.*

Above, he heard the boom of a heavy door slamming shut, then, a moment later, the same door slam again. Then silence.

But which floor were they on? There was no way to tell for sure. He reckoned it was eighteen or nineteen. He'd have to start with eighteen.

Racing upstairs, his hand gripping his side, Shanks failed to notice a gray diskette case lying at his feet, balanced precariously on the edge of a step.

*   *   *

At first Maggie tried every doorknob, hoping crazily that one might not be shut all the way. Allison Delillo, her partner years ago in Kansas City, had once made her living as a "nightcrawler." She would walk the halls of a hotel late at night, pushing against every door until she found one left ajar; then she'd slink inside and boost the occupant's belongings in the dark.

But tonight all the doors were locked tight.

Picking up speed, Maggie turned a corner just as Dreadlocks came through the exit door. There were many more doors on the nineteenth floor than on the penthouse level. Her right arm was numb; she shifted the catalog case and something else slipped out of the torn pillowcase. The chronometer. She didn't stop to retrieve it. It was so goddamn quiet, she thought. Where were the people? She wanted someone to walk into the corridor; she wanted to hear the sounds of a party; she wanted to get where real live people were.

She heard a slight rustling sound, then a crash. She whirled, expecting a knife in her face, then realized the sound came from just ahead, from an alcove. An ice maker. Next to it were soft drink and candy machines. Between the ice maker and the wall was a narrow recess, but maybe just wide enough. She opened the ice maker and set the suitcase inside; it made a hell of a noise, the ice shifting and crashing around under the heavy weight. She squeezed into the space. The opening was very tight but, because of the ice maker, deep enough to allow her room to push back into the corner.

Maggie drew up her legs defensively, pressing her ripped pillowcase and its remnants close to her chest. She felt a hot whiff of exhaust from the refrigerator coils blow across her crotch, exposed from the gaping bathrobe, and thought what a great beaver shot Dreadlocks would get, just before he hacked her to death. The thought let loose a rat in her stomach. She would give all she had in the world, or would ever have, for one cigarette and the time to smoke it. Maybe she should scream, she thought. It would feel wonderful to scream, really let go like she'd done in Wexler's room, scream until help arrived. But she knew it would only bring death that much closer.

Her hand clutched the pillowcase . . . and felt the outline of the derringer. The gun—she had forgotten the goddamn gun. She dug into the case, and there it was, the plastic rig, the toylike gun. She unsnapped the holster strap and held it in her hand. It was tiny, hard to believe it was real, although of course it was. But was it loaded?

She clicked open the pistol's loading gates and both cartridges suddenly slid out. They fell into the folds of her robe and one bounced off onto the linoleum. She clawed her robe and the floor for them.

And then she saw Dreadlocks. Saw his reflection in the glass panel of the candy machine opposite her. Saw him peering into the alcove. Saw his wild face amid the Mars bars and M&M's bags.

The sight of him paralyzed her. She listened to his labored breathing.

Maggie forced her hand to continue its search for the cartridges. Silently, she patted the floor under the ice maker, feeling the grit and dust balls and dead moths.

Dreadlocks stepped into the alcove, coming closer. Then stopped, listening.

At last, Maggie found a cartridge. It made a little *snick* as she dropped it back into the chamber.

Another tray of fresh ice crashed inside the machine. Startled, Dreadlocks jumped to the side, and then he saw Maggie wedged into her hole. His hand held the grisly knife he'd showed inside Wexler's room. He snapped it open. It made an odd ratcheting sound as it unfolded, the serrated blade flashing the light from the fluorescent bulb overhead. He advanced, altering his grip to allow for downward thrusting.

He loomed before her, his spectral face lit with a perverse smile. Maggie tugged at the trigger—but the trigger wouldn't budge. *The safety*. She felt for a safety lever.

Dreadlocks came at her, plunging down the knife. At the last instant, he caught the glint of the derringer and it threw him off just enough. The knife missed its mark by inches, ripping a jagged hole in the dry wall next to her head.

As Maggie flicked back the safety, she saw a sudden blur of red behind Dreadlocks, and heard a heavy *ker-thunk*. Dreadlocks staggered. She watched his eyes glaze over as he reached out for support, falling against the soft drink machine. Shanks stood behind him, holding a bright red fire extinguisher. He raised it again, hoping for a finishing blow, but Dreadlocks dodged the hit, lashing out furiously with the knife. She watched it slice across Shanks's midsection, watched the yellow cotton fabric of his polo shirt split open and a line of blood form at the center. Shanks, already in midswing with the canister, brought it down hard, cracking Dreadlocks's shoulder. He fell backward into the corridor and Shanks went after him, as they passed from Maggie's field of vision.

Maggie squirmed from her hole. As she got to her feet, the second cartridge fell from her robe to the floor.

She went into the hall and they were gone. She set the derringer on the top of the ice machine, opened the lid, and pulled out the catalog case. From beyond the corner she heard a yelp.

Every instinct told Maggie to run in the opposite direction. To safety. Looking that way, she saw a scrawny little man outside an open door. He stood confusedly in his boxer shorts and undershirt. Behind him, someone else appeared—a teenager in an LSU T-shirt; he held a Red Stripe in his hand.

Maggie stepped into the corridor and crept toward the fight. Then heard a terrific bang, like the fire extinguisher connecting with flesh and bone. As she craned her neck around the corner, she saw Shanks open the control valve, releasing spray foam into Dreadlocks's face. Dreadlocks was down on one knee and he jabbed the air with his foam-splattered knife, but he was blinded.

The fight would soon be over. Shanks would survive. But she wouldn't be there for him. She hoisted her loot and scrambled down the hall toward the curious onlookers, toward the elevators.

As if by magic, the car was there, open and waiting for her. The door slid shut and as it did, Shanks turned the corner and saw her.

She barely had time to get it out. "Fuck you, Jack," she said. "And fuck the FBI, too."

It took her a moment to realize she'd left the derringer behind on the ice machine. She very much wished she had remembered to bring it.

Harmon Zander IV was sitting on the hood of his cab and reading an article in the *Daily Gleaner* about the son of a friend of his. The boy had killed a musician on Claude Clarke Avenue in broad daylight and stolen his Fender guitar and his goat. He was apprehended by the constabulary way over in Port Maria. He had had a party and roasted the goat. They were unable to locate the guitar.

As Harmon read the story again, he kept an eye on the front entrance of the Safari Hotel. It was his turn but sometimes the younger drivers attempted to cut in line.

A young barefoot red-haired lady in a hotel bathrobe walked outside carrying a big, scuffed leather suitcase and a white bag of some sort. She waved away a porter. Harmon tucked the paper under his arm and eased down from the hood, requesting if she desired a cab. She said that she did.

He opened the door for the woman and asked where she wished to be taken and she told him to please just start driving somewhere, anywhere. She seemed very flustered but was polite to him. Courtesy was a trait that Harmon Zander appreciated.

She kept looking back at the hotel until they were on the main road, then asked him if he had a cigarette. Harmon did not smoke. She asked him to stop at the first place that sold cigarettes, which he did very shortly thereafter. She rummaged through her bag, which he realized now was a pillowcase, and brought out a fifty-dollar bill. He went inside the Fancy Mart and purchased a carton of Winstons for the lady and a Sprite for himself. She told him to please keep the change.

They drove around for a while and she never told him where to go and he never asked. The air had cooled and it was pleasant driving through the night. They headed east into town, then out A1 past Mahoe Bay and Rose Hall, toward Falmouth, and he kept thinking she would direct him to turn around and go back to Montego Bay, but she never did. Once or twice he sniffed a wisp of ganja from shacks they passed along the way, and, while he himself did not indulge, he always thought the smell was sweet and enjoyable.

Eventually she asked him if he had a screwdriver or a knife. Harmon reached under the seat and produced a fourteen-inch boron steel Stanley, which seemed to please her.

For a moment she was busy in the backseat with the screwdriver. He could not see exactly what she was doing but he assumed she was trying to open her suitcase. He wished he could lower the rearview mirror to get a better view of the lady but he felt that would be rude.

Finally, he heard one of the catches pop open, and then another. Glancing back, he saw her reach into the top of the heavy sample case.

Then he heard her say, "Jesus." He heard her say it over and over again. At first he thought she was praying.

*A*t this hour of the morning, the small terminal of the Sir
Donald Sangster International Airport was virtually deserted, save for Jack Shanks, sitting in a row of steel-tube chairs in
the center of the concourse.

Shanks was looking through the glass toward the passenger arrival
lane and the pitch-black night beyond. Over the intercom a Musak
version of "Strawberry Fields" was playing.

The big brass-and-copper airport clock above the American Airlines counter read three minutes past three. The next flight out was
at seven-fourteen, so there wasn't much point in sitting around the
airport any longer. Shanks knew that, but he also knew he didn't
want to stand; it would hurt too much.

After leaving the hotel, he'd made a couple of stops trying to
locate some tape and gauze. He should have brought along a first-
aid kit; it was one of many things he was thinking he should have
done but didn't. Jamaica wasn't like the States, though; there wasn't
a 7-Eleven on every corner. Eventually he found an all-night tourist
shop downtown and purchased another polo shirt, a dozen plain
white T-shirts, a bottle of rubbing alcohol, and a roll of duct tape.
Back in his room, he cleaned the knife wound as best he could and
dressed it with strips torn from the T-shirts, then taped the mess
in place. As long as he didn't stretch or bend over, he felt it might
hold until he could get to a doctor.

His stomach didn't hurt nearly as much as his side, though. At
first, he'd hoped the rib was merely sprained or even cracked, but

now he was fairly sure it was broken. He really couldn't tell for certain. Every breath was a strain, every motion taxing.

He got up and stood still a moment, gathering strength. Across the concourse an old man was sleeping on the floor beside a shoeshine stand. His chin quivered as he exhaled. Shanks moved on.

Driving back to his room, Shanks considered the angles. Somehow Maggie had learned about the Bureau. He couldn't imagine how. She was a bright girl and now she was an angry bright girl. Still, she had a big problem; she had to get off the island. There weren't many ways to accomplish that, not really. But Shanks had a bigger problem: there was only one of him. He couldn't surveil every boat dock or airport in Jamaica.

On the theory that Maggie needed to put some clothes on her back, he'd asked the shopkeeper at the all-night tourist trap if he'd seen her. He hadn't.

His best bet was to start calling the luxury hotels, asking if any young red-haired guest had just signed in. He could identify himself as a member of the JCF Criminal Investigation Division. The hotel clerks would tell him everything once they heard that.

Shanks tried not to think what would happen if Headache's goons got to her before he did. He hoped to hell that Maggie was bright enough to curb her anger just long enough to comprehend the danger of that situation.

At that moment Maggie was tapping on the door of room 411 of the Sunsplash Inn. She had paid the driver at the street, tipping him another fifty dollars, and watched the old cab rumble off before walking across the big, empty parking lot toward Barry's wing. There was no one around, no one to see her strolling about in her robe.

Before knocking, she had gone to a window and peeked inside through a broken pebbled-glass louver. Maggie could see Barry's legs and bare feet at the end of the bed. The TV was on and he was very still.

Room 411 was at the corner. Maggie picked her way through the bougainvillea and hibiscus along the side of the building until she found a nice spot for what she wanted to do. It took a few minutes until she was satisfied.

Barry was yawning when he opened the door. His new Hawaiian shirt was badly wrinkled and he smelled like a goat, but he was very happy to see her. His eye fell instantly on the catalog case and never left it.

Maggie set the case on the bed and gestured for him to open it. It had overlapping flaps on the top and he greedily peeled them back and reached inside with both arms. She could imagine him at age eighteen, maybe a hundred pounds slimmer and his hair a lot fuller, excitedly peeling off his girlfriend's underwear. The latch of one of the broken locks fell off when he began pulling out the bundles of cash.

"Jeez," he said. "How much, you think?" He upended the case and shook out the remaining money.

"About ten thousand dollars," she said. She knew exactly. Spread before him was eighty-five hundred dollars in bundles of twenties, fifties, and hundreds, double-bound tightly in thick rubber bands. It was considerably less, however, than what she had found when she first opened the case in Harmon Zander's cab. The other $974,500 lay in a black canvas duffel bag she had purchased only minutes before. It was tucked behind a stand of banana trees to the rear of the building. Actually, from where Barry was now standing, it was about thirty inches away, on the other side of the cement block wall.

"That's pretty good," he said. "That's great. Did you get away clean?"

Maggie nodded, lying back in a recliner.

"What about the computer crap?" he asked.

"There wasn't any computer crap."

"No?"

"I think that was the cover."

"I don't get it. What are the Fibbies hanging around for?"

"I'm still working on it myself," she said. "I need some clothes."

"Sure, we'll get them in the morning."

"I need them now. I need you to go get them for me."

"Now?"

"There's a tourist place closer in to Montego Bay, on the right. I passed it coming over here. It's open all night. Get me some shorts, sandals, and T-shirts." She looked at his Hawaiian shirt. "Nothing stupid, Barry. Stick to primary colors, okay? I don't want to stand out, understand?"

Maggie peeled a bill off one of the bundles. Barry took the money but didn't like it. There was a definite shift in their relationship and she could tell he was considering the ramifications of that fact. But she also knew he would realize now wasn't the time to start a fight.

"All right," he finally said. "You'll be here when I get back, right?"

"I didn't have to come here at all, Barry."

"Yeah. Right."

When he'd gone, she went outside to the patio and stood at the low stucco wall, looking down at the ocean below. There was a small, crescent beach, and she watched the waves roll in. It was a cheap motel, she thought, with cheap furnishings, but the setting was nice. And it did have a mini-bar.

Looking at the little refrigerator, she realized how hungry she was. But there wasn't time for that, not now. It would take Barry half an hour, tops, before he was back. In that time she wanted to take a hot shower.

Then maybe she'd give Jack Shanks a call.

Every so often there was a sound in Gordon Wexler's head. Each time it was the same, like a plate smashing. And each time it seemed to flip his brain over, so that he had to start fresh again, figuring out what was going on. It reminded him of what happened when the little bomb icon appeared on his computer screen, telling him there was a system error and he had to boot up again.

For a long time he thought he was dreaming and then he thought he was dead because he couldn't wake himself up. He didn't really care except for the sound and what it did to him. The sound produced a sensation that was very much like pain, but there was no way to find out about it and stop it. He didn't know where his hands and fingers were, or why he couldn't use them.

The cracking sound came again, and the pain, and this time a word: "*What?*"

And he realized the word had come from him. *"What?"* he said again.

It didn't help. There it came again, the goddamn cracking sound, and then the pain. This time, though, he didn't have to start over. He was aware that something was being done to him, something was hurting him. Something might be killing him.

He opened his eyes and saw all that hair hanging down, coils of black hair hanging over a skull face. With a big, ugly bruise above one eye. And then Daniel Poole slapped him again and Wexler felt the pain start at his jaw and reverberate through his head.

"What?" he said. Hands appeared in front of his face, his own hands. He found he could control the fingers but somehow they didn't seem like his real hands. He considered that. It didn't matter whose hands they were, he thought, so long as he could make them do what he wanted, which was to block the slapping. Satisfied with that, he drifted off.

Poole slapped him again. Wexler's hands weren't there to protect his face. He didn't know where they had gone.

"Goddamn it!" he shouted.

"Okay," said a voice. It wasn't his voice, he knew that. He thought maybe it was someone else's voice that he was able to control, like the hands. He opened his eyes to see what had happened to his hands and he found them on top of his stomach. He realized that he was naked in a bright room with people around him.

Then he saw where the other voice had come from. Albert Magliocco was sitting in the big wing chair across from the bed. He was smoking a cigar as big as a baton and had a blue-and-gold captain's hat pulled down low over his eyes. He was not happy.

When Shanks got back to his room the red message light was blinking in the dark. Without turning on the lights, he went to the phone and called the front desk. The message was: *Don't go away.*

Now, sitting in the dark, he stared at the phone, willing it to ring.

Finally, it did.

"How dirty is it, Jack?" she said when he picked up the receiver.

"Where are you?"

"Just tell me how dirty it is, okay?"

"What?"

"What you've had me doing, Jack—your dirty work. You know, taking money that doesn't belong to you. Tell me how dirty—"

"*Wait*—there was money?"

She laughed. "Yeah, Jack, there was a little cash lying around. And I bet you know exactly how much. I bet you have all the goddamn serial numbers scribbled down in your little notebook, huh?"

"What about the disks?"

"No disks, Jack."

That took a moment to sink in. "He didn't have them?"

"Oh, he had them all right. And *I* had them. But then I didn't have them, you know? I was kinda busy. There were a lot of things going on at the time. I imagine they have them back now, Mr. Wexler and his friends."

"Listen to me," said Shanks. "Is there any way they can trace you, any way at all?"

A pause.

"Maggie," he said, "what you think is going on, isn't what's going on. This thing isn't about *money*. If you took their money, there's a blood frenzy going on right this second. If there's *anything* that can lead them to you—anything at all—they'll come after you and eat you up. You have to understand that."

"You're trying to scare me."

"*Yes*. Where are you? Tell me."

Another pause. "No," she said. "I don't trust you."

"Meet me somewhere then, someplace safe."

"Sure. I'm going to take a meeting with the goddamn FBI."

"I'm *not* with the FBI," Shanks said. "I used to be with the Bureau, but no more. I'm in this as deep as you are. Trust me this much, Maggie."

An even longer pause. For a moment, Shanks was afraid she would break the connection.

"Okay," she said. "Let's go swimming."

They wouldn't let him get dressed. Wexler couldn't understand why they wouldn't let him put his clothes on—or why he didn't have any clothes on in the first place. At some point they must have thrown water on him because his hair was wet and the sheets were soaked. The air conditioning was down at the freezer-box level and he was shivering.

Magliocco remained in his chair, staring at him, his flat, slablike face obscured in a cloud of cigar smoke.

He said: "Never realized you had such a little pecker, Gordon."

"What?"

"Little weenie thing, and you liking hookers so much."

Playing with him, trying to frighten him. Headache was good at that.

"What is it?" asked Wexler. "What happened?" Last thing he remembered, he was going to the bar downstairs. He was on the elevator going to the bar. Something must have been wrong with his tabs.

Magliocco said: "Hookers what get you in trouble, you know that? What was this one's name?"

"Her name?" What was he talking about?

"Yeah, her name. The words you call her when you want her to come. *The fuck's her name.*"

His rage was sudden and volcanic; Wexler felt singed by it.

Then he remembered her in a flash: the redhead in the bar. Creamy white skin. Beautiful tits. The slit up her dress. He remembered they got into the elevator . . . but that was it. There wasn't anything after that. A black hole in his memory. Her name, what was her name? Did he even know her name?

Magliocco nodded to Poole, who slapped Wexler so hard this time that it knocked him off the bed and onto the floor. He pulled a wet sheet over himself and found he was crying.

"I don't know," he said. "I *swear* it. I just met her. What did she do to me?"

Magliocco pushed himself up from the wing chair. Although small, he was hard and compact and bullnecked. He came charging around the bed, a grimace on his weathered face. He had something in his hands. Poole eased back.

Magliocco kept coming like he was going to step on him. Wexler could feel the toes of the old man's deck shoes, stained from the saltwater on his boat, pressing against his side. He stood over him and held his hand out. A credit card dropped down, hitting Wexler in the face. *What the shit?* Then another. Then several more. Flopping in his eyes, forehead, neck, all over.

Then some twenty-dollar bills, then a watch—his Gianfranco Ferré chronometer. My stuff, thought Wexler. Why's he doing this?

His gray diskette case was next, hitting him square in the nose. *My God—does he know?* Wexler grabbed it protectively, stupidly, then pushed it away, afraid of showing too much interest. And Magliocco, whose antennae detected every nuance, didn't fail to pick up Wexler's concern.

Then the American Derringer came at him, the butt popping him in the larynx, causing him to cough.

But Magliocco had more in store. A drop of yellowish liquid came trickling down. Then another and another. Wexler cringed with each drop, afraid it might be acid. But the mobster slowly opened his hand, showing a small, clear plastic squeeze bottle. Like a bottle of sweetener or eye medicine. Magliocco raised his hand and hurled it at him.

"Your hooker," he said, "she took something didn't belong to her. I want you should get it back."

The phone rang. Poole picked it up and listened a moment, then spoke into the receiver: "Yeah, you do that. Wait for me there, you hear?" He cradled the phone and smiled at Magliocco. "Hop, he found de cab mon. We know where de woman's at, Cap'n."

"Then go do what I pay you to do," said Magliocco.

21

$\mathcal{S}$hanks walked through the empty lobby of the Sunsplash Inn and onto the veranda, past the softly lapping swimming pool. The underwater lights were still on, casting a rippling turquoise glow. Beyond the pool stood a seawall, where he found a narrow, jagged path of broken cement steps leading down to the beach below. Scanning the shoreline, he could see no one.

He started his descent.

It was obviously a man-made beach, a small, perfect half-circle sliver of sand, enclosed on either side by huge boulders spilling into the ocean. Shanks didn't like the terrain. Too many hiding places. He went to the center of the beach and, as he had been directed, stripped off his pants and shoes, leaving only his Jockey shorts and polo shirt. He hoped she wouldn't be a stickler about the shirt; he didn't want her to see his wound. Feeling like a very inviting target, he folded his arms and felt a breeze brush against his bare legs.

A hundred yards out in the little bay, a small pontoon dock bobbed up and down. A sundeck or diving platform. He could hear the water slosh against its aluminum sides.

Down from him on the beach he saw an object, something white. At first he thought it was a dead gull, but decided it was too big for that. He went over to it and discovered it was a bathrobe, half-buried in the sand. Maggie's robe with the Safari logo. He began to worry that something might have happened to her.

Out of the corner of his eye he caught a movement in the water near the pontoon. A silhouetted figure rose from the sea, climbing the ladder of the float. It was Maggie. She stood on the platform, hands on hips, statuesque. And then she waved him on.

Shanks hesitated, not at all sure he wanted to do this. He glanced back at the rocks, still worried about his exposure. And the last thing he wanted to do with this rib was go for a swim. But he knew he really had no choice. He strolled into the foaming sea and plunged in.

He hadn't been swimming at night since he was a kid, and he found it unsettling. Although there was a three-quarter moon, the light was obscured by cloud cover. And there was virtually no sound, other than the wash of the waves and his steady stroke through the water.

It was farther away than he thought, or else he was in worse shape. He felt himself straining, knowing that he was tearing loose his makeshift dressing. When he could find the time he would have to fashion a tight chest binder. At one point he stopped to tread water. He could see Maggie now sitting yogalike on the platform, observing his progress.

But when he reached the platform she had slipped over the side again and was holding on to the edge on the far end. He started to pull himself up on the ladder.

"*No*," she said. "You can talk from there."

"What do you want to talk about?" He wanted to get closer and read what was in her face.

"The art of lying."

"Interesting spot for it."

"I'm a good swimmer," she said. "I might not be able to outrun or outdrive you, but I'm pretty sure I can outswim you, Jack. And with you in your shorts there, you can't hide any . . . weapon. Out here, there's no one around, no one to sneak up on me. It's perfect."

She was playful. That was good. There was only a slight edge to her voice.

"You have it in your head that I'm with the FBI. I'm not. I left the Bureau six months ago. I didn't lie to you about that."

"About that."

"I didn't really lie to you about the score, either. I just didn't give you all the details. It wouldn't have been helpful."

"Tell me something, Jack."

"What's that?"

"The *truth*. No bullshit, no con. Trust me enough to tell me the truth."

He considered it. He was hanging on to the ladder and his entire right side ached. It would be nice to tell the truth for a change.

"Last year," he said, "the customs service in Hartsfield International Airport in Atlanta picked up a Jamaican smuggler. A freelancer. He brings in heroin, steroids, artifacts, money, whatever. In the course of their investigation, he begins to trade information for a deal. He informs on a middle-level Washington, D.C., coke supplier. The DEA is able to build a nice case. But he also helps them with something else. He gives them the name of a man inside the FBI. An agent receiving payoffs in a money-laundering operation. Me."

He had been speaking in a low voice, hoping she would begin to move closer, and she did. She was just close enough that he could read the surprise on her face.

"Except this is all news to me, you understand. The payoffs were dumped into a special account in a Montego Bay bank. With my name attached to it. The bank wouldn't release its records to the government so they finally come to me. They want me to authorize the bank to release the account history of this account I've never heard about. Which I agree to do. And, lo and behold, there's my signature. I, of course, deny everything. I take a polygraph twice. I pass twice. Then, out of the blue, they discover a checking account in New York—also in my name. Withdrawals from the Montego Bay account become deposits in the New York account overnight. Cash is drawn from the checking account in my name. My signature on the checks. Documents Section 'cannot determine with specificity' if the signature is genuine. So the Bureau has a problem, you see. If the government uses our friend's drug information in court, it means they believe him. Then the question is, *Why don't they believe what he says about me?* After they spend a few months diddling with themselves, the federal prosecutors decide to push the drug case. Me, they aren't so sure about. They have a big meeting with the FBI and the DEA and the assistant attorney general and the

Bureau of Weights and Standards and anybody else who wants to sit in, and finally, these people decide the national interest would best be served if special agent Jack Shanks took early retirement.

"Look," he said. "I'm not as good as you at treading water, okay? Can I just climb up and sit on the edge here? Would that be all right?"

She nodded. "Just keep talking."

It was not easy lifting himself up. He scraped against a rung and the pain jolted him to his toes. "So," he said, settling in on the platform, "letters are now coming in to selected congressmen and newspaper editors from anonymous concerned citizens throughout the commonwealth, asking why the government failed to bring charges against one of its own, a bribe-taker named Jack Shanks. My friends in the Bureau tell me they're going to have to do something. I've been advised to seek counsel."

"So how does this bring you to me?"

"Well, I eventually figure out who's setting me up. It's a hood named Albert 'Headache' Magliocco, an old-line mafioso whose last known address was Atlanta. I put away his brother, Arthur 'Maytag' Magliocco, three years ago."

" 'Maytag'? They really have names like that?"

"They like funny names but they're not funny guys. Maytag washed money for the mob. Headache still does. Headache slipped out of the country before the indictments were handed down. Now he cleans cash through offshore banks, here and in Grand Cayman. At first I thought he was pissed off at me because of his brother, but now I think it's more subtle than that. If I come up dirty, my cases come up dirty, too. My theory is Headache is thinking he can maybe get Maytag busted out, and get his own case dropped, because the government is scared to go to court with evidence I gathered."

She nodded, taking it in.

She said, "They call Maytag 'Maytag' because he washes money, right? So why do they call Headache 'Headache'?"

"Before they became laundrymen," said Shanks, "the brothers Magliocco were juice men. Loan sharks. Headache was the muscle end of it. When they were just starting out in the business, a couple of clients fell too far behind with the vig, so the brothers felt they had to set an example. So Albert cut off their heads. He stored the heads in the urinals of the garage they worked out of, and the boys pissed on them for a couple of weeks. Something like that deserves a nickname, the wiseguys figured. Headache."

A long look passed between them.

Maggie said, "Meanwhile, I'm still sitting in a bar in New Orleans."

"Right. You see, Headache has a young man in his employ, a computer nerd with whom you are intimate."

"Gordon Wexler."

"The same. Gordon Wexler is a high-tech bookkeeper. He wires money back and forth from Magliocco's banks. He set up the frame for Headache. After my retirement party I did a little digging around and discovered something interesting. Gordon keeps all his records—including all the transactions for setting up the various Shanks accounts—on a pair of three-and-a-half-inch floppy disks, which he updates every six months. Apparently, he feels it's insurance against Headache ever deciding to pop his bean. He doesn't know Headache like I know him, though. Gordon keeps the backup set in a safe deposit box outside the country. Guess where."

"Mo Bay."

"And that was one of the purposes of his visit here. Other purposes are emerging. Apparently they were also doing some laundry."

"How did you find all this out?"

Shanks couldn't help but smile. "The thing I like best about you, Maggie, aside from your foam rubber padding, of course, is how you always go straight to the heart of the matter."

He eased his legs into the water.

"Listen to me," he said. "It's important you remember what I'm about to say: I made illegal entry into Gordon's office and put an illegal tap on his phone and hid an illegal wire in the base of his desk lamp. You got that?"

"Yeah. You did something illegal."

"Right. Ex–federal agents aren't supposed to be doing that. If the government finds out, I go to prison legitimately. And now you know this about me. You have something on me."

"So what?"

"It means . . . I can't force you to do things anymore."

During all this, Maggie had edged closer to Shanks. Now, placing her hands on his knees, she pushed his legs apart.

"Does it mean I can force you to do things now?" she asked.

"What do you have in mind?"

Gripping his legs, she pulled herself up out of the water, pressing against him in a fluid motion. Until then, he hadn't realized she was naked.

Shanks took her in his arms as they fell back onto the platform. They embraced and kissed, but their passion seemed unequal, moving on separate tracks. Maggie's kisses were darting and smothering, and immediately, she sensed the problem. She blushed. He was going to think she was too professional at this. Shanks, she realized, was a slow hand; as in all things, he needed to work up to his passion. She could help. Drawing back from him, an embarrassed little schoolgirl smile on her lips, she brushed against his abdomen and Shanks flinched. Her fingers probed the spot, feeling the loose dressing.

"What is it? Oh my God, is that where he cut you?"

Delicately, she lifted the wet shirt and peeled back the bloody dressing. She grimaced. Then she bent over and pressed her lips to the wound.

His hands were suddenly all over her, big hands exploring her body. Big hands having a good time. Very soon they were both on the same track and Shanks had lost all his fear of exposure.

Barry missed the tourist trap on his first pass through town. Once he got outside the city limits, into the countryside, he realized his problem and doubled back. When he finally located it, right where she'd said it would be, it was all lit up like Las Vegas. He couldn't imagine how he'd missed it, except that he knew he had a lot on his mind.

Maggie was running some kind of scam on him. He had no doubts on that score. Earlier, after he'd left her in the lounge at the Safari, he waited across from the hotel for her and watched her come outside an hour or so later and get into a cab, real nonchalant in her bare feet and bathrobe, like that's what everybody did at midnight. Barry tailed the cab and it was clear from the start that she wasn't headed back to his place. But for the life of him, he couldn't figure

out where she did think she was going. The cab just kind of wandered all around the place, through flyspeck towns, up and down
mountains, taking every other pothole backroad it came to, until
Barry didn't know where the hell they were. At one point, thirty
or forty miles east of Montego Bay, the driver cut into an open field
and made a big wide turn, then started back the other way. Barry
had no choice but to drive right past them, looking off to the side,
hoping she didn't see him. Then he made his own little U-turn and
had to press the pedal hard to catch up with them.

But eventually he lost them. They stopped for gas at what Barry
later decided was the only all-night gas station in Jamaica. Barry
held back, aware that his own tank was almost empty. He watched
the old driver gas up his even older Bonneville, watched Maggie
hand him a bill, watched them drive off. As quick as he could,
Barry ripped into the place and pumped half a tank in the Civic,
then ran to the clerk and slapped her a twenty, not even waiting
for the change. But he wasn't fast enough. He raced down the
highway but he couldn't find them again. So he limped back to the
Sunsplash and kicked off his shoes and fell into the bed, realizing
he'd blown it.

Truth was, he was glad. This thing had scared him and he was
happy finally to be free of it. At first, this reaction disappointed
him, because it seemed to reveal something unpleasant about his
character that he didn't really want to confront, but he knew he
was facing a level of fear that he hadn't known since his first stretch
in prison, and he wanted to get out from under it. Now Maggie
was gone and the FBI guy was gone, and the big Jamaican guy in
the hotel corridor was gone. Tomorrow, Barry would catch a plane
out of here for Miami, and then he'd be gone. That was okay with
him.

That was how he was feeling, lying there in bed watching "Smile
Jamaica" on the tube when, boom, in walks Maggie, still in her big
white bathrobe and carting a suitcase of dirty money. And suddenly
he was back in it again, whether he wanted to be or not.

He bought her three T-shirts—yellow, blue, and black. Those
were fucking primary colors, weren't they? Two of them said MON-
TEGO BAY and one said NO PROBLEM. He bought her three pairs
of white shorts. He didn't know her size, so he got two small and

one medium. He didn't know if white was a primary color or not. He bought her two pairs of rubber thongs, also small and medium. They didn't have individual sizes. He wondered what she was going to do about panties, if she even cared. He was pretty sure they didn't sell panties there at the Mo Bay One-Stop Shop-Spot, and he wasn't about to ask.

Barry also bought a six pack of Red Stripe for the ride back to the motel. The Shop-Spot didn't sell hard liquor, but there was plenty of that in the mini-bar in the room.

It was a funny sort of night, he thought. The moon was low and almost full, with tufts of clouds streaming underneath. It looked like the speeded-up skies in those old Lon Chaney, Jr., movies. One minute it was dark, another light. It made Barry think of a pair of grifters he used to work the rare coin scam with, Little Boy Prahl and his wife, Denise. It was back in the early seventies. Spring and summer they'd hit the big cities in the North; fall and winter they'd head south, like birds of prey. But it was always better up north. One day in New York they trimmed two dozen marks and blew out with close to two thousand dollars. Those were good times. He'd stretch out in the back of Little Boy's Fleetwood and they'd pass the bottle and chinwag about all the scams they knew. They even invented a few. Then they'd pull into town and go to work.

It was foolproof. Little Boy would make himself up as a bum, buy a flask, then go up to a well-dressed businessman. He'd show the mark some old coins in plastic wraps and tell the guy he'd found them, and that they belonged to a Dr. Abraham. Problem was, every time he'd try to call him, the doctor would hang up, certain he was trying to rip him off. Little Boy was good at being a bum, Lord Olivier couldn't have handled it better. The mark would take a look at the coins and his brain would start calculating.

Little Boy would ask the guy if he'd call the doctor for him, on his behalf, which the guy would do. Men would fall for this, women usually wouldn't. Women would threaten to call the police if this awful little man didn't leave them alone immediately. Anyway, the mark would call the number and Denise would answer and say, "Dr. Abraham's office," and the guy would explain that he had these rare coins. "Oh, my goodness," Denise would say. "Dr. Abraham has been looking all over for those coins. Just a minute, I'll get him on the line." That was Denise's part.

Then Barry would come on the line and tell the mark, "Yes, those coins are mine, they're very rare, I'm so grateful you've called." Then came the clincher: "I'll pay you a five-hundred-dollar reward this very day if you will be so kind as to return them." Well, the mark would say this other man actually found them—and Little Boy would be off somewhere loafing on the curb, chattering to himself. "Oh," Barry would say, "that fellow is a drunken bum and I'd rather not have to deal with him. Tell you what, why don't you give him whatever he wants and I will reimburse you along with the reward."

And it almost always worked. The mark would buy off Little Boy for fifty or a hundred bucks, and Little Boy would waltz away the happiest bum alive. And the mark would zip over to Dr. Abraham's address on Park Avenue, sure he was coming into an easy five bills, and get kinda soft in the head when he saw the address was a dress shop. He'd go inside and ask if anybody there had ever heard of a Dr. Abraham, and the salesgirls would laugh and say how five or six guys just like him had already been in there asking that same dumb question. Sorry, they'd say, giggling at each other, there's no Dr. Abraham here. And that's when the first glimmer dawned on the mark that maybe he'd been skinned for a hundred bucks. He understood it for a dead cert when he went into a coin shop and found out the rare coins he was holding were worth $1.10 tops. That the plastic covers were worth more than the coins. Sometimes they'd go to the police but most of the time they wouldn't. And even if the bunko squad ever did come around asking questions, Barry would be on the road to Albany or New Haven or Boston.

It was a great life while it lasted. Barry didn't have to do shit, just sit around sipping coffee with Denise in a bus station or bowling alley near a pay phone, that was it.

Denise was a strange woman. She looked like a Pentecostal, always wearing a plain print dress with her hair piled up in a beehive. In the car she was all the time working on her feet: buffing or painting the toenails or rubbing the rough spots with pumice stone. She was extremely proud of her feet, which were big and white and soft. When she wasn't picking at her feet, she'd push back her seat and look up at the sky and tell them what the clouds looked like to her. Barry realized that was what had made him think of her tonight, the clouds. With Denise, clouds never looked like normal things, not like elephants or mountains or whatever. Instead, they always reminded her of the body parts of her relatives. "That one looks like Uncle Jeff's ear," she'd say. Or: "The way that cloud drops down, it looks just like Roberta's brother who had a stump leg." And Little Boy would look back at Barry and wink. Denise was well mannered, she wouldn't smoke or curse or ever go inside a bar, but in the Cadillac she would tank up on Maker's Mark, sucking it straight from the bottle with a straw until she passed out. When she first started out, she'd been a magician's assistant, but she porked up considerably in her later years. At the time Barry partnered with her, she would've dressed out at around three hundred. Denise was dead now. Cancer of the esophagus, 1978. Barry didn't know what the hell ever happened to Little Boy. Probably dead, too. He'd be around seventy-five now, if he was still alive, which was very doubtful. Grifters didn't usually go that long.

Back at the Sunsplash, everything was quiet. Nobody moving anywhere that he could tell. Across the street from the motel, he saw a guy sitting on top of a car. Probably a cabdriver. You couldn't really tell who the cabbies were in this country. They didn't have signs on their cabs, or any meters inside them. They just said they were cabdrivers and they were. This guy had that funny hair some of the Jamaicans had, long and ratty and hanging down to their chest. He was wearing a Lakers T-shirt and just sitting there.

Maggie was gone. The sliding glass door leading to the patio was open, but she wasn't out there. Barry figured she'd skipped on him, was kind of hoping she had. But the suitcase was still there and the money still lying on the bed. It looked to be the same number of stacks as before.

Barry sat down on the sofa and popped open another Red Stripe. He wished he had some pretzels or something, but he'd already eaten the bag in the mini-bar.

Where the fuck was she?

More than anything he ever wanted in life, Barry wanted out of this situation. If Maggie was gone, maybe they came and got her. But why didn't they take the money? Maybe the FBI guy came and got her. Same problem with the money, though. But he couldn't help thinking that all he had to do was pick up all that money and put it back inside the catalog case and then walk outside and get in his car and get the hell out of here. They wouldn't find him because they wouldn't be looking for him. They didn't know who the hell he was.

He realized he was clenching the brown bottle of beer so hard he might split it open. He set it down on the floor and went over to the cash. If he was going to do it, he thought, he'd better move fast, before she got back. She was so crazy, she might just be going for a walk on the beach or something.

He snatched the money and threw it inside the case, then grabbed up his toiletries and dropped them in. He'd ditch the clothes.

She ran out on him in New Orleans, left him high and dry. He was just returning the favor, that was all.

He paused at the door, glancing back for one last look at the room, worried he might have left something behind. Then he opened the door and stared right into the face of the guy with all the hair. Barry made a little squeaky noise that embarrassed him. The guy thought it was funny and smiled. Barry didn't like his smile at all.

The guy thumped Barry hard on the chest, backing him up. Then another guy came into the room, and the air locked up in Barry's lungs. It was the big guy from the hotel.

Both of them looked a little banged up, like they'd been in a fight.

"Hey guys," said Barry. "Come on, no reason for this."

They were looking at the catalog case and Barry held it out for them, but neither of them would take it. Barry scurried over to the bed and dumped the cash onto the bed—along with his Old Spice and his Preparation H and everything else.

"Yours, right? I was just coming to give it to you. I took it from her. She's the one pinched it."

The guy with the hair said: "You missing some, fat boy."

"I am?"

He should have known that; he should have figured it.

"Look," said Barry, "we can do business here. I got some information you need. I can help you find her. We can help each other out, huh?"

The guy shoved Barry backward onto the bed, into all the money. He said, "Talk to me, fat boy," but at the same time he was reaching into his back pocket. A knife. He snapped it open. Barry had never seen a knife anything like it. The long blade seemed to be hinged, so that its full length was over a foot long. Unfolded, it looked more like a miniature sword than a knife.

Barry told the two of them everything he knew, everything, from the time he pulled up in front of the goddamn Acadian Hotel— what?, just last night? Seemed like years ago, something that happened when he was a stupid kid who didn't know shit. He told them the whole story, didn't leave anything out; he tried to joke around with them, embroider it a little, but they didn't laugh once. These were not laughing guys. And at the end of his little story he realized that telling them everything wasn't going to help his case one fucking bit.

22

The first faint streaks of sunlight flashed across the horizon. Lazing on the platform, Maggie and Shanks listened to the water slap against the aluminum pontoons. On the cliff above them a grove of tall coconut palms swayed in the wind.

"We need to go," said Shanks, eyeing the boulders overhead. "The wind is cold."

"It's called the Undertaker's Breeze. It comes from the mountains. In the old days Jamaicans used to bundle up against it, afraid of catching their death of cold."

She looked at him. "I don't want to die," she said.

"Then let's leave Jamaica."

"All right."

With that she swung her legs over the edge and dived into the sea, swimming toward the beach. Shanks stood and observed as she glided gracefully through the surf, taking strong and steady strokes, her bottom naked and lovely and extraordinarily white.

Midway to shore, she glanced over her shoulder and saw that Shanks still remained on the platform. Maggie paused in the water, watching him quizzically. It seemed to her that he was making up his mind about something.

Finally, he climbed down the ladder, taking care not to do any more damage to his body than necessary, and slipped into the ocean and swam after her.

Together, they straggled in to shore. Shanks surveyed the rocky cliffside and felt about as vulnerable as he ever had in his life. The sun was just rising above the rim of the ocean.

"My God," said Maggie, halting.

Instinctively, Shanks flinched, expecting the worst, but he saw her gaze was on the shoreline. Thousands of small crabs were scuttling across the beach. It was a remarkable sight, as though the landscape were alive, a moving blanket of sand. Shanks picked up her robe and his pants, shaking loose dozens of the tiny creatures.

They picked their way across the beach to the steps leading up to the back of the motel. Halfway up, a small footpath veered off toward the open doors of the patio to Barry's room. Maggie turned and grabbed his hand.

"There's something I haven't told you," she said.

He did not reply.

"Barry. He's here, on the island. That's his room."

Suspicion hardened Shanks's face.

"Somehow he followed us down here," she said.

"You two working this against me?"

"*No!* I didn't tell him! How could I? I didn't know myself until just before we left. I swear to you."

Maggie felt the whole thing crumbling in her hands. She took a deep breath. She couldn't let something stupid like this cause any problems now.

"He came into the bar this evening," she said, "just before Wexler got there. He threatened to blow the scam. I promised him money, to get rid of him. He's the one who told me you were FBI. When I ran away from you, I had nowhere else to go."

His eyes frightened her. She could tell he'd returned to an earlier time in their relationship, to where he thought he was dealing with someone . . . untrustworthy.

"Believe me, Jack. Please. I don't have the strength to lie."

"All right. Let's go talk to Mr. Landervaal."

"No. You need to wait here. He's gone, I'm sure of it. I left some cash lying around. I know Barry. I knew he'd take it and run out on me, especially since he thought it was all the scratch I'd scored. But . . . if he's still there, it's better I deal with him myself. I know how to play him."

She could tell she'd lost some points with him, but she felt she was still in the ball game.

"You have to believe me, Jack. I'm not skipping out on you. I called you, remember? I had the money and I called you." She lifted up on tiptoe and kissed him. "Please. Just give me a second."

He grabbed her wrist.

"First, tell me something."

"What?"

"Do you have the disks or not—the truth."

"No. I told you, I dropped them. I'm sorry." Desperation had crept into her voice and she knew it. "You believe me, don't you?"

"Just don't lie to me about this."

"I promise I'm not." She backed away, then turned and jogged up the path toward the patio.

Shanks studied the scenery. Bad guys could lurk from a thousand hidden spots, he thought, behind palms or yuccas or rocks or rooftops. He watched Maggie slip over the low patio wall.

Below him, he could see the tide moving in, the waves now crashing against boulders that had been clear only minutes ago.

He moved a few feet ahead on the trail. From this vantage, he could peer above the rocks and through the narrow, grassy corridor between Barry's building and the next section, glimpsing a small corner of the asphalt parking lot. He could see the trunk of his car, and he scanned the others nearby, looking for anything.

As he was about to shift his attention back to the patio, he caught a small pinpoint of light from inside one of the cars, a maroon seventies-model Chevy Impala. He focused on it. He could make out the shape of a driver, sitting in the dark. The light was the glow of a cigarette.

Shanks dropped to a crouch and backed himself down the hillside. When he was clear of the driver's sight line, he trotted up the trail to Barry's place, moving faster the closer he got.

He stepped tentatively over the stucco wall and onto the patio. Curtains billowed out from the open sliding-glass doors. The patio pavement was wet and sticky under his shoes. Peering inside the room, he couldn't see Maggie—or anyone else. A soft light glowed from the bathroom.

He heard something, a swish. From the bathroom he saw the Safari bathrobe fall to the floor and glimpsed Maggie's reflection in a corner of the mirror. She was naked to the waist, slipping on a yellow Montego Bay T-shirt.

His eyes prowled the bed and living area. He took a step and felt something crack beneath his foot: a thin strip of wood or plastic. He picked it up and saw it was a nametag: HI! I'M DON D. DONALDSON.

"Is that you?" said Maggie, coming out of the bathroom. "You scared the pee out of me."

Something was wrong, he knew it. Something about the texture of the night.

"Be careful," she said. "It's slippery out there. I think it's berries from one of those trees."

"Where's your friend, the habitual offender?" said Shanks. As he spoke, he realized his fingers were slick from where he'd touched the nametag. *Blood.*

"He's gone, like I figured," she said.

Daubs of bright red blood were everywhere on the patio, streaks of it leading to a corner and up the stucco wall.

"You want something to eat?" he heard her say. "I haven't eaten since the plane."

Looking over the edge, Shanks saw the corpse of a man spread-eagled in the bushes. Blood glistened on the leaves like dew. But there was something else . . .

"*Maggie!*"

She opened the door to the mini-bar and the thing came tumbling out, falling to the carpet with a thud, right at Maggie's feet. The mutilated, decapitated head of Bernard Lee Landervaal.

Maggie screamed, slapping at it, falling over backward in her panic.

Shanks grabbed her. She'd stopped screaming but was shaking convulsively. He pushed her down on the bed and ran to the front window. The car door of the Impala swung open and big Ernest Hopper was charging in their direction. Shanks couldn't see anybody else.

"Come on!" he yelled, dragging her toward the patio. They jumped the wall and cut across the path to the ocean steps.

"No!" said Maggie, tearing away. "Wait a minute!"

Before he could stop her, she was running back to a spot along the side where the patio wall met the building. She plucked something—a packed duffel bag—from its hiding spot behind a banana tree.

Shanks put his hand over her mouth and shoved her against the side of the building. Twenty feet ahead of them hurtled the Jamaican, a blur racing for the front door. When he passed, Shanks pulled her along, darting for the next section of the motel.

As they raced past the corner and toward the parking lot, they could hear Hopper kicking open Barry's front door. Shanks's car was parked farther away than he now wished, off by itself in the second row with nothing else around to shield them, but the windows were down and the doors unlocked and he had the keys in his hand. Coming off the sidewalk and onto the asphalt, he took a bad step and shuddered from the pain in his side. Maggie was running well ahead of him.

"Hey!" It was Hopper's voice, somewhere behind them.

She opened the driver's door, leaving it ajar for him, and dived into the front seat. Through the windshield, Shanks could see Hopper coming at them like a heat-seeking missile, almost on top of them. Maggie sank to the floorboard, staring up at him wild-eyed. The car started instantly.

But instead of steering sharply to the right to outrun Hopper, Shanks turned the car directly toward the big man—who suddenly stopped, realizing he was now the object of the chase. He whirled around, but not in time to avoid the Accord bearing down on him.

Hopper jumped to elude the bumper and bounced across the hood of the car, his flat face plastered for an instant on the windshield in front of Shanks. Then he slid off with a crash to the pavement.

Shanks braked sharply and threw the car into reverse, once again aiming for Hopper. Stunned and shaking his head, the big Jamaican barely saw it coming, then rolled desperately to one side.

Having missed on his second try, Shanks peeled out. He ripped across the lot, pulling up to the rattletrap Impala. He got out, leaving his door open and the engine running, and searched under the hood of the Impala for the release.

In the distance, Hopper laboriously got to his feet and squinted bewilderedly at Shanks, then began to trot hesitantly toward his car.

Keeping an eye on Hopper's progress, Shanks dug into the bowels of the engine and yanked out the distributor cap, snapping loose the wiring. He hurled it off into a grassy field, then got back inside the Honda. Now there was no hurry.

Hopper had stopped. He couldn't run anymore.

Shanks started off, skirting the rim of light cast by the streetlamp near where Hopper was standing. Shanks watched him in the mirror, a solitary hulk in the expanse of the parking lot. Then he remembered he didn't want to see him again, ever.

He cut the wheel sharply, throwing Maggie against the door panel.

Hopper was directly ahead of him now, gaping at the car swooping out of the darkness. Shanks hoped he would roll to his right, away from the streetlamp. Then he would have him. But he finally jumped toward the protection of the light pole, a very good leap, in fact. Shanks came as close as he could without hitting the pole, but he felt nothing under his tires. In the mirror he saw Hopper hugging the pole, obviously fearful of a return engagement. But it was time to go.

Maggie scrambled up into the seat, crazy to see what was happening. Holding on to the headrest, facing the rear window, she glanced back and forth between Shanks and the fast-retreating figure of Hopper. Finally, she settled her gaze on Shanks alone. She smiled. But Shanks did not smile, did not change his expression at all.

Suddenly, the image of Barry's bloody, bouncing head careened into her consciousness. She put her hands to her mouth, afraid she might vomit. But she didn't feel sick exactly. She felt cold, if anything. She felt herself icing over, her toes and fingertips freezing, soon to turn gangrenous and rot away. A couple of hours ago Barry had been at her side, working the angles. Now he was a dead thing on a motel carpet. She felt guilty. It wasn't her fault, she knew, but she felt guilty as hell.

Shanks was intent on the road ahead. For a long time she watched his face as he drove, hoping he would look over at her. But he never did. He seemed as inscrutable as ever, and Maggie found herself wondering if maybe everything he'd told her on the pontoon dock wasn't a lie.

23

$\mathcal{B}$irds, the chattering of thousands of birds, woke Maggie with a start. The Accord was parked on a shadowy gravel lane surrounded by dense foliage. Overhead the jungle vines and palm fronds formed a green canopy on which tiny, multicolored birds sang and chirped incessantly, their droppings littering the surface of the car.

Needing air, she rolled down the car window, and the action stirred the entire flock. Through the vegetation she watched a dark, kinetic cloud of birds form, twirl around, vanish.

Where was he?

She rubbed her eyes and looked into the backseat—no duffel bag. She checked the steering column—no keys. Shanks and the money were gone. Still groggy from sleep, she lurched out of the car and down the lane. A wonderful spot, she thought, to ditch me and the car. A little hole cut into the jungle.

Several yards behind her, she could see a footpath. It led to a broken wrought iron gate that opened into a weedy, overgrown cemetery crowded with chalky-white burial vaults and winding, vine-covered walkways. Standing before one of the vaults was Shanks, his back to her. He seemed to be reading an epitaph.

"What time is it?" she said.

He didn't turn around, didn't seem at all surprised at her presence.

"Ten till nine."

"Where are we?"

"Where dead people go." He turned and gave her an odd, appraising look, then strolled down to the next vault.

"We're not dead yet," she said.

"I'm not sure you fully appreciate our situation."

"We have a shitload of money that isn't ours and we're on an island that we need to get off of."

"Maybe you have a better understanding than I thought."

"So let's jump a plane," she said, "fly home and put the money in a bank. Split it."

This was a subject of some concern to Maggie. She was very curious about Shanks's ideas on the split. But he showed no apparent interest.

"Some problems with that," he said. "I don't see you filling out a currency transfer report and notifying customs you're bringing in a million dollars in stolen bills."

"Nine hundred seventy-four thousand five hundred. Where is it, by the way?"

"In the trunk," he said. "With your other things."

He kept going from vault to vault, reading the names and dates like a tourist visiting an interesting historical site, and consequently she was having to talk to his back. Maybe he was having trouble looking her in the eye, she thought. Why would that be a problem for him?

But now he turned and bore right into her: "You plan on smuggling it in? Single, attractive woman, no luggage—you run an eight-out-of-ten chance of a search. They run your name through the network, the odds jump to ten-out-of-ten. You lose the money and several years of your life."

"So what do we do?"

"We give it back."

"You're out of your mind."

"If you want to go on living, it's the only thing to do."

"*No.* I've been waiting all my life for this score."

Shanks turned away from her. The next tomb featured an eight-by-ten color photo of the deceased, a young man named Hollander who had a small, thin mustache, long sideburns, and a happy expression. The photo was encased in heavy plastic and inset into the granite. Mr. Hollander had died in 1974.

Maggie despised graveyards. She wanted to get out of this place, get on the road, get moving.

Shanks said, "Did your boy Barry know your real name?"

"Yes, why? Do you think he told them?"

"He would have told them the theory of relativity if they asked for it. So would you, so would I, in that situation."

The birds were back, furious with their chattering. They seemed all around her now, behind every tree and vault, screaming just at her.

"It's important," said Shanks, "that we don't get in that situation."

"So—let's say we want to hang on to the money," she said. "What's the best way to do that, you think?"

"Your money, you decide."

"*My* money?"

"I don't want any part of it, Maggie."

"Bullshit."

"I've been chasing bad guys for fourteen years. I start taking their money, I'm no better than they are. I become a bad guy. I'm not ready for that."

A fat lizard lazily crossed the path between them. Maggie stopped to let it pass. She said, "It's okay to run an illegal tap on a guy, knock him out, do all this other shit you've been doing, but you can't take money? You have a funny way of drawing the line."

"With Headache, I'm defending myself. They started it. I'm doing what I can to stop it. But if I take money, I'm stepping over the line. I become greedy."

Turning a corner on the pathway, they encountered an old woman bent over on her knees, tending a grave. She was very small and frail, but she was spading the earth savagely. Her presence rattled Shanks; he wasn't expecting company.

Maggie said, "So you're gonna let me have all this money, all to myself, that right?"

"Like I say, my advice is give it back. If you don't, they're going to *kill* you, Maggie. Today, tomorrow, next year." He couldn't take his eyes off the old woman. Something wasn't right, but Maggie couldn't tell what it was. She nodded at the old woman, who ignored her, hacking even more fiercely at the ground.

"Look," said Maggie. "You need to understand something. I get chased bare-assed down a flight of stairs by a Rastafarian. My ex-partner gets his head cut off. I figure I earned that money. It's mine until they take it away from me. Now—you got any ideas or not?"

It sounded good saying it. She felt she'd hit just the right kick-ass tone.

Shanks sighed. "Maybe one or two," he finally said.

Maggie felt terrific suddenly. She'd been afraid since last night, since the cocktail lounge. The fear had seeped into her bones, but now she felt it was beginning to lift just a little. She had faith in Shanks—but why? A minute ago she thought he'd dumped her and run off with the money.

Shanks seemed to read her mind. He gave a little half smile, as though telling her this riddle would be something she'd simply have to solve for herself. He was looking a little frayed, his eyes dark and hollow, his face unshaven and, in the murky light that filtered through the treetops, battered. His hand rested on his stomach, holding his wound. His shirt was dark with dried blood.

Her gaze shifted to the old woman. She had stopped her digging and was glaring at Maggie. She wanted them out of her cemetery.

It had been a bad night for Gordon Wexler. After the phone call and the departure of Poole, Magliocco ordered Wexler to get dressed and fix him a drink, which he struggled to accomplish. The smell of Scotch made him nauseous and he was having trouble moving. His feet couldn't keep up with the rest of him; he had to fight the sensation that he was about to topple forward. But his big problem was his neck; something was terribly wrong with his neck. Every little move hurt like hell.

Magliocco took a seat outside on the balcony where he fired up another cigar and sipped his drink and toyed with Wexler's Nintendo Game Boy. Wexler fell asleep on the bed listening to the electronic beeps and warblings of starships destroying alien invaders.

Sometime during the early morning he threw up over the side of the bed. He expected Magliocco to yell at him or make fun of him or something, but the old man wasn't around. All the lights were on and a soccer game was playing on the tube. Wexler could remember the phone ringing at some point in the night, and Magliocco standing by the bed, speaking into the receiver.

The next thing Wexler knew, it was 10:12 A.M. and his head was pounding. On the TV Hoss was chasing Little Joe around a desk in Pa's study at the Ponderosa.

The good news was that Magliocco was still gone.

Wexler limped into the bathroom. His face and neck looked awful from the touch-up Poole had administered, all blotchy and swollen. He turned on the shower and sat down under the spray until the hot water ran out. Then he changed clothes—jeans and a T-shirt from the Gap, deck shoes, no socks. He went out on the balcony and tried to breathe in the salt air, but the odor of Magliocco's cigars lingered heavily and he felt he was going to be sick again, so he went back inside.

His head didn't have to be too clear, though, to pick up on the fact that he had a major problem. Last night had scared the shit out of him. They'd treated him like he was a fucking bag man who'd lost the receipts, slapped him around like he was a mosquito. Everything was different now; a line had been crossed. He didn't know how he stood with the old man at this point, and he wasn't sure he wanted to hang around and find out.

He needed to do some serious thinking.

He grubbed around in his things on the floor until he found the uppers. He forced down two caps with a handful of water from the tap, praying he could hold them down.

The smell of last night's vomit drove him back to the balcony and he tried to figure out what to do. Twenty-three stories below, people were laughing and talking, going off to have fun in their little rented Jeeps. Outside the gates of the compound the beggars stood in wait.

Every impulse was screaming at Wexler to cut and run.

He wondered: What would Max do?

Mr. Chaudhuri Ayub, general manager of the National Royale Bank of Jamaica, peered over his pince-nez glasses.

"You wish to incorporate a business, that is correct?"

"And open an account at your bank," said Shanks. "I understand you can handle both transactions."

"Oh, yes," said Mr. Ayub. "Yes, yes."

The National Royale Bank was in a nondescript little office on the second floor of a small building off Sam Sharpe Square. There were no teller cages, no ATM machine, no suckers for the kids. Mr. Ayub, a Pakistani, ran the bank with the assistance of his two young sons, who sat primly at two smaller desks to the rear of the office. Across from them, just outside a closed door, a fat Jamaican guard lounged on a wooden chair. Oscillating fans droned at each desk and every few minutes Maggie caught a whiff of incense in the air.

"The name of your firm?" asked Mr. Ayub.

"The Jack and Maggie Company," he said. "She's the president and I'm the treasurer."

Mr. Ayub did not lift an eyebrow. "Just so," he said.

"The thing is," said Shanks, "we'd like as few records as possible. No records, in fact."

Mr. Ayub's thin lips froze in half-smile.

"As we're both aware," said Shanks, "accidents have been known to occur in banks—records misplaced, sometimes even lost entirely."

"Upon occasion," said Mr. Ayub. "Regretfully so."

"And unfortunately," Shanks continued, "when this happens, there's no way to file a report with the government."

"It is very difficult."

"And time consuming. I suppose, though, that if one wanted to avoid all that extra paperwork, some sort of service fee could be charged."

"Possibly."

"Say . . . two percent?"

Maggie was enjoying this, cutting her eyes back and forth throughout the process.

"May I inquire," said Mr. Ayub, "how much you desire to deposit in your new company account?"

Shanks looked to Maggie. "Nine hundred seventy-four thousand five hundred dollars," she said brightly.

Mr. Ayub did not seem particularly fazed by this information. However, he did extend his hand to carefully swivel the oscillating fan around so that it now blew in the direction of his new clients.

"A prosperous business," he said. "My earnest congratulations."

"We work very hard," said Shanks.

"This will be in the form of an American bank draft?"

"This will be in the form of American cash."

Shanks cued Maggie, who raised the duffel bag and dumped its contents on Mr. Ayub's desk.

Shanks asked, "We have an agreement?"

"Just so," said Mr. Ayub. A flickering glance passed between him and one of his sons in the back.

"And can you expedite the articles of incorporation for us?"

"Yes, yes. I am certain of it. Monday would be fitting?"

"Fifteen minutes would be more fitting."

"Ah," said Mr. Ayub. "In that case, the service fee of which you spoke . . . perhaps a more appropriate figure would be four percent?"

His dark eyes fixed on Shanks, judging his reaction.

Shanks said, "More like three, don't you think?"

Mr. Ayub's head ticked to the side and he pressed a button screwed into a corner of his old government-issue wooden desk. Two desks behind them, a buzzer sounded. The taller of the Ayub sons leapt to his feet and hurried over.

"Well, dear," said Shanks, turning to Maggie. "I think the Maggie and Jack Company has found a banker."

"The *Jack and Maggie* Company," Mr. Ayub corrected him.

"That's the one."

Maggie swiveled the fan back around to face Mr. Ayub. His hair ruffling in the breeze, Mr. Ayub whispered to his son, then withdrew a set of signature cards and an ancient fountain pen from a desk drawer and positioned them neatly in front of Shanks and Maggie.

"If you please to sign here and here," he said, pointing to the blanks.

As they signed, he brought out yet another form, with a small bank key, and slid them forward.

"As a valuable benefit to preferred clients, our institution provides a one-year, absolutely free-of-charge safety deposit box for your exclusive usage."

Shanks did not seem surprised at this news. He picked up the key, stood to his feet and began striding toward the back. Alarmed, Mr. Ayub hastened to follow him. The guard, sipping on a bottled Coke, languidly observed the sudden activity.

Shanks opened the door and surveyed the area: a simple vault room containing a wall of deposit boxes protected by a steel day gate. Off to the side were two closet-size private rooms, the doors ajar.

"Excellent," said Shanks, returning into the main office.

"Is there more service our institution could provide?" asked Mr. Ayub, sitting back down.

"Only one other thing," said Shanks. "A bank check. Our company plans to start lending money."

Mr. Ayub's face fell. "And the amount?" he asked sadly.

"Nine hundred seventy-four thousand five hundred dollars—less your fee, of course."

"Just so," said Mr. Ayub. "And the payee would be . . ." He gestured at the two of them.

"That's right," said Shanks. "As I said, we've worked very hard."

Mr. Ayub pressed the buzzer again. He gazed at Shanks and Maggie with a wistful little smile. At the rear door both Ayub sons appeared, looking curiously at their father.

Walking back to the car, Shanks constantly scanned their surroundings like a Secret Service agent. Until she saw him doing this, she hadn't been particularly concerned about the threat of Dreadlocks and his pals descending on them. They were safe, she thought. They were in a crowd. But then she realized she was in a foreign country, that the rules were different. They could be snatched up and taken off and Eyewitness News might not even care.

"So that's all there is to it?" she asked.

"That's it. You lend yourself your own money. And you don't have to strain yourself lugging around a heavy duffel bag. You play it right, you can take deductions for the interest payments you don't make."

"I've never filed a tax return in my life."

"I forgot who I was talking to."

"What's next?"

"You find an American bank and deposit the money. Then you find ways to spend it."

A beggar child came up to Shanks with his hands out. Preoccupied, he shook him off.

"Won't the government come sniffing around," she asked, "a big deposit like that?"

The little boy was insistent. He tugged at Shanks's pant leg. Shanks continued to ignore him.

"Well, of course, it's always best not to disturb our government unnecessarily. They tend to fret about things like this. The trick is to find a friendly American banker . . ."

"At maybe a savings and loan."

"Just so," said Shanks, opening the car door. The little boy stood away from them, finally giving up. "Banks are supposed to report anything over ten thousand dollars but sometimes, like Mr. Ayub, they forget."

"And then I get to go out and buy all the foam rubber padding my heart desires, huh?"

"That and wait for the man who cuts off heads to come after you."

Maggie pulled a twenty-dollar bill out of her pocket, part of Gordon Wexler's pocket change that she'd managed to hold on to. She handed it to the boy, who kissed her hands rapturously. Others appeared from nowhere. Shanks shook his head at her softheartedness.

24

*O*n a back road in the hills above downtown they found a
small café that opened early for lunch. Inside, they took
seats at a rickety wooden table and ordered a platter of jerk pork
and two beers. Shanks didn't eat much. He seemed to prefer watching Maggie dig in.

At one point he went outside to the car and returned with a small
brown paper bag, which he set under the table. He didn't say anything about it and Maggie didn't ask. Shanks liked being mysterious,
she felt. She didn't want to feed his boyish enthusiasms.

As she was finishing up, Shanks handed her a slip of paper.

"What's this?" she asked.

"Your itinerary. Your plane leaves in forty minutes."

"*My* plane? Where are you going?"

"I'm staying over."

"The hell you are."

Across from them a group of old men was playing dominoes. One
of them looked up at Maggie and gave her a toothless grin.

Shanks said, "At the bottom of that paper is the name of a banker
in Miami who can handle the money for you. He'll want about five
percent off the top; give him two. The next number is for the Half
Moon Hotel in Kingston. Call me when you deposit the money.
Ask for Jack Maggie, okay?"

"No, it's not okay. Why aren't you coming along?"

"Someone has to stay here in case something goes wrong at the
bank, not that anything will. Besides, we need to separate, you and
me. They'll be watching the airport and the marina. And don't

forget our friends, the Jamaica Constabulary Force. If last evening's screeching tires and busted doors didn't bring out the management of the Sunsplash Inn, then I bet the maid's discovery of a head on the floor will do the trick this morning."

Maggie flinched at that. She put down her fork and stopped eating.

"Someone may have seen the Accord," Shanks continued, "and noted the tags. Someone may even have seen this American couple cavorting on the pontoon in the early morning hours. The police will be looking for a couple, a guy with a hole in his stomach and a woman with red hair. We need to move very fast to get clear of all this."

"There's something else," said Maggie.

"Yeah, there is. I have some unfinished business down here."

"The disks?"

"The disks. I have some ideas on picking them up from Mr. Wexler."

"We don't know for sure he has them. They could still be lying there in the stairwell for all we know."

"No. I'm sure that Mr. Poole and Mr. Hopper diligently combed every step, picking up anything that fell. Whether they gave it all back to Wexler is another matter, though. I have to hope they didn't have any interest in pieces of plastic, that they turned that back over to him."

"One thing I don't understand," said Maggie. "If you could break in, plant the tap and the wire and everything, why couldn't you just go back and break in again and pinch the disks on your own. Why did you need me? Why all this elaborate scam?"

"When I first broke in, I was fishing. It took me five weeks to get it all down. But by then Wexler had developed even more company he didn't know about. The Bureau was on to him. Agents started pouring in from all over the place. I watched them break in his office. When they found my wire, I had to cut out. But they don't trail him outside the country. They don't have the budget for that. So Jamaica was my only opportunity."

She deliberated over that for a minute. "I can still help you," she said.

"No."

"Why not? You need someone. You can't do it yourself."

"I don't want you along."

"Oh."

"Listen, Maggie. This is something I can do best by myself. As long as you're in Jamaica, it's like a neon sign—*Come and get me*. I appreciate the offer, but no thanks."

"Let's say you pull it off, how are you going to get out of Jamaica?"

"Tomorrow afternoon I'm going to walk aboard the SS *Carla C* cruise ship when it departs Montego Bay. I plan to sit in the bar most of the night. Next morning I will disembark with my fellow passengers at St. Martin, buy a plane ticket, and come see you in Miami."

She smiled.

"You promise?"

Shanks bent down and picked up the paper bag.

"What's that?"

"It's time for you to go back to being a blonde," he said.

The restroom of the café was essentially an open-air toilet, with a clogged drain sunk into the cement floor. Flies buzzed everywhere. Outside the window, devoid of glass, a tethered goat munched away in a bushy thicket. Wisps of smoke from the grill in the back drifted by.

Maggie tried to latch the wobbly door but found the hasp broken. She propped a brick against it and went over to the filthiest lavatory she'd ever seen. Twisting the handle of the faucet, she heard a rumbling sound, followed eventually by a trickle of water from the rusty tap.

Disturbed by the noise, the goat scrutinized her. Next to the empty window frame was a hand-painted sign: GOATS WILL BE SHOT! This one didn't seem to fear the prospect; he returned to chewing the leaves of a hydrangea bush.

Above the sink was a dingy medicine chest with only the lower half of the mirror still in place. Maggie examined herself, touched the strands of her hair.

Again, she thought of Barry. She couldn't shake the horror of it. Barry was a cheat, a conniver, but essentially harmless. He didn't deserve what happened to him. No one did. She thought of her mother lying in the casket in the display room of the Griffin Leggett Healey and Roth Mortuary in North Little Rock, with her drawn cheeks and perfect hairdo. She thought of all the corpses she'd ever seen in her life—her mother, her uncle, a neighbor of her aunt's.

Nobody deserved it.

All eyes were on Maggie when she walked out of the restroom. Her hair was wringing wet—but mostly blond again.

She glanced over for Shanks's reaction but their table was vacant. Again, like earlier in the cemetery, she felt the sudden panic of abandonment.

But she found him outside, leaning against the car. He clapped his hands, applauding her new look. She executed a perfect little curtsy.

By noon, room service had brought Wexler two pots of coffee. Overamped on caffeine, amphetamines, and fear, he was ready to jump off the balcony and fly away.

Instead, he called the airline and discovered there was a flight out to Miami at 1:10. He packed his bags, set them in front of the door, then stood in place, staring at the sheet with the check-out rules, desperately trying to concentrate.

Exactly how much fucking trouble am I in? he wondered.

He went back outside to the balcony. He tried to massage his neck but the least little touch made him want to cry out.

The redhead. As hard as he tried, Wexler couldn't come up with a single thing she had said to him last night, or even what the sound of her voice was like. All he could really remember were those enormous tits. Did he ever get to put his hands on them? Surely to shit he'd remember that, wouldn't he?

What was her game, exactly? Why him? Was it just some random thing, doping up a rich-looking guy in a bar? Wexler didn't believe in coincidences. She must have known he had a safe full of money. But how?

It didn't make any sense.

Now he was back inside the room, pacing. He stepped over a pile of dirty magazines on the floor by the sofa. He'd bought them on the way in from the airport. Sometime during the night Magliocco must have leafed through them. Wexler thought about his brother Bobby. Bobby would fucking love what was happening to him now. He'd always told Wexler his dick would get him killed one of these days. Maybe he was right. First the customs thing, then the redhead. All this trouble, all because of his dick.

A plan, you need a goddamn plan.

The ID. He had to make it to the bank and retrieve his ID for Max. The bank closed at four o'clock and tomorrow was Sunday. If he didn't make it today, he'd have to arrange another trip just for the ID. And he certainly didn't want to come back to Jamaica ever again in this lifetime, not for any reason. But if he left the hotel and Magliocco called, he'd think Wexler was running out on him.

Might even think Wexler was in on the scam with the redhead.

Sure, that's what the old fart was already thinking. That Wexler engineered this thing so he could run off with his fucking cash. That's *exactly* what he would think. A suitcase full of money, that's something a mob boss understands. Offshore accounts and wire transfers, that was something the old *paesano* still couldn't get fixed in his head, not really.

If Wexler made a run for it now, he'd have to return to Atlanta, if only for an hour or so. There were things he needed to get, things he hadn't yet arranged. Then he could pull his little vanishing act. Problem with that, of course, was that Headache picks up the phone, makes a call to Tony Musta, asks him to please send some of his crew over to pick up his runaway accountant. Once he told Tony that Wexler has maybe made off with Tony's suitcase, he'd put every hood in the Southeast on the street.

Artie and George would probably be waiting at Hartsfield for him when he stepped off the plane.

Another option was to just go, go anywhere. Forget about Max, just go. He'd still be able to access the cash; he'd just need to work up a new identity. He'd just have to lay low for a few weeks, that's all.

What it all comes down to, thought Wexler, is just how much danger am I in? How pissed is Magliocco?

Jesus, something's bad wrong with my neck. I gotta do something about my neck.

A plan, a fucking plan.

Take a cab to the bank. Leave a message at the desk. If anyone calls, tell them I had to go out for medicine but I'll be back in a minute.

I'm sick, I need medicine. That makes sense.

That was it. That was a good plan. He felt 100 percent better. Twenty minutes to get to the bank, five minutes inside, another twenty minutes and he's back at the hotel. He might even go outside, hang around the pool, relax. Like he's a guy with nothing fucking whatever to hide.

The phone rang. Bending over to pick it up, he almost screamed from the pain in his neck.

"Someone'll pick you up this afternoon." It was Magliocco. "Don't go nowhere, you hear me?"

"Did you get her?" Wexler asked. "You get the money back?"

Click.

He slumped over on the bed.

This afternoon, Magliocco had said. That meant he had some time, didn't it? A couple of hours at least. Before he made a move, though, he was going to have to do something about his fucking neck. He called the concierge and found out they had a doctor on call. Then he called room service and ordered another pot of coffee.

Under darkening skies, Shanks pulled into a parking space near the loading platform close to the front entrance of the airport. Although not yet one o'clock, the heat was oppressive. Maggie brushed her hair, still damp in places.

A chartered bus approached.

Shanks said, "That tour bus will unload right in front of us. When the passengers get out, you need to jump in with them. Might even want to chat with them"—he smiled wryly—"as you bid adieu to this exotic sun-drenched paradise."

"I get the picture."

He passed her an envelope. "Here's everything you need. It's an open ticket. You just give them your name."

The bus wheezed to a stop in front of them. A flock of happy tourists climbed off, carting huge straw bags and carved masks of lignum vitae.

"So tell me: Am I really going to see you again?" She hadn't planned to ask it, hadn't wished to make herself so vulnerable and needy in front of him. But she wanted the answer.

"Three days at the latest."

"And you're really going to let me wander off with nine hundred seventy-four thousand five hundred dollars. Just like that?"

"You want, we can take it back to the rightful owner. He might give you some kind of reward."

Maggie stared at the floorboard. The tourists were moving toward the terminal.

"You've got to go," Shanks said.

"Don't get hurt."

He nodded, embarrassed. Maggie opened the door, then leaned over and kissed him. Just a light little peck, she thought. Once outside, she stuck her head back through the open window.

"I love you," she said.

Shanks appeared stricken. This was not what he wanted to hear. Maggie began to walk off, then returned.

"I just want you to know," she said, "that I've never said that to anyone before. Except on a job, of course."

She grinned at him and slipped in between two sunburned American women with cornrow-braided hair. She never looked back.

By the time Maggie reached the long line at the ticket counter, she was engaged in a spirited conversation with Jessica Traub and Penny Mott, who were neighbors in the same apartment complex in Mobile, Alabama. Jessica was a claims adjuster for TransAmerica Insurance and Penny was a loan production officer for the Bank of Mobile. Maggie informed them she was chief investigator for the bunko squad of the Chicago Police Department. Her new friends found the particulars of her career fascinating.

As they talked, Maggie surveyed the terminal, checking out every nook. The conversation shifted from fraud to sex. While in Jamaica, Penny had apparently enjoyed the attentions of a man named Jerry from Lafayette, Louisiana.

"He was so *cute*," said Penny.

Jessica rolled her eyes for Maggie's benefit. "Come on," she said, "he was just, you know . . . okay."

Maggie saw him. Daniel Poole. He was leaning against a Coke machine near the duty-free shops, half-hidden in shadow. Maggie inhaled with a suddenness that caused Penny to halt her story about the night she met Jerry at the hotel crab races.

"You okay?" said Jessica.

"Yes."

Poole's eyes swept the concourse like a prison searchlight.

"I really think he's going to call me," said Penny. "He said he sometimes comes over on business."

"Yeah, right," said Jessica.

Maggie saw his line of vision was nearing her. She tried to rein in the panic. She was now a blonde, she told herself. Her bust was considerably deflated, she was wearing sunshades. No slit skirt, no heels. A plain American tourist. One of the girls. She turned away.

"The guy I was with," said Maggie, "he was hung like a donkey."

The other two women were stopped cold. Maggie had their full attention. She wanted them looking at her. Three gals gabbing, as her uncle might have said. That was the picture she was going for.

"Have you ever seen how long a donkey's dick is?" she said. She glanced back at Poole. The searchlight had passed her by, moving toward the arrival lane.

When she turned back to her companions, Penny's mouth was agape. But Jessica clearly wanted to hear more.

Inside the cabin Maggie watched as Shanks pulled out of the parking lot, then waited another five minutes to be safe. When she saw the maintenance crew arriving to remove the ramp, she stood and rushed to the forward compartment and told the flight attendant she needed to get off the plane.

"I've changed my mind," she said. "I'm staying."

"You won't get your money back," the flight attendant said as Maggie slipped down the steps. She walked briskly back toward the concourse as rain began to splatter the asphalt apron. No officials rose to question her reentry. Striding across the concourse, now conspicuously less crowded, she glanced at Dreadlocks's former location by the Coke machine. He was gone.

At the Island Auto counter, she told the rental agent she needed a car. As the woman reached for her pad of forms, Maggie could not help looking back around. There was Poole, now lounging atop a shoeshine stand, getting his needlenose loafers buffed and sipping a Coke. He was looking right at her.

"Your name?" asked the rental agent.

"What?"

"Your name?"

Fighting hysteria, she stared dully at the woman, who regarded her curiously.

"Maggie Rohrer."

"How do you spell that?"

"R-o-h-r-e-r."

She couldn't resist: she turned her head one more time. Poole was paying the shoeshine boy.

"May I see your driver's license?"

"Yes."

She fumbled in her handbag for her pocketbook. One more look: Poole had vanished. She whirled around, terrified for an instant that he was behind her. She spotted him walking through the door of the men's room.

"Please hurry," she said, handing over her license. "I'm in a rush."

The rental agent made a face. *Some people.*

The car was a three-year-old Subaru Justy with manual transmission, and the gears had a tendency to grind when she shifted out of second. It wasn't helped by the fact that Maggie's concentration was focused almost entirely on the rearview mirror. But there was nothing there, only the rain pouring down on a ribbon of winding asphalt.

By the time she made it downtown, great jagged streaks of lightning were skittering across the mountaintops. Each crack of thunder pushed her escalating panic closer to the threshold.

She had trouble finding her destination, and eventually came upon it by accident. Squinting through the rain-streaked passenger window, Maggie happened to see the little sign posted in front: NATIONAL ROYALE BANK OF JAMAICA.

It was the lunch hour and, despite the downpour, the streets teemed with honking cars spraying water. She searched desperately for a parking place. In front of her a car stopped suddenly. Maggie braked the Subaru, sliding to a halt, barely avoiding a collision.

To hell with this, she thought, and made a U-turn, lurching and grinding back the way she came amid horn blasts.

And then she saw Shanks. He was coming out of Ayub's bank holding the duffel bag. It was full. Having no umbrella, he dashed down the sidewalk, his hand holding his side. Maggie watched him move past her, kicking up water as he trotted along.

A truck airhorn brought her back to life. She hadn't been paying attention and had veered over into the right-hand side of the road. Jamaicans drive on the left. She swerved, slamming into a huge pothole. Wildly, she made yet another U-turn, rolling up on a boulevard island.

But she'd lost track of Shanks. She pulled over, double-parking, and opened the car door, standing on the rocker panel, searching for him.

Behind her, cars stacked up. A cacophony of honking horns rang in her ears. Another boom of thunder caused her to bite her lip as the rain streamed down relentlessly.

She climbed back inside her car, drenched, bile rising in her throat.

A mile away she spotted a public telephone near the entrance to a ramshackle grocery store. The gravel parking lot was pitted with pools of water as the downpour persisted.

Mr. Ayub was quick to get on the line.

"This is Maggie Rohrer from this morning. Can you give me the balance on our company account?"

An uncomfortable pause. "The Jack and Maggie Company?" he finally said. He was obviously confused.

"Yes."

"Well . . . at the moment, Miss Rohrer . . ."

"Yes?"

"At the moment, there is, I believe, but a hundred dollars in the account. Mr. Shanks has withdrawn the bulk of the funds, although he has directed us not to close the account. I assumed you were aware of this."

Maggie closed her eyes and felt the blood drain from her face in a rush. Placing her hand on the cement-block wall of the building, she steadied herself.

"And the check?" she asked.

"Payment has been halted at his direction. Is there a problem, Miss Rohrer?"

"No. No problem."

Immediately, she dialed another number taken from the slip of paper she was holding.

A woman's voice said, "Half Moon."

"Can you tell me if you have a Jack Maggie registered?" said Maggie.

"One moment please."

Across from Maggie a small child was banging a grocery cart into the wall again and again. He beamed at her.

"No one by that name is registered here."

"Can you tell me if he has a reservation?"

"No, no one by that name." She rang off.

Maggie set the phone on the receiver. She staggered down the steps and walked stonily back to her car through the torrent.

As she climbed into the car, she realized she was not alone. Daniel Poole grabbed her arm, jerking her into the Subaru. With his other hand he showed his menacing, double-hinged knife.

He said, "Run from me, sweet meat, and I cut you."

She could not take her eyes off the knife.

25

The rain had ended by the time Shanks finished his business at the United Caribbean Bank on King Street, another storefront establishment every bit as undistinguished as Ayub's little place. He paused under the tin awning to slip the new bank draft and deposit receipt into his pocket and check his watch.

Thirty minutes lost, he thought. Too much time gone.

Nevertheless, he tossed the empty duffel bag into the car trunk and drove the six blocks across town. There he sat in the car and waited. Every so often, when another parking space opened up with a better vantage point, he would change locations. By two-thirty he was perfectly situated, across the street about fifty yards down from Ayub's little bank, the National Royale. He had an hour and a half.

Wexler had probably come and gone by now, he knew. But he had no other choices, not at this point. Now he had to play the game all the way to the end.

The pain in his side had eased up a bit, which probably meant he hadn't broken anything. All along he'd been afraid of puncturing a lung with splintered bone, but since he hadn't been spitting up any blood, he felt he was out of the woods there. However, it was still very sore and he was conscious of every breath he took.

The stomach laceration was another story. Once again he was leaking blood, but this time the color was blacker than before. Not a good sign. The wound was very tender to the touch; more than that, it was beginning to putrefy. He knew he needed help soon. If he could pull off this thing with Wexler, then drive to Kingston and get a plane out this evening, then he could walk into an American emergency room sometime before midnight. That ought to be enough time. And if he didn't pull it off with Wexler, he'd either be dead or in the hands of government doctors.

He was thinking about maybe going down the street to a little sundries shop on the corner and trying to find a sewing kit. Years ago in the marines he'd had some survival training, which included instruction on how to suture your own wounds, but Shanks had never had the opportunity to put any of it into practice.

He thought about Maggie, couldn't help himself. She had a lot of the kid in her, surprising in light of her profession. Making love on a pontoon platform under a Caribbean moon was a kid thing to do. Running around with a suitcase full of mob money, thinking she could hang on to it, that was kid thinking. Dirty as she was, she seemed to have a strange purity about her. With her upbringing, the kind of people she hung around with, it was remarkable she had kept the kid in her alive so long.

Well, he thought, it wouldn't last much longer.

At three forty-five a cab pulled up in front of the National Royale Bank of Jamaica and Gordon Wexler got out. He was wearing a neck brace and Shanks could see that his cheeks were puffy and purplish. Wexler said something to the driver, who moved closer to the curb and waited as Wexler walked into the bank.

Shanks gave him two minutes, then headed across the street.

When Shanks entered the bank, carrying the duffel bag, Mr. Ayub looked up with some surprise.

"Mr. Shanks," he said. "Yes?"

One of the sons sat primly at his desk, his dark, wet eyes following Shanks like a watchful bird's. The fat guard was slumped forward in his seat, peering out a nearby window into the street below.

"I want to get into my safe deposit box," said Shanks.

"Just so," said Mr. Ayub. He seemed puzzled.

During their conversation, Shanks did not break stride, moving swiftly toward the back door. As he approached his destination, the taller Ayub son appeared in the doorway, having just finished escorting Wexler to the vault room. Ayub hurried ahead of Shanks and conferred with his son in whispers. The son nodded and held the door open for Shanks.

The boy unlocked the steel-barred gate to the vault room, then cautiously locked it behind him. He went to the rear of the wall of safe deposit boxes and brought out another key ring to open a six-by-six compartment near the bottom. Shanks kept his eye on the two private chambers to his right. The door to one was shut. Inside, Gordon Wexler was busy with his valuables.

After the young Ayub again unlocked and relocked the gate, he produced a small register. Shanks signed it and the boy carefully compared signatures before handing over, with a flourish, the empty metal safety box.

"Do you desire a private viewing?" he asked.

Shanks did. The boy led him toward the other chamber, directly opposite Wexler's.

"You may depress the buzzer when you have completed your viewing," he said.

Shanks entered the room and quickly closed the door.

And then stood there, waiting.

He cracked the door and observed the young Ayub departing.

At once Shanks slipped out the door, carrying his box with him. He put his ear to Wexler's door, and heard a muffled scraping—Wexler's deposit box rubbing the countertop. Shanks delicately placed his own box on the floor, propping it against the doorjamb. He tapped lightly on the door.

"Yeah?" came Wexler's voice.

"A message, please?" He wasn't particularly good at imitating voices but believed he had managed a fair approximation of Ayub's.

On the other side of the door Shanks heard a soft, rustling sound as Wexler stood up. The door opened without hesitation and Shanks suddenly shoved very hard against it, slamming it into the unsuspecting face of Gordon Wexler. Dazed, he fell back against the counter.

Shanks pushed himself inside, easing the door shut. It was a tiny area with little room for two, and certainly no space for a pitched battle. Wexler looked up at him uncomprehendingly, eyes blinking. Shanks chopped him in the larynx, a difficult maneuver with the neck brace, then delivered a beautiful forearm shiver to the temple. Wexler's eyes rolled back and he crumpled. Shanks caught him on the fall, easing him down gently to the carpet. He was forced to smile. He had just executed a technique he'd learned at Camp Pendleton almost twenty years ago from a Sgt. Luis Morales.

"Gordon, old buddy, this just isn't your week," he said.

Still clutched in the accountant's hand was the diskette carrier. Shanks picked it up, dropped it inside Wexler's safe deposit box, then shoved the box under his arm and opened the door—not an easy operation with a body lying on the floor—and retrieved his own deposit box from the floor outside. Trading boxes, he closed the door behind him and returned to his own little chamber.

Just as he set Wexler's box down on his own counter, the rear door opened and the young Ayub appeared.

"Yes?" said the boy. "Is there something the matter?"

"I dropped my box," said Shanks, and he shut the door.

Inside, Shanks raised the metal lid again, and within lay what he'd been searching for all these months—the gray diskette carrier. He parted the Velcro seals and found . . . nothing. No disks, nothing. For a moment he couldn't think of anything to do, felt like slamming his fist through the hollow-core door.

Then he checked the rest of the box. On top lay a plain white envelope, folded once. As soon as he touched it, he knew the disks were there. Two pink-labeled blue disks. For a moment he stared down at his high-tech Holy Grail—pieces of flimsy plastic sandwiching a slice of metal spread with millions of magnetized dots. A puny launching pad for all of this, he thought. A man had lost his life because of these disks, and others might follow.

A brief glimpse told him the box held other items of interest but Shanks had no more time to waste. He dumped all the contents into the duffel bag. Easing open the door, he found the boy poised nervously at the gate to the vault. Reaching back, Shanks closed the lid to Wexler's now empty box and brought it out with him. It was identical to his own. He handed it to the young man and sailed through the door to the main offices, nearly knocking over Mr. Ayub and his other son, who appeared as though they were about to enter.

"Thanks so much," said Shanks, brushing past the two of them.

Now I'm a bank robber, he thought. Add that to my catalog of crime. A headline flashed in his mind: FORMER FBI AGENT HELD IN

JAMAICAN BANK ROBBERY AND ASSAULT. It would require several columns in the *Washington Post*. The guard was still seated in his chair, but now he held a snub-nosed .357 magnum revolver in his hands, turning it over and admiring its parts. His concentration broken, he watched Shanks all the way out the door, intrigued by the wet red stain that had appeared on the front of Shanks's cotton shirt.

Steam rose from the pavement like sulfur fumes from hell and Shanks immediately felt the presence of menace. He had experienced the sensation many times before in his career, and he knew enough not to deny it or question it. Immediately, he turned right on the sidewalk, away from his parked car. Glancing into a store window, he caught an image of the Accord, but saw nothing suspicious. He kept walking.

He wished he had a weapon. He hadn't had the time to arrange a bypass of customs. After he graduated from the FBI Academy, the Bureau had issued him a .32 Walther PPK and, although he'd owned other pieces in his life, including his service revolver in the corps, there was something about the .32 that had instilled him with confidence. He'd hated to give it up. Along with the navy windbreaker with the big yellow FBI initials on the back, and even his Dodge Diplomat. He had turned all that over to his SAIC, who was a good man and was embarrassed to accept it. Shanks *had* managed to hang on to an old ID, one he thought he'd lost and gotten a replacement for; now he carried it in clear violation of federal statutes.

He kept turning down each corner he came to, working obliquely toward St. James Street, never checking behind to give any indication he thought he might be followed. At every store window, though, he glanced back. Nothing.

Still, he couldn't shake his sense of forboding. He knew he needed to get out of downtown fast. And just as fast out of Montego Bay. Right now Mr. Ayub was probably bending over the fallen Gordon Wexler, fanning him and fussing at his sons to call the constabulary and rouse the bank guard to action. Or maybe not. Wexler had had a hard time of it in recent hours but Shanks couldn't believe he'd be dim enough to send the army after him. Wexler didn't want the contents of his safe known to the authorities. Once the police got involved, Mr. Albert Magliocco got involved.

Even so, Shanks didn't want to play cat and mouse with Headache any more than Wexler did. He crossed Church Street to the Miranda, an ancient plantation hotel shaded by bug-eaten royal palms. Heavy cast-iron ceiling fans stirred the sluggish air of the empty lobby, where a dusty oriental rug lay rolled up against a wall. Shanks ducked into a restaurant, the Café Antilles. Cane-back chairs sat upside down on the lacquered black tables and the odor of curry hung in the dusty air. Shanks saw a service door in the back and made for it. Midway there, a young black maître d' hailed him from a dark corner where he was seated, going over accounts and sipping espresso.

"May I help you?" he asked.

"No," said Shanks, not stopping.

This answer did not please the maître d'. "What do you want?" he said.

Shanks pushed open the swinging door to the kitchen.

"You may not go into there!" he heard him call.

Two busboys sitting on bushel bags of rice looked up at him disinterestedly. Next to a grimy old cooler, Shanks saw exactly what he was looking for: an exit door.

Outside he found himself in a gravel alley, pounded once more by the heat. Involuntarily, he put his hand to his stomach and felt blood. He wished now that he'd gone ahead to the sundries store for a needle and thread. He tramped on down the lane.

At the end he came to a crafts market crowded with tourists. Several cabdrivers were relaxing on the front steps. Two of them stood up at Shanks's approach.

"You wanting a cab, sir?" said one.

Shanks nodded yes and made his way to the cab stand. The driver scooted ahead of him and opened the car door. Only when he climbed inside did Shanks turn and look behind him. All was clear, so far as he could tell, but the streets were swarming with people.

"Can you take me to Kingston?" Shanks said.

"Kingston?" said the driver. "Long way, mon!"

He was a tiny, bald-headed man with a big Cheshire cat grin. A thin white mustache ran just above his upper lip.

"How much?" said Shanks.

"Long way to Kingston," he repeated. "T'ree, fo' hour, you must understand. Then I gotta come back, another t'ree, fo' hour."

"Let's talk about it while you drive, okay? I'm in a hurry."

He started the engine. "Sure, mon."

The cab veered into the traffic. Shanks twisted around in his seat, immediately regretting it because of what it did to his side. He surveyed the landscape. No sign of anyone.

The driver was eyeing him in the mirror. "Two hundred dollar, American money? How dat sound?"

"You'll get a bonus of one hundred dollar, American money, if you don't make me talk while you drive."

"Dees words be de las' you be hearing me say, mon," the driver laughed. "Positively."

Shanks did not relax until they were outside the city, rumbling along the narrow highway past the roadside fruit and vegetable stands laden with pineapples and eggplants and cucumbers.

At last he opened the duffel bag and fished out the contents of Gordon Wexler's safe deposit box. He inserted the disks into the carrier, tapped it against his knee for a moment, then peeled back his bloody shirt and shoved the case under his waistband. It felt good pressing against his wound, a serviceable compress. His stomach was a mess, the dressing slipping loose again. In Kingston he would be forced to tend to it; he couldn't board an airplane like this.

Aside from the disks there were two manila envelopes. The larger one was packed with hundreds of photos, most of them Polaroids, featuring Gordon Wexler with various naked women.

The smaller envelope contained, among other things, an American passport. It included a photo of a grinning, squinting Gordon Wexler with short blond hair and a mustache. Underneath was the name *Max A. Zerle*. A host of supporting identification spilled out of the envelope.

Shanks spent some time perusing the documentation, none of

which appeared counterfeit. As he examined it, things fell into sharper focus for him. The more he considered the matter, the more certain he was that Wexler hadn't brought down any new disks this trip. The carrier case was empty because he wasn't *storing* new disks, he was *retrieving* old disks. He was wiping out his safe deposit box.

Wexler was cutting out for a new life.

Shanks came across something else: a folded sheet of accounting paper, very worn at the creases, listing column upon column of numbers. From what he knew of Wexler's accounting practices, and his extreme attention to detail, this was a paper backup to his computer backup—a complete hard-copy record of the bank numbers and access codes and amounts on deposit, stretching back twelve years. Running his finger down the weekly subtotals, Shanks realized that the brothers Magliocco had done very, very well for themselves. Millions of dollars were socked away in assorted banks in Cyprus, Liechtenstein, Barbados, Panama, and Curaçao, but primarily in the Caymans.

Shanks knew what he had in his hands, finally, and it gave him pause. All along, he'd known the disks held more than just the information he needed to clear his name. He'd picked up on that very early in the surveillance.

It had been the easiest bust-in he'd ever known. No Title III search affidavits to file. No federal judges. No daily log reports for the legal counsel division. It was just him and Gordon Wexler.

Shanks had broken into his offices at three o'clock one Sunday morning through a thirty-foot-high casement window in the back of the building. The hardest part was replacing the glass, which took over an hour. The tap took all of two minutes, the wire about a quarter of an hour. He was out of the complex by five.

Day and night Shanks followed the accountant from porn shop to motel room to skin bar as he slinked through his sick and nasty life. Shanks had even rummaged through the man's trash and deciphered the wadded-up faxes and the scribblings on the backs of discarded envelopes.

From all this minutiae, he had gleaned the knowledge that Gordon Wexler documented *everything* on his little blue floppies, including the details of his scheme to eliminate Shanks. And he learned that Wexler was keeping this backup record against the express orders of Albert Magliocco. And, best of all, he discovered that Wexler was skimming off the top.

But somehow Wexler had managed to hide Max Zerle from Shanks's prying ears. He had suspected that Wexler was planning something, he just couldn't determine what. And now that riddle was solved.

Everything resided in the disks. And Shanks had known that his work meant nothing until he had the disks.

All he had lacked was the password, the code that unlocked the floppies and made all those millions of bytes accessible. That was the trickiest part of the plot. It required an overcast day and an eight-hundred-millimeter camera lens. Shanks had flashed his old FBI credentials to the building manager of a company called Tetrek and mounted his tripod and borrowed camera on the roof three hundred yards from Wexler's office window. On the second day he got the light he needed. As Wexler logged onto his computer and keystroked the eight letters of his password, Shanks photographed the reflection of the screen image cast in Wexler's thick glasses. It read: SEX FIEND.

Nothing remained but to break back in, remove the bugs, and take the disks. Wexler kept them in a small, relatively flimsy wall safe inside his home. Shanks was boning up on safecracking when the first Ford Econoline panel vans began pulling in. The federal government had arrived. Agents swarmed over the neighborhood and office park, planting their own wires and setting their own taps and placing their surveillance teams—no doubt scratching their collective heads when they uncovered Shanks's leavings. Wexler's turn with the law had finally come around. Twenty-four-hour-a-day stakeouts made breaking in impossible for Shanks. He had to devise another plan to get at Wexler and the disks, someplace out of the shadow of Big Brother.

Jamaica.

The driver spoke. "Crazy son o' bitch," he said.

Shanks looked up and saw the driver eyeing the rearview mirror with alarm. He twisted around, felt the loose dressing scrape across the nylon of the diskette case, and saw a battered maroon Impala roaring at them.

"Comin' way too fas' for dis road, he is," said the driver.

The Impala didn't slow down. It swooped down upon them like a shark.

Shanks heard the crunch of metal before he felt anything. The Impala had bumped the taxi hard.

"What is dis, mon?" said the driver. "What's happening?"

Shanks had no chance to answer. The image of the frantic driver froze in his vision, then shimmied crazily, as though a fault line had ruptured and the earth's plate had shifted. The cab left the road, smashing through a screen of chicken wire and careening into a field strewn with rock. Shanks felt the undercarriage screech against stone. He gripped the door handle as the Polaroids in the seat flew into the air.

The cab lunged forward, then steeply down. Shanks could see only blue sky, and then an outcropping of boulders. They were dark gray streaked with white and hurtling at them like meteorites. When they collided, Shanks pitched into the front seat, soaring toward the window. His chin caught the metal of the dashboard and he felt a click in his neck as his face twisted. Then burning, his neck burning like a fuse.

Daniel Poole noticed the driver first, his body sprawled halfway through the windshield. Blood poured across the hood in two main streams. Chunks of nonshatterproof glass stood out like little glittering islands in the torrent of red.

One of the passenger doors had sprung open. The backseat was littered with dozens of color photographs. At first Poole thought Shanks had somehow gotten away, there was no sign of him, but then he heard a soft moan in the front. He pulled open the driver's door and saw him crumpled up on the floorboard. Smelling gasoline, he grabbed Shanks by the collar and dragged him out into the grass. He squatted over him, assessing the damage. There was a good deal of blood on Shanks's chin and also on his shirt, about midway down his stomach.

Shanks moaned again, a sigh almost.

Poole slapped him twice, rapid-fire.

Another moan, that was it. He'd live a while longer, thought Poole. Long enough.

Poole stood back up and waved across the field to Hopper, who remained at the side of the road, craning his neck to view the accident. As Hopper started down the hillside, Poole turned back to the comatose Shanks. He said, "Now we got ever'body we need for de party."

There was a noise buzzing in Shanks's ear, like a plane circling and trying to land. It came to him that it was an outboard motor, that he was in a boat.

"*Chum?*" he heard someone say.

A sharp, galvanizing pain swept his brain. He opened his eyes and saw Poole prodding him with the blade of a wooden oar. Shanks was tied hand and foot, wedged into the bow of an inflatable motor tender. In the distance he could see the harbor. His head was directly under the forward seat, half-submerged in saltwater and scum.

"*Chum*," said Poole. "Know what *chum* is?"

Poole was lounging on the rowing seat, smiling down at him. Hopper was aft, steering the tender. No smiles from Hopper. Alongside him was Gordon Wexler. Shanks tried to focus better on Wexler, whose eyes were wide with fear.

"*Bait*, mon," said Poole. "Cut up de little fishes for de big fishes. Big fishes go crazy, mon, smell dat blood. Dat's what de head mon gonna do to you. Cut you up, toss you in de water, watch what happen. *Chum*, mon, dat's you."

Shanks's head lolled back. He felt himself fading out again.

26

As she drove, Maggie felt the knife was a separate, alien presence inside the car. Poole had forced her to take the wheel, after waving off the other guy, the one he called Hop. Hop was in another car and Poole motioned him away, so that it was just the two of them, Maggie and Poole, in her little rental with the grinding gears in the driving rain.

And the knife, the big, weird knife.

Poole sat directly behind her in the backseat, daring her with his glaring eyes to make a move, any move, swinging the knife around like a music baton, keeping the beat to some mad music only he could hear. At a stop sign she gave thought to escape. She moved her hand slightly toward the door release, planning her actions, considering the way she'd duck her head and dive out the door, how she'd tumble and roll when she hit the ground—but he seemed to read her mind. He didn't say anything, just suddenly plunged the knife into her headrest. She felt the blade snag her hair, and in the mirror she could see the knife vibrate with the movement of the car. It was like having another passenger.

Soon they were out in the country, passing candy-colored houses and furrowed fields, and there was no chance to escape, nowhere to run even if she made it out of the car. By then the rain had stopped. At every turn in the road Maggie wanted to ram the car into a stone fence and kill the both of them. She might as well take one of the sons of bitches with her, she thought, since she had no doubt they were going to murder her. No doubt at all. But she couldn't summon the nerve to do herself in, not yet.

Finally, Poole plucked out his knife and directed her off the main highway and down a steep dirt road that opened upon a secluded cove. They got out and walked along a goat trail to the far end, toward a dark shack with a rusted corrugated metal roof. It was what she'd always read about in the newspapers; they take the woman out into the woods and then they do their work on her, and maybe they find the skeleton a couple of years later or maybe they don't.

But that wasn't the plan, not yet. A rotting pier stood on the other side of the shack and tethered to it was an inflatable launch with an outboard motor. Gulls glided overhead and the smell of rotting fish assailed Maggie's nostrils.

The journey to the ship took a while. The seas were choppy and Poole wasn't particularly adept at handling the breakers. At one point a wave tossed the boat high, pitching him backward; he recovered quickly and cursed, then shot a scathing glance in her direction, as if she were somehow responsible. He didn't like losing his cool in front of her. It was a big thing with guys like that, losing their cool. Little else mattered.

Magliocco's vessel was a sixty-foot sport-fishing cruiser. From a distance, it appeared blindingly white, as though freshly painted or washed. It seemed to absorb all the rays of the fading sun. Under normal circumstances, Maggie might have thought it looked beautiful floating there in the emerald and blue waters. As they neared the ship she could make out its name, painted in Gothic lettering: *SHAKEDOWN II*.

On board Poole tied her hands and feet with a length of rope, then pushed her down across a seat cushion on a bench in the cockpit. He rummaged around in a cooler and produced a piece of ripped bed sheet, jamming it deep into her mouth until she began to gag. The cloth was cold and damp and smelled fishy; it had an acrid, bloody taste to it. Poole stared down at her, showing his teeth. He had control over her now. He reached out and cupped a breast and Maggie swung up her head sharply, hoping to connect with his chin. She wasn't close. For a long moment, he continued to stare at her, then lashed out at her with the back of his hand. She felt the stinging imprint of the blow on her cheek and was afraid he'd broken her jaw. Then he very deliberately jerked up her

T-shirt and exposed her bare breasts. Pinning her against the fiber-glass coaming, he pinched a nipple very hard, bringing tears to her eyes.

This is how it's going to be, thought Maggie. She was going to end up raped and mutilated and fucking scared to death all because she tried to pick up a guy in a cocktail lounge and relieve him of his wallet. She had a sudden, grisly image of fish feeding on her corpse at the bottom of the sea, tearing flesh from bone with fierce little shakes.

Poole turned abruptly and went belowdecks. He heard him say, "No problem, Cap'n." A light came on and Poole returned. He sat down opposite her, holding an open bottle of Amstel Light.

Magliocco appeared. She knew who he was without having to be told. He was short and barrel-chested and had a cigar clenched in his teeth. He was wearing a shabby captain's cap, plaid Bermuda shorts, dirty blue Keds, and a T-shirt stained with fish blood from where he'd wiped his hands. His bandy legs were thin and knotted. The mobster looked at her with hard black eyes, then over at Poole. Maggie noticed a scar running from the middle of his forehead through an eyebrow.

He said to Poole, "How the fuck she s'pose to talk with a sock in her mouth?"

Poole jumped up and went over to Maggie and yanked out the rag. She spat on the deck. It was littered with trash.

Magliocco sucked his cigar meditatively, rolling it around in his thick wet lips. Overhead, pennants snapped in the wind.

"Thing I wanna hear from you, thing you're gonna tell me," he said, "is who the fuck's got my money."

Maggie shifted on her seat cushion. She was losing feeling in her hands from being bound so tightly.

"Jack Shanks," she said.

She couldn't tell if he was surprised or not.

After a while, Poole set out again for shore and Magliocco went belowdecks through the salon. When he reappeared, he was holding a quart bottle of Chivas Regal. Sitting back into the center of three fighting chairs, he dropped a line over the boat and took a long pull from the bottle, his feet propped on the footrest.

He didn't seem particularly interested in Maggie. She slipped down to the deck, still bound by rope, pushing herself close against the gunwale to catch the shade, feeling nauseous from the swells. She kept trying to move her fingers but she wasn't feeling much sensation there.

Once she asked him if he'd loosen the rope. He looked over at her drowsily and said, "Fuck you." A moment later she heard him snoring, his cap pulled down over his eyes.

Maggie sat up and watched him for several minutes, suspicious. His lower lip hung out and saliva formed as he breathed.

Her hands were bound behind her and she struggled to slip them down around her ass and up past her legs, twisting about like a sideshow contortionist. She had always been limber so it didn't take much effort to accomplish the trick. With her hands now in front of her she began chewing furiously on the rope. It was triple-braided nylon and tough going. Finally, she switched to just trying to work loose the knots. A moment later, she looked up and saw Magliocco regarding her balefully. She stopped, frozen.

"Go ahead," he said. "I don't give a fuck. You're not going anywhere."

He stood up and yawned and went back below.

Maggie didn't know what to think about that but, after a few seconds, she resumed her labors, gnawing away like a rat. Her hands lacked feeling, they just flopped there, lifeless dangling weights, with sharp pains now knifing down her wrists and forearms. It worried her and she wondered why. What did it matter if her hands died before the rest of her?

Magliocco returned and ambled her way. He stood before her and belched. This time he had a bottle of Amstel Light in one hand and the Chivas in the other. He drank some of the beer, then spiked it with a shot of the whiskey. For a long time he remained there, watching the waves, his knobby knees leaning against the transom door for balance. Finally, he went into the salon and came back with an old rifle. He pulled a long cartridge from his shirt pocket and chambered it, then steadied his aim and fired. As Maggie looked over the gunwale to see what he was shooting at, she heard another retort from the rifle and simultaneously saw a puff of feathers erupt from the chest of a pelican about thirty yards out. The bird dropped to the sea. She watched it flap a wing helplessly in the water. Magliocco coughed up phlegm and spat overboard, then returned the rifle to the salon. Back on the afterdeck he sank into his fighting chair and continued to monitor her progress with the rope.

Finally, Maggie worked herself free. Not moving from her place on the deck, she shook her arms and slapped her hands against her sides, working back the feeling. Magliocco seemed totally indifferent, following her actions as a python might regard a small rodent released in its cage. He wasn't hungry for her yet. But her time would come.

Maggie wanted to untie her feet but she couldn't use her hands yet. She sat back and hoped he would fall asleep again. If he fell asleep, she would go after him. She would go after his eyes.

It was dark when she heard the *rat-tat-tat* of the motor from the returning launch. By then her hands were working right and she'd removed the rope from around her ankles. With Magliocco, she stood and observed the approach of the launch. There were four people in the boat. Shanks was one of them.

They heaved him onto the deck and then secured the launch. When she saw him lying there, crumpled and bloody, she feared they'd already murdered him, certain they'd gotten what they wanted out of him and that now she was utterly alone in this goddamned universe.

Magliocco said, "You didn't fucking kill him?"

"He's faking it, Cap," said Poole. "Boy never felt so good."

He jabbed Shanks in the side with his toe. Shanks groaned.

"He be *real* tender, dat particular spot," said Poole.

They carried him forward and Maggie couldn't tell what they were doing to him. Wexler passed in front of her and said, "You fucking cunt." But she could tell there was something different about him. If anything, he was even more frightened than she was.

"It's a regular cunt convention," said Magliocco, looking off at the horizon. "Lots of cunts aboard tonight."

He went over to the transom and unzipped his fly. Prowling around inside his shorts, he came up with a stubby gray penis, which he pointed in the direction of the ocean. It took him a while to make water, and when he finally managed the feat, he turned and locked eyes with Maggie, who looked away. She heard him whiz into the sea.

"Good stream," he said to no one in particular. "Doc, he's always asking if I got a good stream or not. Not like it was, but good enough. Used to could knock a man down."

Afterward, Hopper weighed anchor and Poole started the engines and took the wheel. Moments later they were cutting through the night sea, with a boom box blaring reggae music. Hopper went into the galley and grilled several hot dogs for himself, then took over the steering. Poole appeared with a marijuana joint the size of Maggie's forearm. He eased into the starboard fighting chair and swung around for a better view of Maggie. His face glowed with each hit. Occasionally, a seed would pop loose and burn a tiny hole into his Lakers T-shirt, but Poole never seemed to notice. He just smiled his heavy-lidded smile and puffed away. It was then that she realized he was wearing a bright new watch, the Benvenuto Cellini Rolex she had taken off Bob Sarcominia in the Warwick. The last time she had seen it was when she handed it over to Barry in the car. She wondered if Poole took it from him before or after he cut his head off.

27

*H*alf an hour underway, Magliocco took off his captain's cap and climbed to the bridge of the high lookout tower. The goons watched his slow progress up the ladder as though half expecting him to fall. Every so often Poole would walk around to the foredeck, where Shanks was fastened to the bow ring with his own handcuffs. Ocean spray whipped at his face. Maggie would watch the Jamaican probe at the prone body, then make his way back.

Then, above the heavy, droning beat of the music and the rush of the wind, Maggie heard the mobster calling out: "Sleeping beauty finally awake, huh?"

Magliocco was standing astride the bridge, his spindly legs planted far apart, looking down toward Shanks. The cigar in his mouth flared like a rocket against the whirling air.

"Hey!" he yelled. "Move sleeping beauty to the back there—what d'ya call it?"

"Aft," said Wexler.

"Right," said Magliocco. "*Aft*. Move him fucking *aft*."

He started climbing down from the tower. His mood had changed. Now he was exuberant, a happy camper. Maggie got up and watched Poole make his way to the foredeck. Shanks was up on one elbow, looking dazed.

"My own fucking boat," yelled Magliocco, "I don't know aft from asshole. Only thing I know's the *head*."

Poole jerked Shanks up and pulled him along. Maggie moved to one of the fighting chairs, passing a glaring Hopper who was now piloting the cruiser from the cockpit controls. Wexler sat numbly off to the side, atop a cushion on the live bait well. Behind thick lenses, his bug eyes tracked Maggie's every move. It was cold and she huddled in her seat, wrapping her arms around her bare legs.

On the boatdeck Poole kicked Shanks's legs out from under him. As he collapsed, Maggie gasped, couldn't help herself. Shanks looked up at her, uncomprehending, confused by her presence. He tried to speak but fell into a hacking cough, then tried again.

"I thought you were flying the friendly skies," he rasped.

"I thought you were human," she said coldly.

But she couldn't look away from him. Shanks was in awful shape. The left side of his face was crusted with blood, and there was a flap of loose skin hanging from his chin. She couldn't imagine what they'd done to him.

Magliocco jumped from the bridge ladder to the deck.

He squatted over Shanks. "Always wanted to meet you, Jack," he said. "Face-to-face. Always wanted it to be this kind of situation, too, where I could talk to you a little bit, then whack you."

He turned to Poole. "Fix him like I told you."

Magliocco got up and settled back into the main fighting chair as Poole began wrapping fishing line tightly around Shanks's hands and cuffs.

"First thing I want to know, Jack, is where's my money? Your whiff here says she don't know. Says you took it to a bank, then you tricked her, took the money out again. That right? What'd you do with it, Jack?"

"I moved it to another bank," said Shanks. Speaking was obviously painful to him. It sounded like he had sand in his throat. Or blood.

"Oh, yeah?" said Magliocco. "Why'd you do that?"

"They were giving away toasters."

Magliocco shook his head, then glanced over at Maggie and winked. "You're a smartass, ain't you, Jack? Heard that about you. That's good, that's good. Smartass is my favorite kind of asshole, this situation. It's the most fun, you know, reaming out a smartass. Boys, catch his act while you can. It won't last." Then his face hardened. "Fucking smartass," he said.

Everyone fell quiet as Poole tied him up with the fishing line. When he was done, he jerked the line harshly, testing his work. Shanks's face constricted in pain.

Magliocco said, "Feeling bad, are you, Jack? A little under the weather? Five minutes from now, you'll give a million dollars to feel half as good as you feel right now. You can't imagine how fucking *bad* a man can be made to feel."

The wind ruffled Magliocco's hair. He kept it combed back flat from his forehead but let it grow a little long in the back. He patted it down with his hand, then looked out across the dark sea.

"But you'll see what I mean," he said finally. "Sit him up."

Poole picked up Shanks and set him on the transom. Maggie saw for the first time that the line wrapped around his hands led all the way back into a rod and reel set in the butt shaft.

"Tell you what, Jack," said Magliocco. "You . . . you're a dead puppy, no way around that. But I got a proposition for you. Your little piece of fluff here—you tell me nice where my money is, I let her live." He winked at Poole. "Okay, Jack? You buy into that?"

As Magliocco spoke, Shanks scanned the horizon, as though searching for a way out.

"She look like she's worth a million bucks to you?" said Shanks.

"What I hear," said Magliocco, "she humps pretty good." Jack, still staring out to sea, seemed to have fixed on something, and Magliocco turned to see what it was. Maggie looked, too, but there was nothing there.

"She's a small-time hustler," said Shanks. "I picked her up in a New Orleans bar a couple of nights ago." He looked right at her, and through her. "Fact is, as long as she's around, she's a problem. She wants part of the take. So if your plan's to trade her for the money, your plan's for shit."

Maggie stared at him. She wanted to jump off the ship and swim, swim until she couldn't swim anymore. The boom-box music pounded in her ears.

"So you don't mind," said Magliocco, "I toss her over the side, huh?"

"Okay by me," said Shanks, his eye still focused in the distance, "except you can't get your money back without her signature on a piece of paper. Mine, too."

"The fuck you looking at?" said Magliocco, once again turning to look. "Think the fucking cavalry's coming to save you?"

Shanks took a moment to smile. It clearly hurt him to do so and, since it was entirely unnecessary movement, the fact that he troubled himself with it seemed to disconcert Magliocco.

"Listen, shit-for-brains," Shanks said, "does the word *sting* mean anything to you?"

It took a moment for the old man to react. "Sting?"

"Have Bob Marley check the calf of my leg," said Shanks, indicating his right leg, "see what he comes up with."

Magliocco stared at him like he was some particularly odd species of fish they'd pulled from the water, something that could fin you bad if you weren't careful.

He nodded almost imperceptibly to Poole. Warily, the Jamaican went over to Shanks and patted down his leg . . . and found something. He pushed up the pant leg. Taped midway up the calf was a lightweight radio transmitter. Poole looked back at his boss.

"The fuck is that?" said Magliocco.

"Experienced man like you," said Shanks, "ought to know a wire when he sees it."

Poole yanked at the radio harness, tearing away the adhesive tape. The wire ran up Shanks's leg. He ripped open Shanks's bloody shirt and discovered the wire trailed across the bloody dressing and connected to a microphone taped in the hollow of his sternum. About an inch of the disk carrier showed above his beltline, but in the darkness they didn't seem to notice that, not yet.

"You're not making any sense, cowboy," said Magliocco. "So you got a fucking tape recorder, so what?"

Shanks looked down at his chest. "It's not a recorder, it's a transmitter. Has an effective range of five miles. Comes over real clear, you'd be surprised. Even better across water. Although I still want you to enunciate as distinctly as possible, Headache, so the secretaries at the Hoover Building don't make any mistakes later when they're transcribing all your colorful language."

Magliocco moved on him like a bulldog. "You out of your fucking head?" he screamed. "You can't do anything to me." He tore at the wiring, snapping it loose and flinging it to the deck. It landed near Wexler, who picked it up. "This ain't the States. We're on the *high fucking seas here!*"

"We couldn't touch you unless the government of Jamaica went along and—believe it or not, Headache—they think you're slime, same as us."

Magliocco kept pushing up against Shanks, engulfed in molten rage. Maggie felt the old man was losing control, was ready to rip into him regardless of anything Shanks told him. He wanted blood and he was a man accustomed to having what he wanted.

"Listen up, Headache," Shanks rasped. "You gotta make some quick decisions here. Right now, a fucking armada of navy ships and helicopters is about to swoop down on you like a fly on a stink."

Magliocco stared at him, dumbfounded.

"Don't you get it?" said Shanks. "*I never quit the FBI.* That was a scam, to fake you out."

Shanks gestured with his hand, pointing off in the distance. Magliocco followed the action—and saw a light.

"The fuck is that?" he yelled at Hopper. "Find out what the fuck that is!"

Hopper grabbed a pair of binoculars and scurried up the ladder to the tower.

Shanks said, "There's only one way out of it for you, Headache. Depends on how smart you are, which is why I figure it probably won't work."

Maggie couldn't get over how much Shanks seemed to be enjoying himself.

"And what's that?" said Magliocco.

"Cut me loose. I'm going to explain it to you. Turn this thing northwest and crank it up. Then knock out the lights. That'll give us a minute or two. It might be enough."

Magliocco was motionless. His eyes were trained on the distance.

At the electronics console, Poole flicked on the combo unit. Maggie saw a split-screen LCD light up. The loran emitted a steady beep. "It's a ship, Cap," said Poole. "Some kind of big ship."

Magliocco moved a step away.

Shanks sat back on the transom. He said, "Your problem, Headache, is you've got a sitcom brain. You really thought the Bureau would fall for that kid stuff your boy came up with? Make them think I was dirty? Nobody bought into it, Headache, *nobody*. But it gave me an idea. You wanted me dirty, well here I am—your Three-Million-Dollar Dirt Hog."

"What are you talking, three million?" said Magliocco. It was an old man talking, a man on the way to the rest home.

"The price of keeping you out of a federal can."

"The fuck. I don't have three million dollars—you crazy?"

"Don't bullshit me, Headache. I've seen your books, I know your banks. Thing is, you don't even have to come up with it yourself. Your boy Gordon can swing me a loan, can't you, Gordon?"

All eyes turned to Wexler. He was as far away from everyone else as he could be and still remain on the boat. He was holding the radio transmitter limply in his hands.

"I don't know what the fuck you're talking about," he said.

Shanks said, "Gordon tell you I bumped into him today at the bank?"

Magliocco's eyes burned into Wexler.

"I didn't think so. See, Gordon's got a little safe deposit box here on the island. He's got them all over. All kinds of neat stuff inside. Lists of numbered accounts. That kind of thing. It's what you always figured, Headache—Gordon's been skimming you. Big time. You just couldn't figure out how. The government knows how."

"That's a fucking lie!" screamed Wexler.

Shanks moved his hands, still cuffed and wrapped with fishing line, down to his bloody shirttail, which he lifted to reveal the disk case stuffed in his waistband. He slipped it out carefully and tossed it at Magliocco.

"Check this out sometime," said Shanks.

Magliocco opened the Velcro straps and stared at the two disks, then looked up dumbly at Shanks.

"Boot it up and you'll find he's ripped off over three million bucks of your money. Fact is, he's better at washing your money than you are, Headache."

Wexler stood up screaming. *"He's fucking lying!* That's not what it is at all!"

Shanks said: "What is it, then?"

Wexler's arms shook with rage. He seemed ridiculous, though, with his brace still in place, keeping his head and neck stiff. His mouth opened and closed but no words came out.

The lameness of his response nailed him and he knew it.

"Look," Wexler said, growing desperate. "I swear to you, this *monzer* is lying to you. He's bullshitting you, don't you see that? He'll tell you anything, make up anything . . ."

Shanks turned to Magliocco. "Another thing your pencil pusher had in his bank box was a passport. His face but not his name. You see where we're headed here? It's Gordon with a cute little blond 'do, only the name isn't Gordon Wexler, it's Max Zerle. He's got credit cards, the whole schmeer. He's worked up a new identity. True or false, Gordon?"

Wexler shook his head. He was wrapping and unwrapping the radio transmitter wire around his fist.

"You got it yet?" Shanks said to Magliocco. "Your boy is planning to take your money and run—soon. That's why the government had to act now. The government wants you, but they also want your money. *All* your money."

Maggie noticed that Wexler seemed to be blocking out the conversation; he was now absorbed with the transmitter.

"They're going to arrest you, Headache," said Shanks. "Can't do anything about that. But I can put the fix in."

"Fix?" said Magliocco dully. He set the disk carrier down on a bench seat.

"Cut me loose," said Shanks, his eye on the disk carrier. "Everything depends on me, Head. It's my case, my evidence. I feel like it, I can testify you and me, we were just having a friendly discussion here on your boat that you so nicely invited me out for a cruise on. No problem. I can find a million ways to turn the government's case into shit. You go free, get to be king of Cobb County again. Even Maytag, he has grounds for appeal. Life is good. But I don't walk into the courtroom unless I have three million dollars in the bank. Cut me loose."

Magliocco's big cigar hung limply in his mouth, the fire gone out. He seemed suddenly a hundred years old. He nodded to Poole— *cut him loose.* Slowly, Poole snapped out his double-hinged knife and approached Shanks, starting to cut into the fishing line.

"No," said Wexler. "Don't."

Wexler stood up, holding the radio transmitter in his outstretched hands.

"This thing can't transmit shit," said Wexler. "See? No batteries."

Poole hesitated, looking over at Magliocco.

From the tuna tower, Hopper yelled down: "Boss!" He tossed the binoculars and began pointing off toward the lights, which now loomed brighter in the night. "Look it!"

Poole caught the glasses and handed them to Magliocco, who took a moment to focus. In that instant, Maggie's gaze shifted to Shanks. He was looking at her hopelessly and it scared her.

"A fucking cruise ship," said Magliocco, lowering the glasses.

"That doesn't mean anything," said Shanks. "All it—"

Magliocco snarled, "*Shut up!* Shut up or I cut out your fucking tongue right here!"

Something went out of Shanks at that moment and Maggie saw it first. Suddenly she knew what it was and it sent an icy jolt all the way to her heart. He'd been working a con on them. He had been running on adrenaline, manufacturing this whole armada and transmitter business out of the salt air, his synapses firing on mist, and now his scam had run out of steam. There wasn't anything left in him. He wouldn't look at her now, she knew, because the time had come to die and he was the one who had brought her to this.

Magliocco grinned. "You got a set of balls on you, I give you that. And now you're gonna have to eat those balls."

Magliocco drew closer to Shanks, cupping his bloody chin with his hand. Pushing him back to the transom, he tightened his hold, his thumb pressing in hard against the flap of skin and exposed bone.

"Know what I'm gonna do to you, Jack? I'm gonna fucking keel-haul you. Know what that is? They did that a lot in the old days. I'm bringing it back."

With his other hand, Magliocco plucked out his dead cigar and cast it overboard. Then he hit Shanks. The blow caught Shanks square in the cheek. It wasn't enough to knock him down and the old man flew into him with both hands, shoving him back. Shanks lost his balance and tumbled backward over the transom. The reel screeched, paying out line.

Maggie screamed.

Magliocco turned to her, smiling. "Thousand-pound test," he said. "We'll see."

Magliocco sat back into the fighting chair and seized the rod. Savagely, he jerked it up. Out in the water, much farther than she would have imagined, there was a sudden splash and she could see Shanks twisting in the waves.

Again, Magliocco pumped the pole. Another spray of water.

"*Stop it!*" she shouted.

"What's the matter, honey? You worried about your john? Don't you think it's funny how he don't give a shit about you?"

Magliocco turned back to his rod. Maggie glanced around, searching the deck for some way out. Hopper was still up in the tower, guiding the ship from the bridge console, Poole was concentrating on the water sport. But Wexler had his frightened, bitter eyes fixed right on her. She was about to make a run belowdecks, to try to find the rifle she'd seen Magliocco use on the pelican, when she noticed something about Wexler. He had pushed himself into the starboard aft corner of the cockpit, with one foot up on a railing stanchion. His pants were bunched along the calf and Maggie realized he was wearing his ankle rig. The one with the derringer.

Maggie charged Magliocco—"*Stop it! Stop it!*" she cried, pounding her fists on his chest. The old man hiked his elbow up, warding her off, while Poole stepped in and hurled her down to the deck. It was a little awkward, but she managed to crash into Wexler, managed to bump against his leg. Kissing the dog, that was what the Goat Man called it.

Wexler didn't realize the gun had been lifted until he saw her flicking off the safety. He opened his mouth to say something, then stopped. She could read his mind. The way things stood now, he would probably fare better with her on top than Magliocco.

But Poole had sensed a change in the current of the night. He turned, saw the gun and smiled. More fun and games.

And finally, Magliocco twisted around in his seat for a look.

Maggie had their full attention. She gripped the derringer tightly, afraid of losing it. It felt absurdly light and inadequate, like she was holding a kid's squirt gun.

For a moment she couldn't think what to do. The wind whipped her hair as, a couple of hundred yards behind, Shanks crashed in the sea. The music from the boom box roared.

"The fuck you think you're doing?" said Magliocco.

"Stop it!" she yelled. "Stop the goddamn boat!"

"Honey, get serious."

She went over to the boom box and hurled it over the side. Then she extended her arms and set her stance like she'd seen them do on TV. She pointed the pistol directly at Magliocco's chest.

"Stop this thing now or I swear I'll shoot you."

Magliocco's eyes betrayed movement above her. Maggie pivoted and saw Hopper creeping down the tower, like a heavy black cloud moving in. She fired. There was a tinny, popping sound and a bright flicker of muzzle flare. Hopper grabbed at his shirt and lost his perch on the ladder. He fell, bouncing off the hoisting pole and hitting the water like a bursting rocket.

Maggie twisted back, again training the pistol on Magliocco. She was aware that she was almost gasping for air; there didn't seem to be enough of it around. Poole had edged a little closer toward her. She motioned him back but he remained where he was, smiling, always smiling. She knew she would fire next at him; he was the one who scared her the most. She hoped to God she hit him.

"*Now!*" she shouted.

Magliocco said, "That popgun only holds two beans, you know."

Maggie made a show of cocking the hammer.

"Okay, okay."

He gestured to Poole, who held his hands up, palms out, having fun with this game they were playing. Keeping an exaggerated distance between them, he snaked around the fighting chairs, moving to the cockpit helm a few feet from where Maggie was standing.

Maggie edged back. She put a hand out to the back of one of the seats, to steady herself.

Magliocco placed the rod in the shaft, letting up on the reel, which screamed as the line raced through it.

Grabbing the throttles, Poole jerked down. The sudden drop-off pitched everyone forward, but Maggie recovered quickly, switching her aim from Magliocco to Poole and back again, afraid of any movement whatever. Wexler sat still, trying to make himself as small as possible.

Poole shifted the engines into idle. Quickly, the cruiser slowed down in the water.

"Okay, honey," said Magliocco, "you're calling the shots."

"Get him back," said Maggie. "Hurry."

With a leisurely manner, Magliocco grabbed the rod—but the line was slack.

"Your boyfriend ain't here no more."

"*Find* him."

Magliocco scratched his ear. He cut a hard look at Poole. He was tired of this crap. He wanted it over.

"Reverse it," he said. To Wexler: "Get up to the tower. Flip on the searchlight."

Magliocco swung the fighting chair around toward Maggie. His bottle of Chivas had been wedged in the seat with him and he pulled it out and took a swig. He playfully held it out for Maggie to share, but she merely stared at him. Sunk back into the big chair with the quart bottle on his chest, he looked like a wizened baby, sucking at the nipple.

28

$\mathcal{S}$he spent the next quarter hour going insane, watching as the beam skimmed the roiling blackness of the ocean, panic-struck that one of them would spring on her at any second. As the waves sloshed against the hull, she directed Wexler where to shine the light. The more Magliocco drank, the funnier he seemed to view the situation.

Maggie had given up hope of finding Shanks alive, but she couldn't think of what to do. Her best approach, she thought, would be to force the two of them over the side, then start the engines. She figured she could handle Wexler until they reached shore . . . wherever the hell shore was. She wondered if Wexler knew how to operate the ship. It didn't matter. She'd take her chances with him at the helm, or her, rather than keep those two rats on board.

Magliocco dropped the empty bottle to the deck. He sat up and made a face at her—*What else can I do?*

Would they do it, just slip over the side like good little boys? She needed his rifle but couldn't think of a good way to get to it.

"*There,*" said Wexler, and she saw it, too. A figure in the water, a body. An ocean swell moved it out of the light and Wexler over-corrected, sending the beam yards away, flashing on emptiness again. Then he found it: it was Hopper, floating on his back, a flower of blood blooming from his white guayabera shirt, his dead eyes open.

Poole came at her then, charging her with that incredible speed. Maggie fired reflexively, out of heart-jarring fear, and her angle was absurdly high, almost straight up. Poole twisted the gun from her hand and slapped her, banging her against a fighting chair, and then again, knocking her to the deck.

"Now we have some fun wit' you, sweet meat."

A spray of bright blood splattered across the deck. Maggie looked up to see Wexler hopping down the ladder on one leg, the other extended and kicking. There was a wound somewhere near his groin. "Help me," he said. "She shot me. Do something. *Help me.*" He slumped to the deck and clawed at his thigh, trying to tear the fabric away. Maggie was surprised at the flow of blood.

Magliocco got out of his chair for a better view of Wexler. "God-damn," he said. "Two for two. I wish I coulda had trigger men shoot as good as you." He crouched over Wexler, studying the wound and the pulsating blood. Wexler looked up at him beseechingly. "I dunno, Gordon, I'm think she musta nicked that big artery you got there." He stood back up. "I wouldn't give piss for your chances, tell the truth."

There was a thumping sound on the foredeck that froze him. To Maggie, it sounded like something knocking on a hatch. The cruiser bobbed in the water, and along with the others she listened to the sound of the lapping sea, the blip of the loran, the low hum of the engines.

"Check it out," said Magliocco in a low voice. He moved quickly to the fishing cockpit. From a cabinet underneath the wheel, he removed a short-barreled twelve-gauge shotgun. Checking the shells, he noticed Poole hadn't moved.

"Go on!" he growled.

Poole brought out his knife and flicked it open. Lifting himself up on an outrigger, he swung onto the side deck, then heard a scream that caused him to slash out with the knife and almost lose his footing.

It was Wexler. "This isn't right!" He was yelling up at Magliocco. "*You can't fucking do this to me!*"

He was squirming in his own blood there on the deck, delirious at seeing more and more of it pour out of his leg. He pressed at the wound with both hands, desperate to staunch the flow. His clothes were soaked in it, but his throat and face were deathly white. His eyes burned in their sockets as he shouted to the old man.

"*I'm too fucking rich to die now!*"

"Shut up," snapped Magliocco. He was packing his pants pocket with more shells.

There was a splash of water. Poole was no longer where he had been standing. From over the side Maggie could hear a furious flailing in the water. Magliocco rushed to the gunwale and, as the craft bucked in a trough, she saw there were two people in the water, Poole and Shanks. Shanks had his cuffed, fishline-entangled hands around the Jamaican's neck, choking him with the handcuff chain. The Jamaican was twisting and turning fiercely, both hands at his throat. He must have dropped the knife when he went into the water. Magliocco put the butt of the shotgun to his shoulder and aimed.

"*Max!*" she heard Wexler scream.

Maggie pulled the throttles, cranking the engines and jerking the boat forward. The old man tried to turn around, wanting to blow her away once and for all, but he stumbled backward and plunged overboard. As he fell, both barrels discharged.

Maggie throttled down. She ran to the transom and looked out—but couldn't see anything, could only hear splashing somewhere in the night.

And then nothing. Only the idling of the engine.

A moment later she saw him—Shanks, attempting to dog-paddle, painfully trying to make his way through the water toward the stern. He didn't seem to be making any progress.

She looked around for something to help him with, a life jacket, anything. In his little corner of hell, Wexler muttered and shook his head, dying, unbelieving. Maggie went for the hoisting pole, then stopped.

What was she doing? Shanks wasn't on her side.

What she ought to do, she told herself, was leave him there, thrashing about in the water with his handcuffs on. She knew she couldn't do that, but she also knew she didn't want to help him.

Shanks grasped at the taffrail. With the cuffs on, it appeared impossible for him to pull himself up. Somehow, he hooked the chain around the rail and raised himself just enough so that his face appeared. His eyes scanned the darkness of the deck. When he at last focused on Maggie, saw her standing in the dark watching him, he actually smiled. His lips were bloody, with deep vertical slits cutting through them. He must have tried to chew his way through the line, she thought.

His head dipped from view. But she could not go to him. She would not help him aboard, not the man who had tried to take her money from her. She would not be his fool.

With his hands still hooked around the rail, he tried to swing a leg up to the gunwale, but couldn't quite manage. He tried again, then seemed to give it up. He coughed and it was a low, rattling cough; he was spitting up. She stood there, biting into her fist, watching his lifeless hands clutching at the rail.

Then, finally, the hands tightened into fists and she heard a groan, and as she went to him, he was able, through some fierce determination of will, to swing himself up the rail. She backed away as he threw half his body across the transom, then paused, then kicked his feet up and over. He collapsed on the deck.

For a time Shanks didn't stir. Eventually, he pushed himself up to a sitting position, his head slumped against the live well. He raised his hands, as if to forestall any talk. Ligature marks showed on his wrists. Slowly, he reached into a pocket and withdrew a folded slip of paper. He held out the paper for her to take.

Maggie didn't move. Shanks dropped the paper to the deck as his head fell back.

She moved toward him, leaned over, and snatched up the paper.

It was a very wet cashier's check. Although the ink ran in places, it was still legible. She read the amount: NINE HUNDRED FORTY-FIVE THOUSAND FIVE HUNDRED DOLLARS. And then: PAY TO THE ORDER OF MAGGIE ROHRER.

Shanks was studying her reaction. He tried to speak, but started hacking furiously, spitting out more saltwater. Maggie held the check to her throat, not sure of anything anymore.

"I figured," he finally said, "it wasn't a smart idea to keep the money in a bank I was going to knock over. So I deposited it in another bank and got another check. I was going to page you in the Miami airport."

"Knock over the bank?"

"Long story," he said. "I didn't knock over the bank exactly, I knocked over Wexler." He forced himself to look at her. "What I told them about you . . . I couldn't make them think I . . . cared, you understand? They would've done things to you, if they knew I cared."

Maggie kept her mouth fixed, her gaze steady. Shanks looked away, over at Wexler, whose eyes remained open although he no longer was moving.

"One thing I don't understand," she said. "Are you with the FBI or not?"

"Everything . . . I told you last night was true." He began to drag himself over to the bench seat.

"And the business about the sting, the shit you were telling what's-his-face?"

"Was shit. A story I cooked up, in case I got picked up. I thought it might be worth a try. Wexler helped it along . . . because I found out today he was planning on taking off. It almost worked. Almost."

"And the wire?"

"I thought it might help the story." He picked up the disk carrier from the bench seat and turned it over in his hands. No apparent damage. He set it back, pushing it close to the gunwale for protection against the elements. "I have a question for you," he said. "Why didn't you take the plane?"

She didn't say anything.

"Let me guess," he said. "Was it because you didn't trust me?" He smiled at her.

Another arm swung over the taffrail—Magliocco.

Maggie grabbed the throttle as Shanks yelled to her: *"No!"* The ship lunged forward and there was a strangled sound, as though they'd hit something. The engines shut down completely.

"What happened?" said Maggie.

Shanks struggled to get to his feet as Maggie crept to the edge. At first there was nothing, only the settling water in the port light, but then a trail of blood snaked to the surface. Just below the water-line a dark shape rose quickly, like the back of a sea turtle. Backing toward Shanks, not at all sure she wanted to see what was coming, Maggie couldn't escape the vision of Magliocco's torso bobbing up. His head was split apart, hinged loosely at the scalp, and she watched as bone and tissue and blood dissolved in the prop wash.

She felt Shanks's hand on her shoulder, then realized it was probably more for his support than hers. She helped him into a fighting chair, growing suddenly fearful that he might die on her, and they watched the mobster's body twist and bob out to sea.

It took them almost an hour to locate Poole's half-submerged body. Maggie manned the grappling hook that snagged the collar of his T-shirt, drawing the corpse toward the boat. Patting down the cold body, half afraid he would suddenly reach out and pull her in, she finally found what she was searching for: a handcuff key. At the last moment, she slipped the Rolex from the Jamaican's wrist. She let go of the body and went over to Shanks, who unlocked his cuffs as she snipped away the bloody, tangled fishing line. He tossed the cuffs into the ocean.

Maggie helped Shanks go belowdecks. Accommodations were surprisingly roomy, she thought, with a nice-size master stateroom done up in teak and brass, plus a smaller guest suite. The problem was that nobody had cleaned up for weeks. The galley was a mess, with garbage strewn everywhere. The stench was oppressive.

She eased Shanks down upon the bed. For a long time, she doctored his various wounds, as he fell asleep. Occasionally, he would suddenly awaken, startled by her ministrations, then nod off again.

When she was finished, she sat and watched him breathe. The sound was heavy and rough, but steady. Satisfied, she pulled a blanket over him and then settled in beside him. She felt herself growing drowsy. She wondered if it was all right to rest, but she couldn't think of anything else she needed to be doing. She listened to the lapping water, thinking that she was alive. So many other people were dead, but she was still alive.

29

*H*er mother was on a Ferris wheel, terrified. She was grossly obese and she cried out to Maggie through tiny, kewpie-doll lips. Every time the wheel dipped down, Maggie would try to reach out and help her, but she could never get close enough. And each time the car would swing back up, lifting higher and higher, as her mother grew smaller and smaller.

Maggie heard a thud, like the thumping of a kettle drum, and opened her eyes. An empty bottle of Chivas fell from a dresser and rolled across the carpet, all the way to the starboard side of the stateroom where it came to rest in a pool of water. She realized everything was tilting in that direction.

Shanks wasn't beside her.

"Jack!" she yelled. She jumped up, faltered, then ran up the companionway and through the galley and the salon to the upper deck.

The ship was foundering; the sea was seeping over the gunwale. No Jack. Somewhere in her consciousness she was aware that the launch was missing; but she couldn't deal with it, not yet.

"Jack!"

How could he have gotten away in the launch without her waking up? He couldn't. Unless he cast himself adrift, and waited until he was far enough away to start the engine.

Something else was missing: the disk carrier. Gone.

She simply stood there, watching the whitecaps rippling in the dark sea, fighting to curb her anger and surging hysteria. Soon the water began pouring in. Maggie felt it licking at her feet, cold and inky black, felt it coming for her.

Against her will, Maggie's attention was finally drawn to the bloodless corpse of Gordon Wexler, so chalky white it looked lit from within, leaning stiffly against the live well.

She raced back belowdecks. None of the lights worked, or the radio; either the generator had already failed or Shanks had deliberately cut the power before he abandoned her. *Abandoned.* The word triggered an awful force inside her, a wild, wailing fear. She wanted to drop to her knees and shriek. It was impossible that he would do this to her. How could she have misjudged him so? What was wrong with her?

In the darkness of the cabin she scoured for whatever she could find to help her out of her predicament. She banged her head hard on an overhead compartment and felt dizzy for an instant. She seized a half dozen seat cushions and a checkered tablecloth; she shredded the tablecloth into strips, tearing off a nail in the process. Hurriedly, she tied the cushion handles together into a ring. The tags on the cushions said they could serve as "flotation devices."

There was a sudden, climactic shift as the stern went under. Water cascaded down the steps into the bedroom and she worried that she was going to be trapped below, that she would go down with the ship to the bottom. A cold rage was mounting inside her, slowly edging out the fear. She must save herself if only to kill the son of a bitch.

Frantically, she searched the cupboards and cabinets, tossing tins of food and candy bars and flashlights and anything else that looked useful into a net bag she'd found. In the closet of the stateroom she discovered a small footlocker; it was unlocked. Inside were bundles of cash, twenties, fifties, and hundreds, double-bound with rubber bands. Maggie knew it was the money she'd left with Barry. Eighty-five hundred. Guilt suffused her; she'd baited him with that money, led the killers to his door.

She found a small Styrofoam cooler and stuffed the cash inside. It was incredible, she thought. Everywhere she went in the Caribbean, there was loose money lying around.

It was time to depart, she knew. The first light of dawn swept across the cloudless sky, but she found herself afraid to take the plunge. But soon, any second now, the ship would upend, and she had no way of knowing how long it would take to sink below the surface and suck her down with it.

Finally, she leapt into the water. It was much colder than she imagined it would be, colder than the night on the pontoon platform in the little bay. The cushions seemed to work, she was staying afloat. Thinking she could somehow repair the leak, she swam around to the starboard side. With a flashlight she saw a gaping, splintery hole in the hull. She realized it must have come from Magliocco's misfiring when he toppled over the side. She couldn't think of any way to fix it.

Maggie kicked away from the cruiser and watched the dawn come up. She had no earthly idea what to do, where to go. She put on a long-billed fishing cap she'd found, affixing a strip of the checkerboard tablecloth to the back, to shield her neck and shoulders.

The sun is coming up over there, Maggie thought as she drifted, so that must be east. So what? How does that help me?

She smeared her face with sun block. It was a fresh tube, never uncapped; she couldn't imagine why Magliocco would have had it on board. He wasn't a sun-block kind of guy, she didn't think.

Behind her there was a sudden rush of sound, like an intake of breath very near her ear. She tensed, fearing some creature from the deep was about to attack, but it was the cruiser, finally upending. There was no delay. The bow shot up, then slipped under, and the ship was gone.

It scared her. Somehow, with the boat nearby, she felt she had a chance. Someone might see the wreck from the air, or from a passing ship. Now she realized she was a speck in the great wash of the sea, about as easy to locate as a floating beer can or a paper plate.

Then something bumped her. It rubbed against a cushion and she screamed as she turned: Wexler's corpse had risen to the surface, trailing after her. It bobbed on its side, limbs frozen in rigor mortis, the hair like seaweed. She gasped for air, kicking away from it. Other debris from the wreck began to pop up around her like mushrooms.

As the light of day spread over the seascape, Maggie saw a small sailboat tacking back and forth against the wind about a half mile away. At first she thought she might be hallucinating, but she knew she wasn't in that bad shape. She wasn't in bad shape at all, really. She moved through the water in the direction of the sailboat. Moments later, she made out the top of a hotel, and then another.

Within ten minutes she was able to slip off her ring of seat cushions and walk in to shore. A man in a parasail floated above her, waving. She waved back. Early morning tourists were strolling the beach, collecting shells. No one paid her any attention. Scanning the shoreline, Maggie detected a dot of yellow far in the distance, just at the edge of the water. She was sure it was the launch from the cruiser. She hiked toward it, wiping the sweat from her face with her makeshift kerchief, which she tossed into the next trash receptacle she came to.

Shanks must have awakened, she thought, and seen how close they were to land. That's when he decided to jump ship. He was a man who took advantage of opportunities when they arose, a character trait she felt they shared. No doubt he had already planned to ditch her and, happily for him, the moment arrived sooner rather than later.

There was nothing in the launch, only the oars. She didn't know what she expected, really. A note? A hint of where he was heading?

Nearby, a wiry old man was sunbathing. She asked him if he'd seen the launch come in, but he hadn't. She went inside the hotel and bought a pack of cigarettes in the gift shop, using the money she'd found in the stateroom. From there she grabbed a cab to the airport.

On the way, she tried to console herself with the thought that maybe Shanks hadn't left her to die, like she first thought. He knew land was close by, knew she was a good swimmer. It took some of the edge off her anger, but not enough.

30

*O*n the morning of October 27, a clammy mist clung to the city of Astoria, Oregon. The air was redolent of mildew and rotting leaves, and the dampness seemed to penetrate the skin and seep into the bones.

The drive up from Portland had taken just under two hours. Although the scenery along highway 30 was spectacular, the driver wasn't in a mood to admire the landscape.

The car crossed the city, making only a brief stop at a coffee shop, before entering a pleasant neighborhood a few miles east of town, along the Columbia River. Coxcomb Hill was a community of beautifully restored Victorian homes, brimming over with curlicues, cupolas, gingerbread fretwork, and broad verandas.

Number 24 Hillcrest Drive was a narrow, two-story frame house with a mansard roof, neatly trimmed hedges, and a small lawn contained by a low wrought iron fence. A big, bushy spruce stood sentinel at the front gate. The name on the mailbox said *Zerle*.

Maggie drove past the house slowly, then pulled into a little park up the block that overlooked the river. She sat on a stone bench and observed the busy traffic of fishing boats and freighters.

It was a strange location for Gordon Wexler to want to spend his post-Mafia days, she thought. Out of the way, sure, but really not his sort of hiding place. She wondered what had provoked him to select this particular spot.

A few minutes after ten o'clock the front door opened and a man in a gray Notre Dame sweatsuit and aviator glasses came outside and locked the dead bolt in place. His blond hair was cut very close, almost a military burr, but he had a full mustache. He performed a brief series of warm-up exercises, then bounded off down the hill for his morning run.

It was him, all right. It was hard to envision him as a runner; it didn't seem right, somehow. But it was him.

The detective had told her his run usually lasted about thirty minutes. He also said that the house appeared very tightly secured, with electric fences and an elaborate and expensive system of alarms. From her vantage in the park, Maggie could observe that the windows on both floors were guarded with burglar bars.

Maggie opened her handbag, just to reassure herself that the little automatic was still inside. A .22 Bumblebee Pocket Partner, purchased from a fence she had discovered in Miami. The serial number was filed away, and the safety was definitely off.

Almost six months had passed, but the memory of her time with Shanks had not receded in Maggie's mind. Every incident was fresh and vivid, and she unreeled the entire experience incessantly, from the cocktail lounge in New Orleans to the beach at Grand Cayman, as she lay in bed at night with the windows open, listening to the pounding of the surf. She analyzed her recollections like an FAA inspector sorting through the debris of a crash site.

Her first surprise after landing in the States was that the check from the United Caribbean Bank was good. She hadn't expected that. Protecting the loot wasn't quite as easy as Shanks had implied, but the banker he recommended was more than willing to show her the loopholes and teach her the system. In the end she was able to hold on to more than $900,000. Not a fortune, not really, but not bad for a weekend's work.

So she took it easy and bought some toys. A little red ragtop, a two-seater with a world-class sound system. A town house by the ocean. A $6,000 pavé diamond ring for her aunt. That was about it.

Most of her money was now sheltered in tax-free offshore bank accounts, but it wouldn't last forever. On the advice of another banker—she'd cut all her ties to the first one, not wishing to leave a paper trail—Maggie was looking into legitimate investments. Right now she had a guy pricing franchises for her, but she couldn't get too excited about that prospect. The more she looked into the business, in fact, the more she wanted to sell them, not buy them. It was one hell of a scam, she thought.

To get a better angle on his approach, Maggie shifted to another bench. She wanted to see his face when he spotted her. Finally, he came chugging around the corner. He was looking up at the sky, as though estimating how much rain the day held in store. He glanced over at the park, then did a little double take, then stopped altogether, hands on hips, chest heaving from his three-mile trek. It took a moment before he crossed the street and ventured toward her, his suspicious eyes searching behind the evergreens and the monkey bars. He was nervous. That was good; she wanted him nervous.

He strolled past a mother pushing her baby in a swing.

"So how'd you find me?" said Shanks. He was looking good, very fit, with color in his face. He didn't try to sit down on the bench with her but kept his distance, probing her expression for a hint of her frame of mind.

"You told me," she said. "Remember? On the boat that night. You told everyone about Wexler's fake ID. You even gave the name. I forgot all about it until about ten days ago, and then it hit me that it was possible, just possible, that you went ahead and took on Wexler's phony identity. Why not? He sure as hell didn't need it anymore. But I couldn't remember the goddamn name. I thought about going to a hypnotist but I was worried about things he might ask me while I was under, you know? Then a couple of nights ago, I'm in bed watching a rerun of 'Get Smart'—you remember 'Get Smart,' with Maxwell Smart? Well, Agent Ninety-nine is talking to him and calls him Max—and I snap my fingers and think, *Max. Max Zerle.*"

He nodded, taking it in. "Must be destiny," he said. Now he was glancing at the parked cars, expecting G-men to pop out any second. "It's still a reach, getting from Max Zerle to Astoria, Oregon."

"No, that was the easy part. I hired a private detective." She watched him wince at that bit of news; he could see his secret spilling out, his fake name suddenly in a computer somewhere. "He's pretty good. He came up with the address thirty minutes after I gave him the name," she said. "I sat out in the lobby and read *The Journal of Police Science and Administration.*"

"But how'd you know it was me?"

"You think the world is full of Max Zerles? I had my detective fly out here and take pictures of you. He faxed them to me. No mistaking those dimples, Jack, even with your hair bleached and buzzed."

He scratched his chest, still a little winded. She knew he was calculating. He was always calculating. *How much time do I have?*

"Tell me something, Maggie. You wearing a body mike?"

"Nope. Or a push-up bra, either."

"You want to go inside, have a cup of coffee?"

All the time, his eyes prowling the rooftops, checking the corners of houses, worried the end was near.

It was great to see.

The living room was sparsely furnished, just a cheap sofa, a matching chair, and a table lamp. Nothing at all in the dining room. The kitchen had a new refrigerator, a Mr. Coffee machine and a case of beer on the countertop. No dishes were out. They sat at a small card table with folding chairs in the breakfast nook. Out the window Maggie could see the river and, in the distance, a desolate spit of land.

"Nice view," she said.

"It's called Cape Disappointment." He was staring at the palms of his hands.

"You're kidding."

"No, that's what they call it." He put his hands in his pockets, then looked up at her. "I'm glad you're here."

"I bet."

"No, I've missed you. Just in the last month, I realized how much. If you hadn't come after me, I'd have come after you."

"That's nice to hear," she said. "You said the words just right, almost like you believed them."

He smiled. "We had something going, Maggie. It took me some time to understand that. I miss it."

She said, "It was never a matter of clearing your name, was it?"

He was back looking at his hands. "At first I suppose it was," he said. "But the more I looked into it, the more money I saw. Money waiting for someone to take. Jack Shanks's good name didn't seem that important to me after a while."

"How much money are we talking about anyway? Five, ten million? What was your price?"

He merely stared at her. She'd seen this face a few times before— his stone killer look.

"So the whole thing," she said, "it was all a big scam, wasn't it? Just another way to fleece somebody."

"Some bad guys."

"Bad guys, right. I forgot." Maggie withdrew a package of cigarettes from the handbag in her lap, careful to leave the clasp open, the gun grip just inside.

She said, "You planned to kill me all along, didn't you?"

"No."

"Sure you did. You were going to do me in that little cemetery right after the job. You were going to take me there after I got you the disks, dump me, then get on the plane alone. The next morning, after things went wrong, you were still leaning that way, but then you came up with another plan, didn't you? I thought it was funny, you having a ticket with no name on it. It was just for you, that ticket, wasn't it? You only had the one."

"Why would I give you a million bucks if I wanted to kill you?"

"I like that. I find the goddamn money, I steal it—you don't know anything about it. And you think you're a sport for letting me keep it."

Again, the killer look, the dead eyes.

"I got a theory about the money," said Maggie. "You let me have it not because you're such a sweet guy but because you figured it might deflect attention from you, at least for a while. You knew the FBI'd start putting the pieces together pretty quick. All those dead bodies in Jamaica, all that dirty money—they'd start wondering whatever happened to Jack Shanks, wouldn't they?"

"They might."

"But a dumb broad like me, flashing all that cash, I'd be sure to draw flies first, wouldn't I? In fact, you've probably tipped them off, given my name to one of your buddies in the Bureau. I wouldn't put it past you. All you needed was a few months. I'm a lucky girl to find you before you vanish for good."

Maggie lit a cigarette and looked around the bare kitchen.

She said, "You're planning to cut out soon, aren't you? This Max Zerle thing, it's only temporary. It's just the name you're using to gobble up all that mob money. Then you'll become somebody else. You'll disappear. You'll be somebody else in some other country, right?"

"Something like that."

She blew smoke in his face, but he didn't seem to notice.

"Only there's this one loose end, isn't there? Me." Maggie laughed. "Yeah, I bet you are goddamn glad to see me. I bet you've been giving me a lot of thought lately. The only living witness. The only one who knows the score. Someday, somehow, I could be a problem. See, I think your second plan—the one you thought up that morning in the cemetery—was to let me spend a little of the cash until you were finished with all the work you had to do, then you'd hook up with me again. You'd retrieve what was left of the million, then bury me somewhere deep. Then you'd be free forever. No more worries."

Shanks rubbed his jaw and started to frame an answer but she cut him off.

"And you didn't figure I'd be too much trouble to find, did you? Low-life hustler like me. You found me once, you could always find me again."

Shanks got up with a suddenness that caused her to jump forward in her seat, and went around behind her, into the living room. She slipped her hand inside the purse, feeling for the automatic. A moment later he returned, setting a small metal ashtray in front of her. Mr. Neat.

Very softly, he said, "Why did you come here, Maggie? What do you want?"

"Reason I came, Jack, was to do you before you did me." She raised the pistol above the top of the table and watched him take in the sight.

"Don't worry," she said, stubbing out her cigarette. "I'm not going to shoot you. I changed my mind. In Jamaica I killed three people, Jack, and I didn't like it. I don't want to kill anybody else, not even you. This is just to make sure I get back to the car okay. If you don't mind, I'm gonna leave you now. You can come after me if you want, try to find me. That's up to you, of course."

Getting out the door was no problem. He was careful to give her a wide berth. Outside there were enough people in the street and the park that Maggie felt confident he wouldn't attempt anything. Still, she didn't put the pistol away, not yet.

As he followed her to the car Shanks seemed disconcerted, as though he wasn't sure he'd read the situation right. Like maybe there was another angle he wasn't considering. She wondered what ever happened to his little leather notebook.

Maggie was eager to leave. She climbed into the car and started the engine quickly. She caught him surreptitiously glancing at the license plate, memorizing it. It wouldn't do him any good trying to trace it.

He drummed his fingers on the roof of the car. "You're wrong," he said. "You don't have to be afraid of me, Maggie. I wouldn't hurt you. I plan to stay here two, three more weeks. Give me a call. I want to see you again. We could have some fun, you and me."

She looked deep into his face: the dark eyes, the new scar on his chin. The blond look didn't work for him, she thought. Made him look too Nazi.

It was hard to understand the hold he'd had on her. She only knew him for three days many months ago, but it seemed like they'd been married for years, had a couple of kids, a messy divorce, gone on to other lives.

"I don't think so."

"But that's why you came," he said. "Don't you see that?"

"No, I just had to see if I was right. I had to see it in your face, so I'd know for certain what a shit you are. So long, Jack."

She threw the car in gear, leaving him standing in the middle of Hillcrest Drive. She didn't look back. She wanted to get out of Astoria as fast as she could.

Mr. Zerle didn't know it yet, but other unexpected guests would soon be paying a visit. At the coffee shop in Astoria, Maggie had placed a phone call to the Portland office of the FBI and spoken anonymously to the assistant agent in charge. Although he'd never heard of former agent Jack Shanks, he seemed fascinated with the story she had to tell. Maggie had gotten the distinct impression that the Bureau would be following up quickly on the information—within hours, she suspected—and she didn't want to be around when they barreled down the street.

She wasn't worried that Shanks might eventually roll over on her. Like him, Maggie had taken special precautions. The difference was that he didn't know what her new name was, or where she resided.

But once on the open road, Maggie found she wasn't in any hurry to return home. Now that she was here in the Pacific Northwest, she told herself, she ought to do some sight-seeing. A few miles outside of town, U.S. 101 swung south along the coast, all the way through California. Her guidebook said the highway offered the traveler a host of exquisite panoramas, and she wasn't a girl who could pass up an exquisite panorama when one presented itself.

She had unlimited mileage on the rental, so she might as well make a trip of it. Maybe stay in some nice hotels along the way, the kind with mini-bars in the rooms. Who knew, she might even throw on her black dress and go downstairs to the cocktail lounge for a Ladystinger. It was always a good idea, Maggie felt, to keep your hand in. You never knew what might happen.